"You might want to call DeFore."

Lakesh's eyebrows rose. "Why?"

Grant didn't answer. Grimly he returned to the cloud-filled chamber. The vapor showed no indication of thinning, which was definitely unprecedented. He made his way to Kane and painfully went onto one knee beside him.

He saw only one Kane now. He still wore Grant's Mag-issue, Kevlar-weave coat, and he noticed the bulge of the holstered Sin Eater beneath the right sleeve. But his eyes were closed, his face slack. Grant did not see any signs of respiration.

Shrugging off the tentacles of dread that clutched at his heart, Grant placed a forefinger at the base of Kane's throat to check his pulse.

His finger passed through Kane and touched a metal floor plate.

Other titles in this series:

Exile to Hell
Destiny Run
Savage Sun
Omega Path
Parallax Red
Doomstar Relic
Iceblood

JAMES AXLER

OUTLANDERS™

HELLBOUND FURY

THE LOST EARTH SAGA
BOOK 1

A GOLD EAGLE BOOK FROM
WORLDWIDE®

TORONTO • NEW YORK • LONDON
AMSTERDAM • PARIS • SYDNEY • HAMBURG
STOCKHOLM • ATHENS • TOKYO • MILAN
MADRID • WARSAW • BUDAPEST • AUCKLAND

First edition March 1999
ISBN 0-373-63821-3

HELLBOUND FURY

Special thanks to Mark Ellis for his contribution to the Outlanders concept, developed for Gold Eagle Books.

And Time, a maniac scattering dust,
And Life, a Fury slinging Flame
—Tennyson

The Road to Outlands—
From Secret Government Files to the Future

Almost two hundred years after the global holocaust, Kane, a former Magistrate of Cobaltville, often thought the world had been lucky to survive at all after a nuclear device detonated in the Russian embassy in Washington, D.C. The aftermath—forever known as skydark—reshaped continents and turned civilization into ashes.

Nearly depopulated, America became the Deathlands—poisoned by radiation, home to chaos and mutated life forms. Feudal rule reappeared in the form of baronies, while remote outposts clung to a brutish existence.

What eventually helped shape this wasteland were the redoubts, the secret preholocaust military installations with stores of weapons, and the home of gateways, the locational matter-transfer facilities. Some of the redoubts hid clues that had once fed wild theories of government cover-ups and alien visitations.

Rearmed from redoubt stockpiles, the barons consolidated their power and reclaimed technology for the villes. Their power, supported by some invisible authority, extended beyond their fortified walls to what was now called the Outlands. It was here that the rootstock of humanity survived, living with hellzones and chemical storms, hounded by Magistrates.

In the villes, rigid laws were enforced—to atone for the sins of the past and prepare the way for a better future. That was the barons' public credo and their right-to-rule.

Kane, along with friend and fellow Magistrate Grant, had upheld that claim until a fateful Outlands expedition. A displaced piece of technology...a question to a keeper of the archives...a vague clue about alien masters—and their world shifted radically. Suddenly, Brigid Baptiste, the archivist, faced summary execution, and

Grant a quick termination. For Kane there was forgiveness if he pledged his unquestioning allegiance to Baron Cobalt and his unknown masters and abandoned his friends.

But that allegiance would make him support a mysterious and alien power and deny loyalty and friends. Then what else was there?

Kane had been brought up solely to serve the ville. Brigid's only link with her family was her mother's red-gold hair, green eyes and supple form. Grant's clues to his lineage were his ebony skin and powerful physique. But Domi, she of the white hair, was an Outlander pressed into sexual servitude in Cobaltville. She at least knew her roots and was a reminder to the exiles that the outcasts belonged in the human family.

Parents, friends, community—the very rootedness of humanity was denied. With no continuity, there was no forward momentum to the future. And that was the crux—when Kane began to wonder if there *was* a future.

For Kane, it wouldn't do. So the only way was out—way, way out.

After their escape, they found shelter at the forgotten Cerberus redoubt headed by Lakesh, a scientist, Cobaltville's head archivist, and secret opponent of the barons.

With their past turned into a lie, their future threatened, only one thing was left to give meaning to the outcasts. The hunger for freedom, the will to resist the hostile influences. And perhaps, by opposing, end them.

Chapter 1

The first thing Kane heard upon returning to the gallery beneath the tower was a woman weeping piteously. The girl Trai sat on one of the paving stones at the rim of the depression, huddled in a little ball of grief, hugging herself, rocking back and forth. To his surprise, Brigid sat beside her, patting her back, speaking to her soothingly in her own language. They were alone, the bodies of Gyatso and the slain triplet nowhere in sight.

"What's with Zakat's bitch, Baptiste?" he demanded. "She'll have more to cry about once she hears about where he ended up."

Brigid glanced at him reproachfully. "She knows already, somehow. She felt the link she shared with him disappear."

"Good. I wasn't sure if the son of a bitch was dead or not."

"What about you?" she asked.

He rubbed the back of his neck. "Just don't ask me to stand on my head for the next couple of days."

Brigid got to her feet, a hand on Trai's shoulder. "She's just a child, not really to blame. She was a servant in the monastery and the monks, particularly the high lama, treated her badly. Zakat seduced her with kindness—and probably his psi-abilities."

Kane shrugged disinterestedly. "Where's Balam?"

"Attending to the body of his son."

"His son?" Kane echoed, startled.

"The triplets are his children, born of a human woman nearly four hundred years ago. Like he said, they are the last of their particular breed."

Kane shook his head and covered his eyes for a moment. He tried to loathe Balam again, even tried to pity him, but he could find neither emotion within him.

"Kane."

At the hoarse whisper, he dropped his hand and saw Balam, flanked by the drooling twins, stepping into the depression. "You recovered the facets of the Trapezohedron."

Balam wasn't asking, he was stating. Kane removed them from his pocket and held them out. Balam made no indication he even noticed. He inclined his head toward the ebony cube laced within Lam's fingers.

"Take it and go."

Kane's blood ran cold and his flesh prickled. "And end up like Gyatso? Offhand, Balam, I can think of a hundred easier ways to check out."

"The new human was responsible for his fate. The energy he directed into the stone was strong, but it was of an incompatible frequency. It was deflected, turned inward, and it destroyed him. Take the Trapezohedron, Kane."

He looked into the face of Lam, eyes closed again

in placid contemplation. He stepped into the depression.

"Kane!" Brigid spoke warningly, fearfully. "What if—" She bit off the rest of her question.

"If the 'what if' happens, you know what to do," he replied.

He heard the overhung firing bolt on her Uzi being drawn back, and he threw Balam a cold, ironic smile. It wasn't returned.

Reaching out, he touched the black rock in Lam's hands, feeling his pulse pound with fear. He tugged gently, experimentally. The Trapezohedron came away easily. Without resistance it nestled in Kane's hands.

Almost as soon as it did, the flesh on Lam's face and limbs dried, browned and withered. His eyes collapsed into their sockets and his body fell, his robe belling up briefly as he joined the skeletal remains around the altar.

Kane froze, the hair lifting from his scalp, his mind filling with primal, nameless terror. He gaped wild-eyed at Balam.

"His vigil is complete. Yours begins."

Kane despised the tremor in his hands and voice. "My vigil for what?"

"To find a way for your people to survive, as mine did."

Kane swallowed with painful effort. His throat felt as if it were lined with sandpaper. "The only way is to displace the barons, you know that."

Balam nodded.

"What do you want in return?"

"Nothing in return. I have returned to the old, old ways of our forebears when we passed on truth rather than burning it."

"But you *did* burn it," Brigid said accusingly.

"To preserve ourselves," Balam replied. "A sacrifice made for an appointed period of time. That time is over. Our blood prevails."

Kane shook his head in frustration. "I don't— Are you betraying the barons, blood of your blood?"

"They are blood of your blood, too, Kane. I no more betray them than you do."

"A state of war will exist between our two cultures again," Brigid pointed out. "Rivers of that mixed blood will be spilled."

"If that is the road chosen," Balam said faintly, "then that is the road chosen. Blood *is* like a river. It flows through tributaries, channels, streams, refreshing and purifying itself during its journey. But sometimes it freezes, and no longer flows. A glacier forms, containing detritus, impurities. The glacier must be dislodged to allow the purifying journey to begin anew."

"And what of you?" Brigid asked quietly. "What will you do?"

Balam stood, swaying slightly, his huge fathomless and passionless eyes fixed on them. Then he flung up one long, thin arm in an unmistakable gesture, pointing to the entrance to the gallery. "I will do nothing, and you must do what you can. Go."

Then he turned and walked away, trailed by his sons.

For an instant, Kane grappled with the desire to go

after him, but he knew there was no reason and no point to it. Taking him back to Cerberus served no purpose. What Balam actually was Kane could not know, but a strange, aching sadness came over him as he watched him stride gracefully away.

He didn't know why he felt such a vacuum within him, then he realized he was reacting to an absence of hate.

Kane turned toward Brigid, and she saw the confusion, the uncertainty in his eyes. "Now what do we do?"

Brigid looked from Kane to Trai and to the black stone nestled between his hands. "We wait for tomorrow."

Kane shot her a glance, an irritation borne of stress, pain and exhaustion glittering in his gray-blue eyes. "It's tonight I'm worried about, not tomorrow. It's full dark outside the caverns, and the temperature will be well below freezing."

Brigid nodded thoughtfully, then ran a hand through her tangled, red-gold mane. She cast a furtive look toward the retreating backs of Balam and his twin sons. "I don't want to be the one to ask if Balam can put us up for the night. Do you?"

Eyeing the skeletons scattered in the depression on the floor, Kane repressed a shiver. "No, I don't. We can try to make our way back to the entrance and make camp there until dawn—and hope our horses haven't frozen to death."

He took a long, last look around the oval gallery whose walls, floor and ceiling seemed coated by a lacquer of amethyst, reflecting the light cast by flames dancing in a huge bowl brazier. He shoved the black stone into his coat pocket, ran a hand through his dark hair and announced, "Let's go."

Brigid gestured to Trai, spoke a word to her and the three of them left the chamber by the way they had entered it, ascending the flight of small rock steps to a narrow corridor. The passageway curved past a pair of power generators. Twelve feet tall, they resembled two solid black cubes, a slightly smaller one placed atop the larger. The top cube rotated slowly, producing a murmuring drone and the odor of ozone. Although Kane and Brigid had seen similar generators twice in the past, they still had no idea of their operating principles or the form of energy they produced.

The three people emerged from the base of a stone tower that formed the hub of a wheel, the city of Agartha radiating out around it. All the squat, windowless buildings were of black basalt, quarried from the walls of the cavern itself.

From the high, arched roof spilled a ghostly blue luminescence, tiled as it was with square light panels. The outskirts of the settlement sloped gently upward toward a broad shelf of stone forming a natural doorstep to a tunnel.

Yal, the Dob-Dob soldier from the Trasilunpo monastery still sat at the base of the boulder where Kane's fists and feet had battered him. He hung his shaven head despondently, making no effort to wipe away the blood dripping from his flattened nose. It mixed with the froth flecking his loose lips.

"Tell him Zakat is dead," Kane said to Brigid. "Ask him if he wants to stay or to go."

Brigid repeated Kane's words in the Tibetan's language, but he made no response. Trai spoke to him sharply, and the man slowly lifted his head. His eyes were wide and showed no recognition of the girl. His teeth gleamed in a grimace of pain behind his writhing lips, and a low moan bubbled up his throat. He poked at the gravel-strewed ground with the point of a *khanjarli* dagger.

Kane's flesh prickled with horror at the madness glittering in the Dob-Dob's eyes. The man's reason was broken, shattered into a thousand pieces that could never be put together again. He reached out and took the mini-Uzi from Brigid. His own side arm, his Sin Eater, had been damaged in his brief struggle with Yal.

"Tell him to drop the knife," Kane whispered tensely, resting his finger on the trigger of the subgun.

Brigid snapped out a few words, but Yal's only response was a high-pitched tittering. His madness-clouded mind didn't allow him to recognize the Uzi as a weapon—or if he did, he simply didn't care.

"Let's move away slow," Kane said to Brigid from the side of his mouth, taking a careful backstep.

At his motion, Yal gave a sobbing cry. He launched himself to his feet, the double-curved thorn of steel glittering in his right hand. His eyes rolled back in his head, displaying only the whites as he rushed toward Kane, the dagger held high.

Kane quickly stroked the trigger of the autoblaster.

The staccato drumming of the 3-round burst sounded obscenely loud in the cavern, the echoes rolling and rebounding.

Yal catapulted backward from the triple center punch to his chest. Robe flapping, he crashed to the ground, the dagger blade chiming on the rock. Trai shrank against Brigid, too shocked by Yal's behavior and his swift execution even to scream.

In a low, quavering tone, Brigid said, "This was all too much for him. The mental link with Zakat was probably the only thing that kept him from fusing out long before."

Kane only nodded, silently agreeing with Baptiste's assessment. Either through the Russian's own psionic abilities or with them enhanced by the two facets of the black stone in his possession, Zakat had achieved some kind of mental link with his followers. When it was broken, so was Yal's mind. Reared in a land bound by the ancient traditions of Agartha, the holy abode of the eight immortals, when Yal realized he had followed a path of blood and greed to reach it, he was overwhelmed by guilt and horror. Kane felt no particular sympathy for him. Brigid had told him Dob-Dobs, the soldiers of the monasteries, were recruited from the ranks of convicted Tibetan criminals.

Bending over the man's body, Kane searched his robes and found a bulky hand torch with a box-battery attached to it. He guessed it was of Russian manufacture.

"We've certainly brought more than our share of

death and bloodshed to the sanctuary of Balam's people," Brigid murmured.

Kane threw her a swift, hard-eyed glare. "What's that old phrase Lakesh uses—quid pro quo? Balam's people came to within a hair of exterminating *our* people. I'm not going to feel ashamed over this little bit of payback."

Despite his harsh words and tone, Kane did feel shame. Judging by the knowing light in Brigid's emerald eyes, she felt it, too.

He nodded to Trai. "Ask her if there are more Dob-Dobs waiting outside the cavern."

Brigid translated the question, receiving a sad head shake in response.

Kane took point as always, the white rod of the flashlight piercing the gloom. The three facets of the black stone in his coat pockets seemed to weigh very little, but he was acutely aware of their burdensome presence all the same.

He still had no clear idea of the nature of the stones, and he wasn't sure if he could comprehend it if one was offered to him. According to Balam, they were pieces of an inestimably ancient artifact predating humanity's rule of Earth. The existence of the black stone had been hinted at through all the ages of man, whispered about since the dawn of recorded history to the near-annihilation of the species in the nukecaust nearly two centuries before.

The stone had been known by many names, by many peoples of civilizations both primitive and advanced—Lucifer's Stone, the kala, the Kaa'ba, the Chintamani Stone, the Shining Trapezohedron. Always it had been associated with the concept of a key that unlocked either the door to enlightenment or madness. It had served as the centerpiece, the spiritual focal point of Balam's people, even after it had been fragmented and the facets scattered from one end of the Earth to the other. He claimed that through it, they glimpsed all possible futures to which their activities might lead.

But the black stone was far more than a calculating device that extrapolated outcomes from actions. Balam had said, "It brings into existence those outcomes."

He had referred to the stone as a channel to "sidereal space," where many tangential points of reality lay adjacent to one another, the parallel casements of the universe. He had also called it a something else, a doorway to "lost Earth," and the memory of those two words still sent a chill down Kane's spine. He found it almost impossible to grasp the concept of a multitude of realities coexisting with his own. He couldn't wrap the fingers of his mind around it. The notion turned to smoke and drifted away.

It took a great mental effort not to replay the vision he had glimpsed upon first touching the primary facet of the black stone. He had seen himself dying on a street. He watched himself sprawl across a cobblestoned gutter, and the cadaverous Colonel C. W. Thrush nudged his body with a booted foot.

Even after that demonstration or vision, he still didn't understand what Balam had meant by a "lost Earth."

Neither had Grigori Zakat, but that ignorance hadn't prevented him from embarking on a quest to recover all the pieces of the stone, following a path so many others had trod before him. His life was dedicated to the accruing of personal power, according to an esoteric religious tenet he practiced.

The Russian assumed if there were people of great power, then it stood to reason there were objects of equally great power, perhaps far older than humanity itself, swirling with forces that defied any attempts to measure or evaluate them.

Zakat's dreams now lay entombed with him in the eternal darkness of a subterranean abyss, deep beneath the mountains at the border of Tibet and China. Kane couldn't help but wonder if the fragments of stone that so obsessed Zakat should join him there.

They continued on through the tunnel, the crunch of their feet on gravel sending up a steady echo. The passageway opened into a wide cavern, a city of stalactites and stalagmites, and rock arches and formations.

Kane led the way through it, past the signpost that Balam's folk had erected ages before—an erect-standing statue, about fifteen feet tall. It depicted a humanoid creature with a slender build draped in robes. The features were sharply defined, the domed head disproportionately large and hairless. The eyes were huge, slanted and fathomless. One six-fingered hand pointed toward the shadow-shrouded end of the cavern from which they had just emerged.

The three people continued along the trail to the bank of the underground river, more of a stream at the point where Kane and Brigid had left the boat. The craft was made of yak-hide and wood, and they carefully climbed into it, not wanting to rupture the ancient seams.

Kane relegated the task of poling the boat against the current to Trai. He felt more than justified because of the various aches and pains the girl's former master had inflicted on him only a short while ago. Besides, she was sturdily built and very strong.

It was hard, laborious work, and Trai grunted and gasped with the exertion. The stream widened into a seventy-foot-wide waterway, and Brigid directed Trai to pole toward the opposite bank, where she and Kane had first launched the boat. The girl's arms trembled and sweat glistened on her face, despite the dank, chilly air.

After they beached the boat, Kane allowed Trai to rest a few minutes before they moved on again through the tunnels. None of them spoke much. Trai remained silent except for a few sniffles, in mourning over the death of Zakat.

Kane didn't voice his own worries to Brigid. He feared that if the horses they'd left in the valley wandered away, the return trek to the Trasilunpo monastery and the mat-trans gateway there might be too rugged to make on foot. The arduous journey from the Byang-Thang plateau on horseback had required a full day, from sunrise to sunset. Their supply of concentrated foodstuffs and water had been in a pack, which Balam had dropped before entering the so-called kingdom of Agartha. He prayed it would still be there.

The tunnel became little more than a curving ledge, with a rock wall on one side and yawning, impenetrable blackness on the other. It inclined, and the three people inched their way along it, flattening themselves against the wall.

Finally, the ledge stopped slanting upward, widened and leveled out. They made their way through the passageway to a natural foyer, and the beam of the flashlight illuminated the tiny steps carved out of rock that led to the mouth of the entrance tunnel, about ten feet over their heads. Pursued by Zakat and his party through the tunnel, Kane and Brigid had suffered bruising falls because they hadn't known the crude stairway was there.

Kane handed her the flashlight. "Stay here with her. I'll make a recce."

He quickly scaled the steps, wincing as flares of pain ignited all over his body. The spill he'd taken and the brutal hand-to-hand fight with Zakat made his limbs feel as if they were sewn together with barbed wire.

On hands and knees, he crawled down the tunnel, heading toward the indistinct glimmer of light at its nether end. Pushing aside clumps of dry grass, he climbed out of the cleft in the base of the mountain, grateful of the fresh air, as cold as it was. Standing at his full six-foot-one-inch height, he stretched in relief and surveyed the area. The frosty stars shining above snow-gilded peaks cast the box canyon into a stark vista of shadow and light. After hours of silently suffering the claustrophobic fear of being buried alive, he immediately felt better looking up at the open sky.

Bulwarks of granite stood like huge tombstones all around, providing something of a break from the icy gusts of wind that howled down from the mountain passes. He sighed with relief when he saw the pack still lying where Balam had dropped it, but he saw no sign of the ponies, either the ones he and Brigid had ridden or those belonging to Zakat and his party. On impulse, he whistled and an answering whinny floated from behind the upstanding slabs of stone.

All of the horses were there, grazing on the scrubby grass and chewing the stems of underbrush. The squat, sturdy bodies of the five animals were covered by pelts of shaggy fur. Kane figured they would have no trouble withstanding the low temperatures for the rest of the night if they remained behind the windbreak. Consulting his wrist chron, he saw with a slight start of surprise that it was only a few hours shy of dawn. His sojourn in the underground galleries of Agartha had seemed to comprise a lifetime and a half.

He hobbled the ponies as best he could with their reins, then returned to the tunnel with the pack of provisions. Carefully climbing backward down the steps too small for normal human feet, he announced, "The horses are still there, so come daybreak we ride instead of walk."

Brigid translated his words for the benefit of Trai, and the girl ducked her head in relieved gratification.

Kane distributed the self-heat ration packages and bottles of distilled water. They were a poor substitute for a meal, particularly after what all of them had experienced. But nobody dared complain, even though Brigid had to show Trai how to work the self-heat tabs on the rations.

Chewing a mouthful of chicken à la king that had the flavor and consistency of paste, Kane said, "By this time tomorrow, we'll be back in Cerberus. Lakesh will have his precious rocks, but he probably won't feel they were much of a trade for Balam."

Brigid shook her head impatiently. "We learned more about Balam and the Archons in the past three days than Lakesh found out in three years. He won't criticize us for leaving Balam here. We always know where to find him again."

Kane grunted. "Yeah, well, I never intend to come back here." He paused to wash down a mouthful of food with a swig of water and asked, "How much of what we learned do you think we can actually believe?"

Brigid shrugged. "The multiverse hypothesis is very old. You and I already experienced something close to an alternate reality when we went down the Omega Path. Remember?"

Kane smiled wryly. "I might not have a eidetic memory like you, Baptiste, but I'm not likely to forget that. But even you have to admit the idea of alternate realities isn't an easy one to accept."

She shrugged. "Maybe there *is* only one reality. We just haven't figured it out yet, but Balam's folk did."

Kane found her response unsatisfactory. "Balam and his people have been lying to humanity for twenty thousand years or more,'' he argued. ''Why should he start telling the truth now?''

Brigid nodded, slowly and reflectively. ''I suppose we'll find out.''

''When?''

Smiling wanly, wearily, she replied, ''Like I said, tomorrow.''

Chapter 2

Like a massive battleship somehow beached there, Cobaltville loomed high on the grassy bluffs overlooking the Kanab River. The white stone walls rose fifty feet high, and at each intersecting corner protruded a Vulcan-Phalanx gun tower. Powerful spotlights washed the immediate area outside the walls, leaving nothing hidden from the glare. On the far side of the winding river, tangles of razor wire surrounded cultivated fields.

As in all the fortified villes, a narrow roadbed of crushed gravel led up to the main gate, passing two checkpoint stations. The first, at the mouth of the road, was a small concrete block cupola, manned only by a single Magistrate. Past the cupola, pyramid-shaped "dragon's teeth" obstacles made of reinforced concrete lined both sides of the path. Weighing a thousand pounds each and five feet tall, they were designed to break the tracks or wheels of any assault vehicle trying to cross them.

A dozen yards before the gate, stone blockhouses bracketed either side of the road. Within them were electrically controlled GEC Miniguns, capable of firing 6000 5.56 mm rounds per minute. Past the blockhouses was the main gate itself—twenty feet wide by fifteen high, with a two-foot thickness of rockcrete sheathed by cross-braced iron. The portal was opened by buried system of huge gears and cables.

Inside the walls stretched the complex of spired Enclaves. Each of the four towers was joined to the others by pedestrian bridges. Few of the windows in the towers showed any light, so there was little to indicate that the interconnecting network of stone columns, enclosed walkways, shops and promenades was where nearly four thousand people made their homes.

In the Enclaves, the people who worked for the ville administrators enjoyed lavish apartments, all the bounty of those favored by Baron Cobalt.

Far below the Enclaves, on a sublevel beneath the bluffs, light peeped up from dark streets of the Tartarus Pits. This sector of Cobaltville was a seething melting pot, where outlanders and slaggers lived. They swarmed with cheap labor, and the random movement between the Enclaves and Pits was tightly controlled—only a Magistrate on official business could enter the Pits, and only a Pit-dweller with a legitimate work order could even approach the cellar of an Enclave tower.

Seen from above, the Enclave towers formed a latticework of intersected circles, all connected to the center of the circle, from which rose the Administrative Monolith. The massive, round column of white rockcrete jutted three hundred feet into the sky. Light poured out of the slit-shaped windows on each level.

Every level of the tower was designed to fulfill a specific capacity—E Level was a general construction and manufacturing facility; D Level was devoted to the preservation, preparation and distribution of food and C Level held the Magistrate Division. On B Level was the Historical Archives, a combination of library, museum and computer center. The work of the administrators was conducted on the highest level, A Level. Up in the top spire, far above even the Enclaves, Baron Cobalt reigned, unapproachable and invisible.

Beyond the office suites and the reception areas, A Level was a labyrinth of concealed chambers and secret corridors. One particular corridor led through a confusing array of rooms and archways, ending finally in a large chamber, illuminated by the sickly gray glow from an unseen light source.

Six men stood in a semicircle in the center of the enormous Persian carpet that covered the floor. Several of the group were administrative members of the various divisions, one was the highest-ranking Magistrate administrator and four were from Baron Cobalt's personal staff. The Cobaltville Trust, or what was left of it, had assembled.

Each of the nine villes in the continent-spanning network had its own version of the Trust. The organization, if it could be called that, was the only face-to-face contact allowed with the barons, and the barons were the only contacts permitted by the Archon Directorate.

The Trust acted more or less as the protectors of the Directorate, and its oath revolved around a single theme—the presence of the Directorate must not be revealed to humanity. If their presence became known, if the technological marvels they had designed became accessible, if the truth behind the nukecaust filtered down to the people, then humankind would no doubt retaliate with a concerted effort to wipe them out—or the Directorate would be forced to visit another holocaust upon the face of the earth, simply as a measure of self-preservation.

The measured, reverberating tones of a hidden gong sounded, and as one, the six men turned to face a patch of murk. In the gloom, a door slowly opened. Behind a filmy gauze curtain, a golden light, suffused in pastel hues slanted down from above. The gong struck thirteen air-shivering strokes, and the shaft of muted golden light became a glare. Right before the glare faded to its previous soft hue, a dark figure appeared within it.

The baron had arrived.

Only a few members of the Trust had ever gotten a clear, unobstructed view of Baron Cobalt. With their eyes still recovering from the sudden glare, they blinked toward the blurred figure behind the curtain and received the same impression as always—a gaunt, man-shaped figure under six feet tall, with unusually long arms and unusually short legs, head bowed as if in intense concentration, one hand under the chin, the other behind his back.

The baron's face was in shadow, but the men glimpsed a long, narrow head and a domed, hairless skull that seemed just a bit too large. Most of them had no idea of the color or shape of the baron's eyes.

"Nothing is as it was." Baron Cobalt spoke, and his contralto voice, pitched to a sibilant whisper as always, vibrated with a tone none of the men had ever heard or expected to hear. "Nearly three months have passed since my adviser and your comrade, Lakesh, was abducted. In that time, what has the search for him accomplished?"

No one responded to the question. Since every one of them knew the answer, they assumed the baron did, too. All of the nine villes had engaged in a cooperative search, not only for Lakesh, but for the renegade Magistrates who had taken him. Since they had used the baron's own personal gateway unit to escape Cobaltville, it stood to reason they had rematerialized in one of the many Totality Concept redoubts, scattered across the face of America.

The subterranean installations were constructed two centuries before to house the most advanced scientific miracles of the day under the aegis of the Totality Concept. They had been sealed for generations, since the Program of Unification.

Over the past few months, the redoubts located in ville territories were methodically visited and inspected. More than one had shown signs of recent occupation, as if Baron Cobalt's quarry knew they were being sought and jumped from redoubt to redoubt to escape capture and confuse the trail.

But other events had occurred during the search for Lakesh and the seditionists who abducted him. A squad of Sharpeville Magistrates was obliterated in Redoubt Papa, and Baron Sharpe himself was seriously wounded—by a man in the black Magistrate armor.

A few weeks after that, a report was filed from Baron Samarium's territory in Louisiana, stating that several swamp-dwellers had encountered Kane. Shortly thereafter, Baron Ragnar in Minnesota was assassinated in his own private chamber by a woman, though the reports of the incident were garbled. The true identity of the woman had yet to be determined, but the names of Kane and Grant figured prominently in reports filed by a pair of Mags who had secured a redoubt in Ragnarville's territory.

The attempted homicide of one baron coupled with the successful assassination of another was more than distressingly unprecedented—the two events were blasphemous on a scale not witnessed since the institution of the unification program, eighty-some years before.

The baronial hierarchy ruling the nine villes was more than the governing body of postnukecaust America—they were god-kings, hybrids of human and nonhuman, genetic material melded with the sole purpose of creating new humans to inherit the Earth. The barons served as a bridge between predark and postdark, the plenipotentiaries of the Archon Directorate itself.

Therefore, in order to prevent another apocalypse, maintaining the secrecy of the Directorate and its work was a sacred trust. It was a sworn and solemn duty, offered to very few.

No secret as complex and as wide-ranging as this one could be completely hidden. Rumors abounded about the Directorate and the Totality Concept even before the nukecaust, though they were relegated to the status of conspiracy theories. During the century and a half following skydark, some of the secrets were discovered. Humanity, what was left of it, was too scattered even for the Directorate to control. The near annihilation of the race hadn't annihilated the race's inborn sense of curiosity, the drive to search in strange places for strange things.

Many of those strange places were penetrated, the strange things uncovered, but humankind was too concerned with day-to-day survival to reason out the whys and wherefores behind them. It required only a generation to reduce the knowledge of strange places and things to mere rumors, and another generation to fanciful legends. Only members of the Trust and a few select subordinates were aware that the legends were anything but fanciful. There were, however, a handful of others who suspected a hard and very real foundation lay beneath the legends.

Some thirty years before, a junior archivist in Ragnarville had found an old computer disk purporting to contain the journal of a woman scientist by the name of Dr. Mildred Winonia Wyeth. Allegedly Wyeth had been cryogenically frozen before the nuking, and she had survived skydark and the long winters. Revived a century later, she had traveled Deathlands with the legendary Ryan Cawdor.

Sometime during her wanderings she found a working computer and recorded her thoughts, observations and speculations regarding the postnukecaust world, the redoubts and the wonders they contained.

Apparently a very educated woman, Wyeth had no inkling of the true nature of the redoubts or even the presence of the Directorate, but a number of her extrapolations came frighteningly close to the truth.

The Trust suspected the *Wyeth Codex* had been downloaded, copied and disseminated like a virus through the Historical Divisions of the entire ville network. There was no solid proof of this, of course, only anxieties that gave rise to the fear that a renegade group of historians-insurgents, labeled Preservationists by the intel section, might know far more than the Trust or even the semidivine barons themselves.

Recent events had cast doubt not only on the semidivine status claimed by the baronial oligarchy, but the existence of the Archon Directorate itself. Every man standing before Baron Cobalt had been conditioned to believe that the Directorate allowed humanity to survive at its sufferance. If they did not obey the edicts of the baron, or perform their duties to the exacting standards established by the Directorate, another apocalypse would be the sure result.

Now, a baron's authority had been blatantly flouted, one had been wounded and another lay dead. And the Archon Directorate had not visited another holocaust upon the Earth, had not intervened, had not even made its displeasure known. There was not even a hint that the Directorate was even aware of the appalling events rocking ville society.

No member of the Trust dared wonder aloud about the lack of action on the part of their hidden masters. They continued to stand silently and wait for Baron Cobalt, their god-king, the ambassador of the Archons to speak again.

Usually, the baron paced back and forth beneath the arch, his graceful movements suggestive of a bizarrely beautiful dance. Now he stood as stiffly immobile as the men facing him.

"Nothing has been accomplished," he said in his lilting whisper. "I have been failed, and when a baron is failed, then the Directorate is failed. Can any of you imagine their grief when they are forced to render a judgment upon us?"

The members of the Trust did not reply, but pudgy Ojaka shifted his feet uncomfortably on the carpet.

"I asked a question!" Baron Cobalt's voice sounded like the snapping of a whip.

"Yes, my lord baron—"

"We do, my lord—"

"Forgive us—"

Baron Cobalt cut off the murmured litany of shame and humiliation with a scornful laugh.

"'Forgive us,'" the baron repeated, adopting a whiny falsetto. "Everything we have built since the nukecaust, the order that has been restored since the Program of Unification, all of the boons granted to us by the Directorate, is threatened by a handful of renegades. And you beg forgiveness."

Stepping forward, Baron Cobalt thrust aside the gold-dusted veil with a savage gesture. He approached the assembled men with a measured, haughty stride, and they were too stunned recoil. For most of them, it was the first time they had seen the baron's true appearance, and they gaped in mingled awe and fear.

A golden bodysuit encased the baron's slender figure, matching the almost translucent tint of his complexion. The smooth, almost poreless skin was stretched tight over protuberant facial bones, all sharp angles of cheeks, brow and chin. The elongated skull tapered from a high, round, completely bald skull down to a pointed chin.

No lines marred the face, not even on the tall forehead. Below them, large, slanting golden-brown eyes stared out from deep sockets. The thin slash of the mouth showed authority, and the tiny nostrils in the fine, thin nose flared with angry contempt.

"Has every redoubt in all of the baronies been inspected?"

Abrams, the gray-bearded Magistrate Division administrator, cleared his throat, making a sound like chips of pottery grating against one another. "My lord, I received the final report this morning. Every redoubt on the continent that is equipped with an indexed mat-trans gateway has been visited and searched. Some of the recording instruments indicated activity, though most did not."

Baron Cobalt drew in a long, contemplative breath. "They escaped via the Cerberus network. Logically, they would have materialized in another mat-trans unit...therefore, that particular unit would have a record of their arrival. If that record has not been found in any of the redoubts, only a single conclusion remains—at least one redoubt remains to be searched."

The baron cocked his head at a quizzical angle toward Abrams, his big eyes slitting suspiciously. "Do you have any feedback to my hypothesis?"

Although Baron Cobalt's voice was pitched low, the undertone of a challenge vibrated within it.

Abrams forced himself to meet the baron's gaze,

trying not to lean too heavily or obviously on his walking stick. His crippled right leg was an ever-present reminder of his one face-to-face encounter with the murderous Kane.

"My lord, there is indeed one redoubt that has not been searched." Abrams spoke matter-of-factly. "It is listed on the records as Redoubt Bravo, in Montana."

"Why was this redoubt not investigated, since it is within Cobaltville's territorial jurisdiction?" The baron's question was the sibilant hiss of a serpent.

Abrams continued to meet Baron Cobalt's intense, unblinking gaze. "Lakesh himself reported the installation as completely unsalvageable. The nuclear generators are down, all of its operating systems have been off-line for nearly a century. Other than that, though technically within our sphere of jurisdiction, Redoubt Bravo is in an exceptionally inaccessible area—on a mountain peak in the Bitterroot range."

Baron Cobalt's eyes finally blinked, in mild surprise. "The Darks?"

Abrams nodded. "Just so. The weather at that altitude is dangerously unpredictable, and it is inadvisable to make an aerial recce. After all, we have yet to replace the Deathbirds lost over the past few months. Under the circumstances, I saw little need to risk what's left of our fleet to investigate an installation that one of our own declared derelict."

Baron Cobalt inclined his head in a short, grim nod. Employed by the Magistrate Division, the Deathbirds were modified, retroengineered AH-64 Apache attack gunships. Two of the aircraft had been lost, and one had sustained severe damage in the recent past. Kane, Grant and the archivist-turned-seditionist, Baptiste, had been involved in each incident.

"Then overland is the only option left to us," the baron announced.

"My lord," Abrams said hesitantly, "it will require a long journey through the Outlands, and according to the report Lakesh wrote, only one treacherous road leads to the redoubt."

"And you don't feel the risk is worth it?" Baron Cobalt inquired mildly.

Squaring his shoulders, Abrams declared stolidly, "No, my lord, with conditions being what they are, I do not. Men and matériel will have to be removed from Cobaltville for an unknown but definitely extended period of time. If indeed a rebellion is brewing, and after what happened in Ragnarville I think that's likely, the ville will be underprotected."

"I see." The baron's response was quiet, almost disinterested. "Your point is well taken."

He began to turn away, drawing a weary breath through his delicate nostrils. Then, in a blur of inhuman speed, Baron Cobalt pivoted on his heel, eyes wide and wild, face upturned toward Abrams's. "You will do as I bid!"

The command burst from the baron's mouth in a high-pitched shriek of rage, amid a spray of spittle. His hands knotted into fists, the knuckles straining against the finely textured skin so tightly, it appeared as if they would split the flesh.

"You, Abrams, *will* take a contingent of Magistrates into the Darks! You *will* thoroughly investigate Redoubt Bravo personally and you *will* return here with a definitive report!''

Abrams drew on his well-spring of self-control to keep from flinching from the baron's paroxysm of frustrated fury. He had seen the baron displeased and even angry before, but never hysterical. In that moment, Abrams feared less for his own future than for the future of all of the baronies. If the barons lost control, first over themselves, then over their villes, anarchy and chaos would engulf all that had been built since unification.

Trying to ignore the icy hand of terror that stroked the buttons of his spine, Abrams ducked his head to break eye contact with the baron. He murmured, ''As you so wish, so shall you be served, my lord.''

A sneer twisted the baron's features, turning his sculpted face into an ugly mask of contempt. ''Humanity serves only its own venal needs, its most base whims. You serve me because you fear to lose what I have given you. Your life, being first and foremost.''

Wheeling, Baron Cobalt stalked back toward the veiled archway, snapping over his shoulder, ''I do not wish to hear from you again until you are prepared to embark—and I expect that report within twenty-four hours.''

The light haloing the arch disappeared, and the shadows that replaced it claimed the baron's figure.

Abrams turned away, not surprised or even ashamed by the weakness in his knees or the tremor in his hands. He trudged across the carpet, leaning on his cane for support. He paid no attention to his fellow members of the Trust—not that they drew any attention to themselves. All of them were stricken, shocked speechless by Baron Cobalt's wild outburst.

Abrams even ignored the pair of Baronial Guardsmen who appeared to escort the Trust from the chamber. Huge men wearing white uniform jackets, red silken leggings and high black boots, they lived only to protect the barons. Abrams had heard they were products of genetic engineering, with a focus on physical prowess and a disregard for the intellectual, but at the moment he would not have cared if they were stickies.

Nearly thirty years had passed since he had worn the battle armor of a hard-contact Magistrate or gone out into the field. Despite his apprehension at the prospect, he suspected he would probably be safer in the Darks than within the walls of Cobaltville.

Chapter 3

If Kane thought the journey down from the monastery was arduous, the trek back up the mountain passes was no less rugged.

Starting out at first light, with the sky still mantled with the cold gray gloom of dawn, Kane and his pony took the point. Ahead and above, the terrain was a forbidding array of serrated black crags, towering cliffs and broken black rock. The narrow trail looped up through the slopes, wending its way around stone bastions and granite pillars.

Brigid and Trai followed him, the tethered horses of Zakat's party bringing up the rear. He and Brigid had argued the merits of bringing the other ponies, but when he reminded her that Balam's steed had plunged over a precipice the day before, she conceded the point. It was better to have spare mounts and not need them than need them and not have them.

Although the temperature was low and the wind chill uncomfortable, the weather held, with no signs of a snowstorm of the kind that had assaulted them the day before.

Kane had repaired the minor damage inflicted by Yal on his Sin Eater, and it was now securely holstered to his right forearm beneath the sleeve of his Kevlar-weave coat. The magazine of the big-bored,

Mag-issue handblaster carried twenty 9 mm rounds. When not in use, the stock folded over the top of the weapon, lying perpendicular to the frame, reducing its holstered length to ten inches. When needed, all Kane had to do was tense his wrist tendons, and sensitive actuators activated a flexible cable in the holster and snapped the weapon smoothly into the hand. The stock unfolded in the same motion. The Sin Eater had no trigger guard or safety, and the blaster fired immediately upon touching the crooked index finger.

The snowy crests of the Cherga mountain range loomed high above them, making for a jagged skyline. For the first two miles, the trail was a fairly level, gradually ascending a parapet of basalt. Kane had noticed the day before that it was largely hand hewn, and in some places it appeared as if demolition charges had done the construction work. But after that, the path became rougher, more narrow with sharp, zigzagging upward turns.

The path was like a sharp-edged causeway butting up against a rock wall on the right and a sheer drop slanting steeply down for hundreds of feet on the left. They skirted ledges that hovered over chasms so deep the bottoms were lost in shadow.

The only sound was the keening of the wind and the steady clopping of the horses' hooves on the gravel-strewed path. After an hour of slow, steady traveling, Kane glanced back to see Brigid swaying in the saddle, head bowed in sleep, hair covering her face like a screen. He himself was desperate for sleep—he was now approaching his thirtieth hour without so much as a catnap. He managed to keep himself awake only by an effort of will that was almost painful.

He called out to Brigid, and she roused only when he half shouted her name. She came awake with a start, dizzily reeling on her mount's back. For an alarmed instant, Kane feared she would fall from the saddle, but she snatched at the reins and recovered her balance.

"We'll take a rest when we reach the tunnel," he told her. "You've got to keep your eyes open, or you're liable to be dozing here permanently."

She glared at him, then self-consciously averted her face. Her mane of hair was a wild, unbrushed tangle, her face smeared with grime and her forehead encrusted with the dried blood from a cut that had scabbed over.

Kane couldn't help but be reminded of how she looked when they made their escape from Cobaltville. Those memories seemed to belong to another person entirely.

"Sorry," he said. "I'm worn-out, too."

Brigid didn't speak, but she nodded in acknowledgment of his apology.

Kane turned in the saddle. Brigid Baptiste was actually one of the toughest women—people, for that matter—he had ever met. For a woman who had been trained to be an academic, an archivist, and had never strayed more than ten miles from the sheltering walls of Cobaltville, her resiliency and resourcefulness never failed to impress him. Over the past eight months, she had left her tracks in the most distant and alien of climes and walked in very deep, very dangerous waters.

Both of them had come a very long way, in distances that could not be measured in mere miles from the night of their first meeting in the residential Enclaves. As a sixteen-year veteran of the Magistrate Division, Kane was accustomed to danger and hardship, but nothing like he and Brigid had exposed themselves to since their exile.

Kane occasionally wondered how his regimented, ville-bred mind had managed to adapt to all the new, and on the face of it, insane situations he had found himself in over the past eight months. But, he reminded himself sourly, when Lakesh had admitted to interfering in his genetic makeup, he had also claimed to have bred superior adaptive traits into him, as well.

Superior traits were certainly needed after the nukecaust of January 20, 2001. The world lay wasted, nature violated and outraged, transformed overnight into a contaminated shockscape littered with the shattered aspirations of humanity. Much of the United States became the Deathlands, a continent-sized hell on Earth where vast tracts of deserts replaced forests, lakes either boiled away or became inland seas, and great cities were reduced to towering man-made cliffs of vine-hung ruins. Then there were the first strike targets, and the passage of time had not cleansed them of hideous, invisible plagues.

Kane shivered, and not from the cold, when he thought of the hellzones of Washington Hole and Newyork. He had visited both fairly recently. It was in Manhattan, in the ruins of the Museum of Natural History, where he had intersected with Grigori Zakat's obsession with gaining power through the Black Stone.

Sometimes, Kane thought bleakly, that was all life had been reduced to after skydark—the drive to gain power at whatever the cost.

For the survivors of the nukecaust, the price of power was tragically high, but dreams of gaining it did not die. In the century following the atomic megacull, what was left of the world filled with savage beasts and even more savage men. They lived beyond any concept of law or morality and made pacts to achieve power, regardless of how pointless an exercise it seemed.

Survivors and descendants of survivors tried to build enclaves of civilization around which a new human society could rally, but there were only so many people in the world, and few of these made either good pioneers or settlers.

It was far easier to wander, to lead the live of nomads and scavengers, digging out stockpiles, caches of tools, weapons and technology laid down by the prenuke government, and building a power base on what was salvaged. The scavengers knew that true wealth did not lie in property or even the accruing of material possessions. Those were only tools, the means to an end. They knew the true end lay in personal power. In order to gain it, the market value of power had to stabilize, to be measured in human blood—those who shed it and those who were more than willing to spill it.

As the second centennial of the nukecaust approached, the anarchy and barbarism that had ruled Deathlands for nearly 150 years was curtailed, if not completely banished. The price of power changed, and the legal tender was no longer human blood, but the human spirit, the seat of the soul. If the soul could be controlled, then humanity could be bound in a heavy harness.

Power existed for its own sake, not to accrue wealth or luxury or long life or happiness, but only to gain more power. Everything else—love, honor, compassion—was irrelevant. Those who controlled its price controlled not just the world, but every human being who lived in it and was born into it.

Kane, Brigid and Trai pushed on, doing their best to fight off weakness and exhaustion. All of the injuries Kane had suffered over the past few days were like little fireballs igniting all over his body.

His jaw throbbed from where Zakat had butt-stroked him with his rifle in Newyork, the cut on the tender lining of his cheek stung and his neck ached from the full nelson the Russian had put on him. He resisted taking any of the pain medication in the survival kit. He was already groggy from lack of sleep and the high altitudes.

As the trail ascended, the wind cut into them like whetted steel. All of them, the horses included, dropped their heads against it. Kane tugged up the winged collar of his heavy Kevlar-weave coat, trying to cover his ears. The overcoat could turn any projectile from a knife to a .38-caliber round, and was insulated against all weathers, even chem storms.

When his cheeks and ears went numb, he thought he might prefer a shower of acid rain to the incessant, icy slashing of the wind.

As he shifted in the saddle, he became aware of the weight of the stones in his coat pockets, and he contemplated the wisdom of chucking them into the abyss. But after what he and Brigid had gone through to get them, it seemed like a fairly futile gesture.

The mountain holding the Byang-Thang plateau and the Trasilunpo monastery loomed gigantically above them, so distant that it seemed they could never reach it in a week, much less a day. It was a dark mass of dizzy escarpments and crags, with a snow-clad peak dominating it all.

As the sun rose higher, they climbed through deep shadows cast by abutments and overhangs. All morning and into early afternoon the party of people and horses threaded its way along the treacherous trail. The path turned and twisted over great heights, up turreted ridges and around wind-scoured bastions the size of houses.

Kane began to feel a quiver of unease as the afternoon wore on. The day before they had taken shelter from a storm in a tunnel that had been enlarged out of a natural cave. He thought to have come in sight of it by now, though, of course, climbing uphill was slower going than down.

Almost as soon as the thought registered, he caught the scent of smoldering tamarisk root and roasting meat, borne on the wind. Reining in his mount, he gestured behind him for Brigid and Trai to do the same. The path twisted around a massive gray shoulder of stone, and the smells wafted to him from the other side of it.

He dismounted, gritting his teeth against the spasm of pain in his crotch. Seeing Brigid and Trai sniffing the air, he commented quietly, "Hell of a place to have a cookout. We'd better recce."

The two women dismounted and followed him as he edged around the broad base of the rock. Pressing his back against it, Kane hazarded a quick look and glimpsed what he had been hoping to see for the past hour.

The trail entered a gash in the cliff face and ascended through a tunnel. What he hadn't hoped to see were the five short, stump-legged men in fur caps and girdled caftans swaggering around a cookfire. A small animal roasted on a spit, seared by the flames.

There were no women or horses with the men, and scant luggage. He did see short swords and match-lock muzzle-loaders. Behind him, he heard Trai's breathy whisper: "Khampas."

Kane cast Brigid a quizzical glance and she translated. "Bandits."

He wasn't surprised. The men had the same feral, predatory look about them as Le Loup Garou's band of Roamers he had buried beneath an avalanche a couple of months before.

Stepping back around the abutment, he said, "It looks like they plan to stay there for a while."

Brigid cast her eyes skyward. "We can't take too much time to wait them out—not if we want to reach the monastery by nightfall."

The notion of spending the night on a mountain

pass didn't appeal to Kane at all, mainly because the temperature plunged to well below zero once the sun set. And night came early to such high altitudes.

Brigid spoke to Trai in a hurried whisper. The Tibetan girl responded with vehement head shakes, gestures of negation and a torrent of fearfully spoken words.

"Like I figured," Brigid said grimly. "The Khampas are poor. They used to make a living exacting tribute from the lamasaries, but now they live only by murder and theft. Trai claims we're too rich for them to simply let us pass by. They'd rape us—me and her, I assume, though she wasn't really clear if you were excluded—and sell us and the horses to other Khampas."

Kane gusted out a slow sigh. "In other words, to get to the plateau, we've got to chill them."

Brigid nodded. "That was the advice Trai gave."

Swiftly, Kane scanned the terrain, although there was not much to see or use as cover if they decided to sneak up on the bandits. Clambering around the rocks would be more dangerous than facing them head-on.

"Looks to me like our best chance is to march right in, act friendly and blast them." He angled a questioning eyebrow at Brigid.

"Are you waiting for me to contribute something to that strategy?" she asked. "I don't see any other option than your favorite tactic—to brazen it out."

Kane smiled, but it had no humor in it. "All right. Keep your blaster hidden. We'll leave Trai and the other horses here. If the slaggers start jabbering at us, do you think you can understand them?''

Brigid shrugged. ''It depends on their regional dialect. But if they're as nasty as Trai says they are, they probably won't waste much time on polite chitchat.''

Brigid conveyed instructions to Trai, and the girl seemed only too happy to follow them and remain hidden from the bandits.

Remounting, Kane and Brigid heeled their ponies into a leisurely pace around the stone shoulder. As they circled it, an alarmed yell went up from the men in the tunnel. They snatched at their weapons, but a bearded man with a face the color and texture of badly cured leather shouted commands at them.

The three rifle barrels pointed their way drooped a little, but a man holding a glowing ember snatched from the fire to light the matches held his ground. The muzzle-loaders were crude weapons, and Kane guessed their design was based on the old *bandukh* template.

Kane and Brigid approached at an unhurried gait. When they reached the mouth of the cave, the bandits crowded close, eyes full of curiosity. Looking past them to the far end of the tunnel, Kane saw no signs of other men. As it was, their rank, unwashed odor was nearly as strong as that as of the cook fire.

The chief was puzzled and suspicious, but the gaze he directed toward them was primarily full of lust—for the animals or the woman, Kane couldn't be sure.

They reined in just inside the tunnel mouth. The chief stared at them for a long moment before demanding, "What do you do here, outlanders? Speak quickly before my warriors flay the flesh from your soft pink asses!"

He contorted his face in a ferocious grimace, which might have been intimidating if he wasn't toothless. When Brigid translated his threat, Kane didn't even try to repress a disdainful laugh. The Tibetan bandits were about as much warriors as the most motley bunch of slaggers in the deepest squats of the Pits. They were back-shooting scavengers, and Kane felt the old Magistrate sense of righteous superiority rise up in him.

Eyes fixed on those of the bandit chief, lips creased in a contemptuous smile, Kane said to Brigid, "Inform him that we have no quarrel with him, that we're pilgrims on the way to the monastery. All we want is to pass unmolested."

Brigid nodded. "I'll tell him, but I don't think he'll care."

"Me either, but I want to give him a chance to think it over and stay alive."

Brigid spoke to the short man in sibilant syllables. The Tibetan listened, then grinned gummily. He made an expansive gesture, waving to them with his left arm. Kane noted that his right hand never strayed far from the sash wound about his waist. His reply contained an undertone of mockery.

Brigid exhaled wearily through her nostrils. "He doesn't believe us. He claims it's his family's tradition to guard the road leading from the plateau to the holy land of Agartha and exact tribute from all who wish to pass. He says if we were truly pilgrims, we would know this and not argue with him.''

"Let me guess," Kane ventured. "If we give him a horse and all our belongings, we can go on our way."

"No, we have to give him *both* horses. He didn't mention anything about letting us go on our way."

Kane glanced surreptitiously toward the men with the matchlocks. The fuses of the rifles could only be lighted one at time, and there was a several second interval before the powder in the pans ignited. It would make more sense for the bandits to use their muzzle-loaders as clubs.

The chief's black, flesh-bagged eyes bored in on Kane's face. He asked a question.

"He wants to know who you are," Brigid translated.

Casually, Kane shifted the position of his right arm. "Tell him I'm the man who has death up his sleeve."

Brigid repeated the reply, and the Tibetan's posture instantly tensed. He opened his mouth as if to reply, then closed it again.

"He's thinking it over," Brigid whispered. "But he's got his reputation to consider."

The man's right hand casually inserted itself among the dirty folds of his sash as if he were absently scratching at a flea bite. Then he yanked out a big-bored revolver and leveled it at Kane's breast, his thumb pulling back on the hammer.

The Khampa chief's move was smooth, obviously the result of long years of practice. It was probably the only profitable habit he had developed in his life. His eyes didn't catch the lightninglike blur of motion in Kane's right hand.

Motion and the earsplitting boom of a shot were simultaneous. The bandit chief kicked backward from the tunnel floor, as though he were trying to put as much distance between him and the blaster that had magically appeared in the outlander's hand as he could.

He fell into the cook fire, bits of white-gray matter spraying from the cavity in the rear of his skull. A mist of blood surrounded his head like a halo. The revolver clattered end over end across the rocky ground.

Before the four Tibetans recovered from the shock of seeing their leader fall into the fire—taking their meal with him—Kane had them covered with his Sin Eater. A faint twist of smoke curled up from the barrel.

"Tell them to drop their weapons," Kane said flatly.

Before Brigid repeated the command in their language, the bandits hurled their matchlocks to the cavern floor and dropped to their knees, babbling in sheer terror.

A mirthless smile lifted the corner of Brigid's mouth. "They think you're a Dré, a demon, a messenger of death come to test them in the form of a man."

Kane looked at the men trembling in paroxysms of fear and went frosty with disgust. "Give them this message—have them put out their chief and step aside for us.''

Brigid interpreted, and two men, averting their faces from Kane, tugged the corpse off the fire and smothered the flames dancing along his ragged clothes. They dragged their chief to one side of the tunnel and clustered around him, trembling and moaning.

Turning in her saddle, Brigid called Trai's name. After a few moments, she rode around the shoulder of rock, leading the ponies. She joined them in the cave, eyeing the Khampas impassively.

In a stentorian voice, Kane announced, ''Tell them to find another job. They aren't worth shit at this one. Tell them that if they don't, I'll return, and death will once more speak from my sleeve.''

In a cold, hard tone, Brigid translated Kane's command. The bandits ducked their heads repeatedly and murmured, cupping their hands before their faces in a peculiar gesture.

''Do you still feel like taking a rest?'' Kane asked.

Wrinkling her nose at the acrid stench of burned cloth and scorched flesh hanging in the air, she shook her head. ''Not if we have to share this place with them.''

Kane hefted his Sin Eater. ''I can always run them off.''

She shook her head again. ''I've had my quota of violence for the week.''

As the three people rode past the huddled Khampas, Kane heard them whispering three words over and over, in hushed tones of awe, like a mantra.

"What does Tsyanis Khan-po mean?" he asked, stumbling over the pronunciation.

Stolidly, Brigid replied, "The king of fear."

Kane hitched around in his saddle to stare at her in surprise. "The king of fear?" he echoed. "Isn't that what Zakat was called hereabouts?"

Casting a backward glance toward the four Tibetans, Brigid replied, "It was. They just bestowed the crown on someone more deserving. The king is dead. Long live the king. You're earning quite the reputation in the far corners of the world."

Kane wasn't sure how to take her comment, so he said nothing more.

Chapter 4

Lakesh returned the red-eyed glare of the three-headed hound and said softly, "'Hence loathed Melancholy of Cerberus and blackest Midnight born, In Stygian cave forlorn, most horrid shapes and shrieks and sights unholy.'"

He looked reproachfully over the rims of his spectacles at the illustration of the slavering black hound painted on the wall. Three snarling heads grew out of a single corded neck, their jaws wide open, blood and fire gushing between great fangs. Beneath the image, written in exaggerated, Gothic script was a single word: Cerberus.

Before reaching for the control lever, he murmured, "I must say you've done a piss-poor job of guarding the gates of this particular Stygian cave."

His reedy voice sounded strangely hushed in the high-ceilinged, vanadium-walled corridor. Grasping the lever, he pulled it to a midpoint position. With a rumble and whine of buried hydraulics and gears, the massive sec door began folding aside, opening like an accordion. It was so heavy, it took nearly half a minute for it to open just enough to allow him to step out onto the mountain plateau that housed the Cerberus complex.

The early-morning sun flooded the broad plateau

with a golden radiance, striking highlights from the scraps of the chain link enclosing the perimeter. The air smelled fresh, rich with the hint of spring growth wafting up from the foothills far below. He inhaled it gratefully.

A wizened apparition of a man, Mohandus Lakesh Singh looked very old, but nowhere near his true chronological age of 250 years. He had spent a century and a half of those years in cryogenic stasis and, after his resurrection fifty years earlier, he had undergone several operations to further prolong his life. His malfunctioning heart had been traded for a healthy one, his glaucoma-afflicted brown eyes exchanged for bright, albeit myopic blue ones, his weak lungs changed out for a strong new pair.

Calcified arthritic joints in his shoulders and legs were removed and built with ones made of polyethylene. None of the reconstructive surgeries or physiological enhancements had been performed out of Samaritan impulses. His life and health had been prolonged so he could serve the Program of Unification and the baronies.

From a technical, strictly moral point of view, Lakesh had betrayed both, but he found no true sin in betraying betrayers or stealing from thieves. He could not think of the hybrid barons in any other way, despite their own preference for the term ''new human.''

New perhaps they were, but whether they deserved the appellation of human was still open to debate. However, if their numbers continued to grow, his own personal definition of humanity would vanish and the self-proclaimed new humanity would take its place.

Lakesh stepped farther onto the tarmac, forcing himself to inhale the fresh, unrecycled air. He had spent most of his adult life cloistered in installations like the Cerberus redoubt, and he couldn't help but sourly note the irony that it was only after the Earth had become a nuke-blasted shockscape had he come to appreciate the small things about it.

Still, he retained a certain fondness for the Cerberus facility, good old Redoubt Bravo. Built in the mid-1990s, no expense had been spared to make the seat of Project Cerberus a masterpiece of concealed impenetrability. The thirty acre, three-level facility had come through the nukecaust with its operating systems and radiation shielding in good condition. When Lakesh had reactivated the installation some thirty years before, the repairs he made had been minor, primarily cosmetic in nature. Over a period of time, he had added an elaborate system of heat-sensing warning devices, night-vision vid cameras and motion-trigger alarms to the plateau surrounding it. He had been forced to work in secret and completely alone, so the upgrades had taken several years to complete.

The redoubt had housed Project Cerberus, a subdivision of Overproject Whisper, which in turn had been a primary component of the Totality Concept. At its height, this redoubt had housed well over a hundred people, all devoted to manufacturing the Cerberus gateway units in modular form. Now it was full of shadowed corridors, empty rooms and sepulchral silences, a sanctuary for thirteen human beings. It was possible that the handful of people who lived in the installation would be the last of their kind.

Lakesh had tried many times since his resurrection to arrest the tide of extinction inexorably engulfing the human race. First had been his attempts to manipulate the human genetic samples in storage, preserved in vitro since before the nukecaust to provide the hybridization program with a supply of the best DNA. He had hoped to create an underground resistance movement of superior human beings to oppose the barons and their hidden masters, the Archon Directorate. His only success had been Kane, and even that was arguable.

Still later, upon discovering the journal of Dr. Mildred Wyeth on a computer disk, Lakesh had seen to its dissemination throughout the Historical Divisions of the villes. At the same time, he wove the myth of the Preservationist menace, presenting a false trail made by a nonexistent enemy for the barons to pursue and fear. He created the Preservationists to be straw adversaries, allegedly an underground resistance movement that was pledged to deliver the hidden history of the world to a humanity in bondage.

Not that there weren't postskydark precedents for groups like the Preservationists. A century or more before, a loosely knit organization called the Heimdall Foundation had been formed to keep alive the science of astronomy and astrophysics.

And there was Ireland's Priory of Awen, whose origins could be traced back over a thousand years, to its reputed founding by Saint Patrick.

Other, smaller enclaves dedicated to various pre-dark sciences had existed in the century following the nukecaust, but Lakesh was fairly certain few of them survived the purges of the unification program. Of course, there was no way to be sure.

When it got right down to it, Lakesh wasn't certain of much of anything anymore, even of the human race's survival for another generation.

Over the past few months, Lakesh had embarked on the most audacious and desperate plan in a double lifetime filled with scheming. He had constructed a small device on the same scientific principle as the mat-trans inducers, an interphaser designed to interphase with naturally occurring quantum vortices. Theoretically, the interphaser opened dimensional rifts much like the gateways, but instead of the rifts being pathways through linear space, Lakesh had envisioned them as a method to travel through the gaps in normal space-time.

He had hoped to open a rift that intersected with the home dimension of the Archon Directorate, if indeed the entities were pandimensional rather than extraterrestrial. The interphaser had not functioned according to its design, and due to interference caused by Lord Strongbow's similar device, the so-called Singularity, its dilated temporal energy had sent Kane, Brigid, Domi and Grant on a short, disembodied trip into the past.

Although the interphaser had been lost, its memory disk had been retrieved, and using the data recorded on it, Lakesh had tried to duplicate the dilation effect by turning the Cerberus mat-trans unit into a time machine.

Such efforts were not new. A major subdivision of the Totality Concept had been devoted to manipulating the nature of time. Operation Chronos was built on the breakthroughs of Project Cerberus, but it had not been as successful.

The Operation Chronos scientists employed a practice they termed "trawling," focusing on subjects in the past and pulling them forward to the twentieth century. Although not directly connected with the time-travel experiments, Lakesh had heard rumors of their many attempts and failures.

Without access to the specs and data of Operation Chronos, Lakesh could not duplicate what they had done, so he determined to circumvent it. He saw to the creation of the Omega Path program and linked it with the mat-trans gateway.

The concept was sound—to dispatch Kane and Brigid back through time to a point only a month before the nukecaust so they could hopefully trigger an alternate event horizon and thus avert the apocalypse.

The Omega Path had worked, at least insofar as translating them into a past temporal plane, but they came to learn it was not their world's past, but another's, almost identical to it. Any actions they undertook had no bearing on their world's present and future.

Lakesh could only engage in fairly futile speculation on what had happened, and on the system of physics at work. Operation Chronos had functioned on the "chronon" theory, that time was not continuous but made up of subatomic particles jammed together like beads on a string. According to the theory, between each bead, each individual unit of time might exist in an infinite series of parallel universes, fitted into the probability gaps between the chronons.

The man—or creature—calling himself Colonel Thrush had said as much to Kane and Brigid when they encountered him on New Year's Eve, 2000. He had also hinted that versions of himself existed in every one of the infinite number of probability gaps to prevent what the Omega Path program had been created to do—to bring about alternate event horizons and divert the stream of time.

After that failure, Lakesh had essentially given up hope, though he masked his despair behind a cheery, "try-try-again" facade. Then Balam, the redoubt's Archon prisoner for the past three years, had suggested another way, and it took the form of an inestimably ancient black stone.

At the sound of a steady thump, alternating with a dragging scrape from behind him, Lakesh turned and saw without much surprise, that Grant was making his laborious way down the corridor. From instep to just below his knee, a fiberglass cast encased his right leg. Domi followed close behind him, holding a pair of crutches. Grant was a big man, well over six feet tall, while Domi barely topped five. The crutches were almost the length of her entire body.

Grant's dark brown, heavy-jawed face was knitted in a fierce scowl. Black stitches were barely detectable beneath his downsweeping mustache at the corner of his mouth. He winced with each step he took. The tibia and talus bones of his leg had been fractured less than five days before. He was also suffering from strained ligaments, abrasions and internal bruising. The injuries had been inflicted by, of all things, the preserved carcass of a blue whale.

As far as Lakesh knew, DeFore, the resident medic, had prescribed a full week of laying flat on his back for Grant. But then, almost none of the redoubt's personnel obeyed DeFore's medical edicts, including himself.

"Friend Grant, darlingest Domi," Lakesh said as they stepped out of the doorway onto the plateau. "Nice day for a stroll, isn't it?"

Grant snorted and waved away the crutches Domi offered him, leaning against the sec door to take the weight off his injured leg. Domi slitted her ruby red eyes in irritation and allowed the crutches to drop, clattering loudly, to the tarmac.

"Not your body slave," she said doggedly. "You want 'em, you pick 'em up."

Grant began a stern rebuke, but when he saw the genuine anger flaring redly in her eyes, he turned it into a grunted, "Sorry."

The small albino girl nodded shortly. Domi was a curvaceous white wraith, her flesh the color of a beautiful pearl and her ragged mop of hair the hue of bone. Though petite to the point of being childlike, she was exquisitely formed.

Due to that exquisite form and her unearthly beauty, she had been trapped in sexual servitude by Guana Teague, the former boss of the Cobaltville pits. Memories of those six degrading months floated very near to the surface of her mind. She tended to overreact to any situation, no matter how trivial, which reminded her of that time.

She viewed Grant as her savior, her gallant black knight who had rescued her from the depraved lusts of the man-mountain, but in point of fact, the reverse was true. Of course, if Teague hadn't been preoccupied with crushing the life out of Grant, Domi would have never been able to get the drop on him and cut his throat. She kept the knife that had done the deed as her most treasured momento.

"It's been three days," Grant said in his lionlike rumble. "Bry told me last night that there was still no signal from the transponders."

The subcutaneous biolink transponders were nonharmful radioactive chemicals that bound themselves to the glucose in the blood and a middle layer of epidermis. Based on organic nanotechnology, the transponders transmitted heart rate, brain-wave patterns, respiration and blood count. The signal was relayed by a Comsat satellite uplinked to the Cerberus redoubt. Every member of the installation had been injected with them.

Although Grant spoke matter-of-factly, as if Brigid and Kane were only acquaintances, Lakesh knew it was his coldly professional, hard-contact Mag persona speaking.

Lakesh smiled encouragingly. "You should've checked with him this morning, as I did. Their transponders began transmitting again a few hours ago."

Grant didn't sigh in relief, but the broad yoke of

his shoulders sagged just a bit. "What accounted for the interruption in the signal?"

Lakesh shrugged. "Any number of things. Severe weather fronts or perhaps they were in an area that blocked transmission. At any rate, they're back online, though the vital signs monitor receives occasional spikes, as if they're exerting themselves."

He paused, eyed the position of the sun and added, "There's a ten-hour time difference between here and Tibet. Presuming they're undertaking an overland journey, I wouldn't expect them back for some little while yet."

Grant nodded, making no reply, but Lakesh could guess at the kind of emotions racing through him. Grant and Kane, although they had served for many years as highly decorated Magistrates in Cobaltville, had been anomalies in the ranks of ville enforcers. Teamwork, acting as cogs in wheels was encouraged, but true friendship between Mags was frowned upon. Devotion to duty, to serving the baron was paramount. Kane and Grant had broken this cardinal rule. Grant in particular had sacrificed everything that had given his life purpose in order to save his partner and, more importantly, his friend.

Although he would never voice it, Grant felt terrible not being on hand to assist Kane and Brigid with whatever difficulties they might be undergoing. Still, he was levelheaded enough to realize that there were very few situations Kane wasn't equipped to handle.

Pushing himself away from the sec door, Grant

asked, "Do you think Balam is coming back with them?"

Lakesh frowned slightly. He thoughtfully tugged at his nose before saying, "I wish I knew. All things considered, I would have to say no. As Kane himself pointed out, Balam no longer served a purpose here, either as a hostage or a source of information."

"It's because Kane pointed that out is why I'm mentioning it."

It took a moment for the implications of Grant's comment to sink in. Swiftly, he brought his head up, eyes wide in sudden alarm. "You're not suggesting that Kane might kill him, are you?"

"That possibility occurred to me," Grant admitted. "Kane can be a hard man, as you know."

Lakesh forced an uneasy chuckle, acknowledging that Grant wasn't telling him anything new. "I guess we won't know about Balam until Kane returns."

Grant nodded. "What about the agreement with Sky Dog? We ought to be putting together a tech team to send to his village."

Lakesh frowned in annoyance at the unwelcome reminder of the pact Kane had struck with the band of Sioux and Cheyenne. Only ten days before, Grant, Brigid and Kane had established diplomatic contact with the redoubt's nearest neighbors, a group of Amerindians living on the flatlands beyond the foothills. A great deal of hostility and suspicion had to be overcome, since in the years after the nukecaust, the native tribes had reasserted their ancient claims over lands stolen from them by the predark government and returned to their ancestral way of life.

After Kane had gained a fragile trust, their shaman, a Cobaltville-bred Lakota by the name of Sky Dog, showed them the reason why he and his people had settled in the area. Nearly a hundred years before, Indian warriors had come into possession of a predark mobile army command post—refurbished and reengineered into an armored war wag.

Sky Dog was perceptive enough to realize that the wasicun living in the superstition-haunted Darks were hiding from the forces of the villes. He proposed that if the war wag was made functional again, his people would be the first line of defense against an assault that might be mounted against the installation.

Kane accepted the proposal unilaterally, on his own initiative without consulting Lakesh or anyone else. Lakesh couldn't deny Kane's decision was logical, but he was still peeved he hadn't been allowed any input.

"I think," Lakesh replied after a moment of deliberation, "it would be best if we wait until dearest Brigid and friend Kane return. He seems to have set himself up as our informal ambassador to the indigenous tribes."

Grant suppressed a smile at Lakesh's unsuccessful attempt to hide his annoyance. "Whatever you say."

Bending, he picked up the crutches, tucked them under his arm and limped back inside the redoubt.

Chapter 5

Despite the cast on his leg, Grant's stride was still long, and Domi had to take two steps to his one to keep up with him. In a low, grumbling tone, Grant said, "I'm sorry about that back there. I wasn't thinking."

She flashed him an impudent grin. "I'm used to you not thinking."

As they reached the T junction in the corridor, they saw Beth-Li Rouch approaching from the opposite direction. The slender young woman's gait was determined, and her lovely Asian features set in a grim mask. Grant instantly sensed Domi stiffening beside him. The two women were similar as to height and build, but the resemblance ended there. Rouch's mouth was wide and sensuous, her skin the color of ivory and her almond-shaped eyes very dark. Shiny, raven's-wing black hair fell nearly to her waist.

She glanced at Domi, but said nothing to her, fixing her intense gaze on Grant. "I'm looking for Lakesh."

Grant bristled at her autocratic, imperious tone, but he managed to keep his anger from showing on his face. Hooking a thumb over his shoulder, he replied evenly, "Back there, taking the air."

Without a word of thanks or a nod of acknowledgment, Rouch stepped around them and stalked purposefully down the wide, vanadium-sheathed corridor, hips swinging arrogantly.

"Bitch," Domi growled.

Grant knew Domi didn't like Beth-Li Rouch for several reasons. First and foremost, Rouch could barely disguise her contempt for the half-feral albino girl from the Outlands. Second, Domi considered Brigid Baptiste her friend, and she viewed Rouch as her friend's enemy. By her simple outlander logic, Rouch was therefore her enemy, too.

Grant bore the young woman no particular dislike, since the reason for all the enmity was pretty much Lakesh's fault. Rouch was the newest arrival among the exiles in Cerberus, only three or so months out of Sharpeville.

Lakesh had arranged for her exile to fulfill a specific function among the men in Cerberus, but he had made it quite clear that Kane was the primary focus of his—and Rouch's—project to expand the little colony. Kane had refused to cooperate, and that refusal had triggered all sorts of tension and wounded feelings.

Grant began walking again, feeling a hot, throbbing ache spreading up from his injured leg. He had disobeyed DeFore's orders about staying off it for a week, and he was loath to stop by the dispensary and ask her for a pain reliever. She'd give it to him certainly, but a tedious lecture would go along with it.

Ever sensitive to his moods, Domi asked, "You hurting again?"

He forced a smile, despite the twinge of pain when the stitches stretched. "It's tolerable."

"You say that about everything," she retorted with a grin. "You could be up to your ass in shit and all you'd say is, 'It's tolerable.'"

Taking him by the arm, the girl steered him down the corridor to her quarters. Grant resisted for a moment, but figured Domi wouldn't renew her attempts at outright seduction when he was at less than peak physical condition.

Despite her many invitations, Grant had never visited Domi's living quarters before. He had vaguely pictured them as a pigsty because of her impulsive, undisciplined nature. He was pleasantly surprised when she opened the door and ushered him in. The two-room suite was tidy, the bed made and the floor clean. A spray of wildflowers added color and scent to the Spartan furnishings.

Grant sat in the nearest chair, and Domi pulled over a stool from the dressing table, placing a pillow on it so he could prop up his leg. She seemed very happy he was there, so she could look after him, and Grant felt a pang of regret over his decision to keep the relationship platonic. It wasn't the first time he had felt such pangs.

Domi was younger than he, but he had no idea how much and neither did she. The girl could be as young as sixteen or as old as twenty-six, but he knew making the ambiguous difference in their ages an issue was simply an excuse, and a feeble one at that.

The real reason was he could not look at Domi's white skin and crimson eyes without the image of

Olivia's café au lait face, deep brown eyes and black hair superimposing itself over the girl's features.

There had been women since Olivia, but no real passion and certainly no love. As a Magistrate, whenever he felt the need for sexual release all he had to do was make a trans-comm call and a woman would be sent up to him. In the four years since he had lost Olivia, he never spoke of her and did his best not to think of her. He had deliberately frozen the softer emotions within him.

Domi was a painful reminder of those emotions, although she was as different from Olivia physically and temperamentally as it was possible for a woman to be. An uninhibited, loving animal with no shame about her desires, Domi still resisted invitations from the other men in the redoubt. She wanted only him.

Grant sat silently as Domi bustled around him, chattering gaily about nothing in particular. Despite himself, Grant found her monologue soothing and for the first time in days, he felt himself beginning to relax. Still, he couldn't help but notice how the points of her small, pert breasts showed through the tight bodice of her bodysuit.

Domi stood behind him and her fragile-looking fingers kneaded the muscles at the base of his neck with surprising strength. He began to voice an objection, then decided there was no reason. He would hurt the girl's feelings again, and there had been enough of that, not just today but over the past eight months.

"Don't be so tense," she said quietly, and he felt the soft brush of her breath against his right ear. "Try to relax for once. I won't bite you."

Grant did as she said, leaning back into her strong, massaging hands. Domi bent forward, pressing her smooth, satiny cheek against his.

"Better?" she whispered. Her breath, either from exertion or arousal came in soft pants.

Slowly, Grant turned his face toward hers. Her eyes were fierce crimson slits. He said quietly, "It's tolerable."

Her lips met his, careful to avoid the laceration. Her tongue stretched out, exploring gently.

Bry's voice rasped over the public-address transcomm. "Lakesh, we're registering activity on the mat-trans net. It's the signal you've been waiting for."

LAKESH SHOOK HIS HEAD in dogged determination. "I'm afraid that's impossible. Quite, quite impossible."

Beth-Li planted her fists on her flaring hips and tilted her head at a defiantly inquisitive angle. "Why? You smuggled me out of Sharpeville. It shouldn't be any more difficult to smuggle me back in."

"The logistics are different now," Lakesh replied reasonably. "Due to Baron Sharpe being seriously wounded, coupled with Baron Ragnar's assassination, all the villes are on high alert. The administrators are exceptionally paranoid and will continue to be. Your mysterious reappearance after such a long absence would make you the focal point of an intense—and very unpleasant—investigation."

The breeze gusting over the plateau caught Beth-Li's hair, and it streamed behind her like an ebony banner. Coldly, she stated, "There's no reason for me to be here any longer. Your breeding program failed. You might as well accept it. I have."

Lakesh shifted his feet uncomfortably and averted his eyes from the woman's penetrating gaze. His plan to improve the breed and turn Cerberus into a colony had met unexpectedly stiff resistance from Kane. He viewed it as continuation of sinister elements that had brought about the nukecaust and the tyranny of the villes.

The Totality Concept's Overproject Excalibur dealt with bioengineering and one of its subdivisions, Scenario Joshua, had sprung from the twentieth century's Genome Project. The project's goal was to map human genomes to specific chromosomal functions and locations in order to have on hand in vitro genetic samples of the best of the best, the purest of the pure.

Everyone who enjoyed full ville citizenship were the descendants of the Genome Project. Sometimes a particular gene carrying a desirable trait was grafted to an unrelated egg, or an undesirable gene removed. Despite many failures, when there was a success, it was replicated over and over, occasionally with variations. Lakesh had wanted to insure that Kane's superior qualities were passed on, and mating him with a woman who met the standards of Purity Control was the most logical course of action. Without access to the ectogenesis techniques of fetal development outside the womb, the conventional means of procreation was his only option.

"Just because Kane won't cooperate doesn't mean

it's a failure," he said defensively. "There are other men here."

Beth-Li's lips worked as if she were going to spit at him. "Their genetic profiles are questionable. Only mine and Kane's have a perfect matchup of desirable traits. And if you think I'm going to spend my life being passed around from man to man, popping out their brats every year, you're completely fused out."

Lakesh tried to dredge up anger at the young woman's defiance, but he could feel only a weary resignation, a tired acceptance that yet another one of his plans had failed miserably.

"I can't send you back," he declared firmly. "You were told at the time your exile was permanent."

She gestured in the general direction of Cobaltville. "Then send me to another ville."

"That's no solution. In fact it would be worse than if you showed back up in Sharpeville."

"Do you think I'd betray you, talk about this place?"

Choosing his words carefully, Lakesh replied, "I think you might be compelled to talk. I've experienced firsthand the methods Magistrates use to wring information out of prisoners."

"And what am I here but a prisoner?" Beth-Li demanded angrily.

"I know. And I am sorry. I'll shoulder all the blame as long as you don't direct it at Kane and Brigid."

The remark had the opposite effect than Lakesh intended. The spark of anger in her dark eyes became a bright flame of fury. In a low, venomous tone, she said, "You promised me that Baptiste would stand aside and leave my way to Kane open. You lied."

"I didn't lie." Lakesh dropped his voice to a whisper, looking around guilty before saying, "I underestimated the strength of their bond. I spoke to her and she agreed. I went along with your plan to test his feelings for you. It might have worked."

A short time before, Beth-Li had proposed a scheme to put herself in jeopardy in order to prove Kane's feelings for her. Lakesh hadn't cared for it, since it involved duping Auerbach, another exile. His approval of the plan had been grudging.

"Yes," she said bitterly. "It might have worked if Baptiste hadn't been along."

Lakesh sighed, shaking his head dolefully. "You know I couldn't object to her participation in the search-and-rescue mission for you without arousing suspicion."

"You could have stopped her, told her what was going on."

"And that would have aroused Kane's suspicions. He still doesn't trust me. It was a childish plan anyway, doomed to failure. Perhaps something could have been salvaged if you hadn't made the capital mistake of threatening Brigid."

"And Kane threatened to chill *me!*" Her voice rose to a high pitch of humiliation mixed with rage. "Me! That son of a bitch treated me like a gaudy slut he found in some pesthole!"

Lakesh cut her off with a sharp gesture of one hand. "It's my fault. I didn't understand the depth of his feelings for Brigid, and frankly I still don't."

Beth-Li inhaled a deep breath through her nostrils, trying to calm herself. "They don't act like they're in love, and when they're together here in the redoubt they don't even eat dinner together, much less fuck."

Lakesh winced at the woman's choice of words. Intellectually, he realized the term had lost its obscene connotations two centuries earlier, but as a man raised to be an academic, he still found it offensive.

Still, he sympathized with Beth-Li's confusion over the relationship between Brigid Baptiste and Kane. He didn't understand the bond they shared, so different than the one Kane had with Grant but seemingly stronger.

Beth-Li's observation was true. In between missions, Kane and Brigid spent very little time together, and it wasn't surprising, since they were so different as to personalities. Brigid was cool, analytical as a former archivist should be. Kane, on the other hand, was so high-strung and unpredictable as to be unstable. Lakesh had wondered more than once if Kane unconsciously relied on Brigid to keep him sane and she, just as unconsciously, relied on him to keep her human.

His own relationship with Kane stretched back decades, to the man's grandfather. His involvement with Brigid Baptiste's forebears didn't go back quite as far, but it was far more personal and intimate. Lakesh had gone to great lengths to conceal that involvement.

"There's no way I can stay here with Baptiste laughing at me, thinking she beat me," Beth-Li continued.

"This wasn't a competition," Lakesh said, forcing a solicitude into his voice that he didn't feel. "I miscalculated and you paid the price. I'll try to make it up to you."

Beth-Li narrowed her eyes. "It *is* a competition, even if you don't see it. If I stay, the competition won't be over. And in every competition there has to be a winner and a loser. "

She paused and added in a flinty voice, "I don't like to lose, Lakesh. Think about it."

She wheeled and stalked back into the redoubt. Alarmed, Lakesh followed her. Then Bry's voice blared over the trans-comm wall unit, "Lakesh, we're registering activity on the mat-trans net. It's the signal you've been waiting for."

Chapter 6

Black space peeled back on itself as great blossoming explosions of color poured through from behind it. Faintly at first, as through rolling multicolored clouds, shapes began to materialize, sliding into sharp focus.

Kane's ears were struck by a distant blast of sound, and the clouds seemed to burst into flame, as if a thunderstorm of unparalleled fury had swallowed him, shredding him molecule by molecule. Then came a wave of dazzling white flares and variegated lightnings that streaked and blazed.

A monster-shape hove out of the glare. With a long, pointed steel prow, a tapering stern and roaring funnels belching smoke and sparks, it had the shape of a warship. A half dozen treaded tracks, each ten feet long, were arranged along the sides of the huge machine, bearing it forward in a series of clanking lurches. The grinding rumble was as of a hundred locomotives.

Kane watched it, straining and grappling with invisible chains enwrapping his memory. Finally, a link snapped, and he remembered dimly arriving back at the Trasilunpo monastery on the Byang-Thang plateau an hour after sunset.

He recalled how he and Brigid had made straightway for the gateway unit in the subterranean vault. Brigid entered the destination code for Cerberus and he closed the door, which initiated the automatic jump mechanism.

He knew he should be opening his eyes and seeing the brown-tinted armaglass of the mat-trans chamber in Cerberus, in Montana—not on a scene wrested from a nightmare.

The war wag rumbled forward over rocky ground, dark tubes curving from its rivet-studded hull shooting out flashes of red and white lightning. The treads plowed up the soil, beating it into ridges and furrows like the waves of a stormy sea. A mountain thrust up from the near horizon, and by a burst of dazzling light Kane saw a grouping of carved faces staring out from the high granite cliffside.

He was surprised when he recognized the five colossal stone effigies that represented the greatest leaders in American history—Washington, Lincoln, Jefferson, Roosevelt and Hitler.

Hell-hued blossoms bloomed from spots all over the vehicle's dark bulk. Mortar rounds burst from ports in the war wag's hull and exploded among the rebels on the rocky slopes. Brutal detonation after detonation bloomed in a line, ripping open the stony soil, flinging maimed bodies through the air like disjointed puppets.

People fled wildly from the advance of the huge machine, scattering in panicky flight in all directions. A crooked finger of lightning flicked from a tube, caressing the running men and women. They screamed in agony, engulfed by licking flames, their hair igniting into coronas of fire.

The dark leviathan shuddered to a clattering halt, and a vent in its undercarriage released a hissing cloud of vapor. Out of the billowing mist, down a ramp, plunged a horde of armed and armored figures, all black clad from crown to heel. They wore tight black breeches and high black boots, and ebony uniform jackets with silver piping tight to the chest and shoulders. Broad belts held half a dozen objects sheathed in pouches. Bulky black breastplates enclosed their upper torsos.

One of them held a banner aloft with a black design emblazoned on a bloodred background. Kane recognized the symbol—a thick-walled pyramid, enclosing and partially bisected by three elongated but reversed triangles. Small disks topped each one, lending them a resemblance to round-hilted daggers.

A black-uniformed man shouted commands that were drowned out by the hissing of the vent and the mechanical roar. Though his features were partially obscured by a coal-scuttle helmet, Kane glimpsed a flat, sallow face that was almost round and a pair of mud-colored eyes. It was Salvo, his former commanding officer in the Cobaltville Magistrate Division, his genetic twin and a man who had lived only to hate him.

Another uniformed man stepped from the steam and joined Salvo. Kane recognized him, too. It was himself, standing shoulder to shoulder with a man he himself had chilled months before.

He suddenly had the sensation of plummeting forward in a wild flight, heading directly for himself. Kane felt a brief struggle as the ego, the essence of the other Kane melded within his own.

Then he sniffed the hot, electric smell sizzling in the smoky air and his stomach lurched at the thick stench of roasting human meat.

The troop of soldiers marched forward. All of them had paper-pale faces and eyes that were larger than normal. Their builds were slender and graceful, and they moved with danceresque, mincing steps.

Men appeared, climbing over the rocks a hundred yards distant, leaping from them, scrambling in a terrified retreat. Machine guns opened up, the bullets crashing against the rocks, the stream of autofire tearing them to blood-streaked ribbons.

"Cease firing," Salvo shouted into his helmet comm-link. "It's over."

A man staggered up from a declivity near one of the war wag's treads, thin trails of smoke streaming from his hair. He started to run, stumbled, fell, dragged himself to his feet, took a step, then fell again. This time, he did not get up.

He raised a raw, blackened travesty of a face. His blistered, leaking lips writhed and he croaked, "I surrender. Help me."

Salvo fired from the hip, a short burst from the subgun slung over his shoulder. The man's burned features dissolved in a wet, red spray. The bullets knocked him backward into a tread-dug ditch.

Salvo chuckled. "So the rebellion ends with a whine for mercy, not a bang." He threw a grin at

Kane. "A little anticlimactic, isn't it, Brother? Move in."

"Those aren't Field Marshal Thrush's orders," Kane replied. "He told us to set up a perimeter around the Rushmore zone, to keep the Roamers from escaping—"

Salvo cut him off with a sharp, savage gesture. "Do it. I'm in command here. You take point."

Kane moved forward, using hand signals to tell the troopers to fall in behind him. He strode quickly over the rocky ground, and it wasn't until he had crossed ten yards when he noticed the soldiers had hung back. He turned around, opening his mouth to shout an order.

A small, round object arced overhead, dropping between Kane and the troopers. A flash of fire and the shock of a concussion slammed into Kane with the force of a giant sledgehammer and bowled him away into blackness.

THE GRENADE DETONATED on the first-floor landing. The concussive wave crashed down the steps and lighted the marble-floored foyer with a bright orange flash. Kane felt the shock and the heat on the back of his head.

The rest of the interdiction team had taken up positions around the embassy reception hall, deploying like well-oiled parts of a machine, subguns leveled to cover every possible avenue of either escape or opposition.

Kane looked up the stairway, noting that the four members of the embassy's security detail had been incapacitated by the stun grenade. His helmet comm-link buzzed, and Grant's voice filtered into his ear. "The west wing is secure. Nobody's here but a couple of hybrid grunts. The diplomatic staff must have been evacuated."

"Resistance?"

"A little. Some of those bastards are armed with infrasound wands."

"What about the ambassador?"

"No sign of Thrush at all. He might have been tipped off."

Kane grunted, not wanting to contemplate the possibility. "Stand by."

He ran up the stairs, keeping close to the curving, elaborate balustrade, taking three steps at a time, holding his Spectre autoblaster in a two-handed grip. The corridor was filled with astringent smoke. Through its shifting planes, he glimpsed four figures stirring feebly on the floor, their white faces streaked red from the blood oozing from hemorrhaged eardrums.

Kane stepped carefully around them, turning right, beneath an arch into a long, carpeted hallway. Almost at once, a door opened at the far end of the hall, and a hybrid was framed there, with a fragile-looking infrasound wand in his hand. It flicked toward him, the three-foot silver length shivering and humming.

Kane threw himself against the wall, raising his side arm. Even with the special shielding inside his helmet, he wasn't sure he could take a direct hit, so he fired once. The ultrasonic burst swept high, a barely detectable blur peeling long splinters from the wall above his head. The round from the Spectre caught the hybrid in the chest, hurling him backward amid a flailing of arms and a kicking of legs. The wand clattered to the floor.

"So much for diplomatic immunity," Kane muttered beneath his breath.

He carefully moved down the hallway and paused by a window. He peered out past the broken glass. The grounds of the Archon embassy were filled with running, falling and shooting figures. Smoke boiled from a corner of the building, and flames licked out of a ground-floor window. An armored car trundled through the wreck of the wrought-iron gate, spouting 30 mm shells in a jackhammer rhythm. A recoilless rifle thumped several times, and sparks danced from the heavy metal hull of the car as the rounds ricocheted away.

He saw a Cerberus specialist surrounded by a pack of hybrids, their infrasound wands humming and popping viciously. The ultrasonic waves pulverized the man's joints and crushed the bones in his face. He opened his mouth to scream, and his teeth blew out of his mouth in a cloud of splinters.

Kane put his blaster out of the window and depressed the trigger, firing a long, full-auto burst. Hybrids squealed as the high-velocity rounds struck them, knocking them down like puppets.

An explosion filled the hallway with rolling, thunderous echoes. A sheet of flame erupted, and the concussive roar broke the world behind him.

THE LIGHTS on the control deck flickered in a strobing pattern. A blinding flare of crimson-and-white light burst from the main monitor screen. The *Sabre* shuddered brutally as the artificial gravity and inertia-dampers fluctuated. Rubbing the flash-induced spots from his eyes, Kane shouted, "Status!"

It was as Baptiste had warned—if it was a Dreadnaught they were tracking, a GRASER blast would result in negative engine control, jammed communications frequencies, shields and sensors operative only on a nominal level.

The *Sabre* was a cruiser, Rapier Class, larger and more formidable than ships used for system patrol duty. But the craft and its crew had a dual mission, and the high command of the Sol 9 Commonwealth wasn't exactly sure what they might encounter. First and foremost, she was supposed to get information back to the Ranger Division on the *Parallax Red* station. But if the *Sabre* encountered hostile Directorate vessels, the standing orders were to attack, then run.

Kane had ordered a brace of Shrikes fired at a distant sensor hit, beyond the range of the visual scanners. Less than a minute later, the fire had been returned—by a gamma-powered laser projector.

The *Sabre* rocked again. Kane had to grab the comm-console to keep from staggering into Grant at the helm board. "Tactical. Give me a 360 view. Adjust for the flux. Thrusters at station-keeping until we establish another target lock. "

"A moot point, Commander," Baptiste said. "I believe our target has found us."

On the screen, outlined by regularly placed running lights, a massive, ominous shape slid into view, blackly outlined by the distant red light of Mars. The weapons emplacements bristling the huge, disk-shaped craft were clearly visible.

"Grant!" Kane yelled. "Hard to port. Evasive maneuvers, thrusters at maximum!"

Grant's hands never reached the controls. A streak of hell-hued light erupted from the Dreadnaught and impacted blindingly on the *Sabre*'s aft deflectors. The deck jumped underfoot. Kane's comm-console squirted a shower of sparks, and the *Sabre* lurched ten degrees on her starboard side. All lights flickered, came up, flickered again and finally flashed on dimly.

In the semidarkness, Kane struggled to find and punch the comm-link button. "Bry, engine status."

"Checking," came the strained reply.

"Our aft shield generators are down," Baptiste said. "Enough of the GRASER beam leaked through to make glancing contact with the hull."

"Weapons status."

"Shrike pods unaffected and operable," Domi said from the fire-control panel.

"Bry, bleed some power from our fore shield generators to cover our ass," Kane ordered.

"There's no point in that," Baptiste said. "At full strength, our screens were easily pierced. A weakened deflector won't resist a second GRASER shot of the same intensity."

Kane gritted his teeth. From engineering, Bry said, "That shot made confetti out of the thrusters. We're not going anywhere for a while."

"Do we still have maneuvering ability?" Kane asked.

"The wing gyros are still operative," Grant answered, "but without the main thrusters, we'll just wallow like Venusian Doughpots."

"Deploy them anyway. Give me a controlled burn."

Grant's fingers touched a series of buttons. A moment later, ribbed wings of alloy unfolded on either side of the craft. They were designed to allow the *Sabre* to make an atmosphere entry like a jet plane, not be used for deep-space maneuvering. The small rocket tubes tipping the wings spit narrow tongues of blue flame, and the cruiser slowly rotated.

Cold fingers of terror knotting the inside his chest, Kane looked at the screen. The Dreadnaught hung on it, like a vulture poised over a dying victim. He found himself laboring for breath and realized the oxygen recyclers were at half-power. "Divert our remaining power to the environmental systems," he said to Baptiste.

The Dreadnought slid closer, halting at one kilometer from the *Sabre*'s port bow. Its dark bulk completely filled the monitor screen. On the hull, a running light haloed an inverted triangle containing the stylized silhouette of a bird of prey, crested head thrown back, beak open, claws outspread, wings lifted wide. Kane clamped his teeth on a groan of despair. The Dreadnought was the personal warship of Colonel Thrush.

The *Sabre* was a good ship. Nothing in the system was any faster or more maneuverable. But the Directorate's Dreadnoughts had all the other pluses—their defensive screens were more sophisticated and their gamma-powered lasers could slice through a meteorite like cardboard.

"If only we could get off one missile," Kane muttered.

"Pointless," Baptiste replied. "The Dreadnought's pulse shields would detonate it before it reached its target."

An aperture on the Dreadnought irised open. A coruscating rainbow radiance spilled out, seething with energy.

Grant stiffened in his chair. "They've got their molecular destabilizer powered up."

A wavering ribbon of scarlet light whiplashed from the port, and Kane gripped the armrests of his chair tightly. Scarlet light flooded the control deck and an extended thunderclap filled his ears.

THUNDER POUNDED, surrounding the mat-trans chamber with a steady kettledrum beat that could be felt in the bones. Behind the brown-tinted armaglass walls, bursts of light flared and flashed. The characteristic hurricane howl of the gateway cycling through a materialization was drowned out by the hammering.

Lakesh stood in the anteroom doorway at once electrified and petrified by the sights and sounds. Behind him, at the master mat-trans console in the control complex, Bry shouted, "Power fluctuations across the scale!" Circuit switching stations clicked with a castanet-like rhythm

Glancing over his shoulder, Lakesh saw the needle

gauges on the boards ticking back and forth. Lights on all of the readout consoles flashed erratically.

On the far side of the big, vault-walled room, he saw Grant and Domi hurry through the open doorway. Both them looked around anxiously, fearfully at the electronic chaos erupting in the complex. They made their way quickly down the aisle between computer stations and joined Lakesh.

"What the hell's going on?" Grant demanded, squinting against the light strobing within the jump chamber.

"I don't know," Lakesh answered, raising his voice to be heard over the constant, surflike throb. "It began as soon as the autosequence initiator engaged. According to Bry, the phenomenon is similar to what happened when the interphaser was used to transport you back here from England."

Grant wrestled with a sudden surge of unreasoning fear. He remembered all too well the side effect of that particular jump, which shunted all of them, he, Domi, Brigid and Kane, off into the past in the form of disembodied ghosts.

He glanced over his shoulder at the huge Mercator relief map of the world sprawling across the expanse of the facing wall. Pinpoints of light shone steadily in almost every country, connected by a thin glowing pattern of lines. They represented the Cerberus network, the locations of all functioning gateway units across the planet.

"How can that happen again?" Grant half shouted into Lakesh's ear. "This was just a normal gateway transit, right?"

Lakesh didn't answer, keeping his eyes fixed on the six-sided chamber.

"I *hate* these fucking things," Grant growled.

As suddenly as they began, the pulsing of sound and the display of pyrotechnics ended. Everything was calm and quiet again, except for the muffled whining of the materialization cycle beneath the jump platform.

Pushing past Lakesh, Grant crossed the room and reached for the heavy chamber door. He ignored Lakesh's word of warning and heaved up on the handle, pulling the door open on counterbalanced hinges. Smoke and mist swirled within the chamber, so thick he could see nothing.

The mist was a byproduct of the quantum interface, a plasma wave form that only resembled vapor. Usually, it dissipated within seconds of a successful transit, but he had never seen it so heavy before, like an ocean fog trapped within the armaglass walls. Thread-thin static electricity discharges arced within the billowing mass.

Grant hesitated only a moment, then plunged into the clouds, fanning his hand in front of his face. He heard a faint, feminine groan from underfoot, and he bent low, narrowing his eyes. He barely made out the prone figure of Brigid Baptiste, stirring feebly on the hexagonal floor plates.

Crackling light flashed again and he recoiled, but it limned for an instant the figure of Kane—or rather what appeared to be *four* Kanes. He lay sprawled on the platform floor, as motionless as a corpse, his body sheathed in a cocoon of sparkling energy, like a miniature aurora borealis.

Around him floated three hazy, shadowy duplicate Kanes, lying exactly as he did. They flickered like images on a faulty vid tape. Grant was reminded of wavery mirages produced by shimmering heat waves rising from a sunbaked desert.

He stared in shocked denial, knowing his eyes could not possibly be conveying accurate information to his brain. As he stared, the aura faded away completely, and the mist swallowed Kane's body again.

At his feet, Brigid uttered another low groan, then attempted to hike herself up on an elbow. She blinked up at him unfocusedly. In a faint voice she called out, "Kane?"

Grant put a hand under her arm and gently lifted her up. "It's me, Grant. You made it back."

Brigid swayed on rubbery legs. She staggered as Grant led her to the jump-chamber door. Domi and Lakesh moved forward to help her. She looked completely disoriented, her green eyes glazed and blank, skin very pale beneath the scattering of freckles over the bridge of her nose.

"Kane?" she asked again, hoarsely.

"I'll see to him," Grant said, more to Lakesh than to Brigid. "You might want to call DeFore."

Lakesh's eyebrows rose. "Why?"

Grant didn't answer. Grimly, he returned to the cloud-filled chamber. The vapor showed no indication of thinning, which was definitely unprecedented. He made his way to Kane and painfully went to one knee beside him.

He saw only one Kane now. He still wore Grant's Mag-issue, Kevlar-weave coat, and he noticed the bulge of the holstered Sin Eater beneath the right sleeve. But his eyes were closed, his face slack. Grant did not see any signs of respiration.

Shrugging off the tentacles of dread that clutched at his heart, Grant placed a forefinger at the base of Kane's throat to check his pulse.

His finger passed through Kane and touched a metal floor plate.

Chapter 7

Grant's heart gave a wild lurch, and he snatched his hand away with such speed and force he sat down hard. A gasping curse tore from his lips. "What the fuck—"

Lakesh heard him and called out, "Grant! What's happening?"

He was too numb to reply, his vocal cords frozen, his thought processes paralyzed. He realized he gaped goggle-eyed and openmouthed at Kane's body. Conjecture and terror careened madly through his mind, staggering off the walls of his skull.

"Grant!" Lakesh's voice was tight with fear and impatience.

"Stay out for a minute," he replied, dismayed by how shrill his voice sounded.

"Why? Answer me!"

Grant ignored him and the pain in his leg. He shifted position, getting to all fours. Tentatively, he stretched a hand toward Kane again. He looked solid, he argued to himself, so he had to *be* solid.

Without warning, a skein of energy, like cobwebs of voltage sprang up and surrounded Kane's body. It touched Grant's fingers, danced up, crawled along his arm. His skin prickled, as if a million electrified ants marched along his flesh. He had no chance to cry out or pull away before the crackling display ended. When it did, a handful of Kane's coat was gripped in his fist.

Simultaneously, Kane's eyes flew open, wide and wild. Convulsions shook him, racked him violently from head to toe. He dragged in a great shuddery breath as if his lungs had been deprived of oxygen for a long time. He clawed out with his right hand, finding Grant's wrist and closing his fingers around it as if it were an anchor to life. His pale, glassy eyes asked a silent, beseeching question.

"You're back," Grant told him. "You made it back."

Air rasped in and out of Kane's throat as he tried to sit up. He managed only a flailing spasm of arms and legs. The lack of coordination deeply disturbed Grant. A characteristic of Kane was his wolflike reflexes.

Grant pulled him to a sitting position by the collar of his coat, and Kane shivered, inhaling and exhaling with deep gasps. He clasped his head with both hands. Finally, he managed to say, in an aspirated whisper, "Baptiste."

"She's here," Grant said quietly. "She seems okay. What about you?"

"Head hurts."

"Can you stand?"

Kane lowered his hands, glanced up at him and tried to grin, but it looked more like a grimace of agony. "Try."

Grant heaved him to his feet and like a pair of drunken dancers, they lockstepped through the mist to the open chamber door. Lakesh's face registered his relief when he saw them. Brigid sat on the edge of the long table in the ready room and though she looked weak, her eyes were no longer glazed. She fixed them on Kane.

"Are you all right?"

As he carefully stepped forward, he husked out, "Yeah. Head feels like a frag gren went off inside of it, but other than that, I'm fine."

Grant released him, and Kane immediately fell flat on his face. Almost as immediately, he started pushing himself up by trembling arms, cursing under his breath in embarrassment.

Domi instantly moved to his side, offering him support as he tried to climb to his feet again. Grant hauled him erect by the collar of his coat. Kane met the troubled gazes of Lakesh and Brigid and muttered, "Piece of shit Russian gateway. Should have known."

The mat-trans unit in the Trasilunpo monastery had been part of the Soviet Union's Sverdze project, their analogue to Cerberus. Months before, he, Grant and Brigid and undergone an exceedingly unpleasant jump to a Russian gateway. It had become a given with him that all units of Russian manufacture were faulty.

Neither Lakesh nor Brigid agreed with Kane's contemptuous assessment. "Nothing like this happened when we made the initial jump," she declared hoarsely. "Nothing like this has ever happened on *any* jump."

"That's not quite true," Bry announced from the doorway leading to the control complex.

Before the slightly built tech could elaborate, he was forced to step aside to admit DeFore and her aide, Auerbach, as they rolled in a gurney. Kane eyed it with distaste, and DeFore regarded him similarly.

"Somebody in here better need medical attention," she stated in a menacing tone. A stocky, buxom woman with deep bronze skin, braided ash-blond hair and liquid brown eyes, she was one of the first Cerberus exiles and accustomed to speaking her mind.

Lakesh gestured to Kane and Brigid. "An examination is in order."

Leaning on the edge of the table, Kane said defensively, "I'm feeling better."

"Me too," Brigid added.

Shaking his head, Lakesh declared, "Not good enough. Go with DeFore to the dispensary." His tone brooked no debate.

"Which one of you wants to ride?" Auerbach asked, nodding to the gurney.

Neither Kane nor Brigid answered him. Brigid slid off the table and began walking with a slow determination toward the door. Kane hesitated before following her. DeFore passed a small, handheld rad counter over both of them.

"Low-end green," she announced. "No immediate need for decam."

As Kane moved around her, Lakesh said, "Friend Kane, three of you left here. Only two returned. Is there a reason for that?"

Kane flicked narrowed, pain-filled eyes toward him in irritation. With a cold sarcasm, he answered, "Yeah. One of the three didn't come back. Satisfied?"

"By no means." Lakesh fell silent, staring at him with unblinking expectation.

"If you want to know if I chilled Balam, just ask me."

"Did you?"

"No." He started walking after Brigid, putting his feet down with such care it was as if he feared the floor would open beneath them.

"And the Chintamani Stone?" Lakesh demanded.

Without pausing, Kane shrugged out of the long coat and tossed it atop the table. It landed with a solid clunk. "Look in the pockets."

Lakesh opened his mouth to voice another question, but Grant caught his eye, favoring him with a disapproving scowl. "We can have a formal debrief after he and Brigid are checked over and get themselves back together.

In a whisper, he added cryptically, "And in Kane's case, that might take a while."

If Lakesh found the comment puzzling, he gave no indication. He busied himself patting and then groping through the pockets of the long black coat. From them he pulled three black stones. Two were nearly identical, roughly the size and shape of a man's fist. At first, and even second glance, they appeared to be chunks of obsidian, or some other dark mineral. Only by careful examination could the eye discern the marks of tools on them, or faint scratches that might be inscriptions.

The third piece was much larger, cube-shaped, the surfaces so perfectly smooth it was as if they had been polished and lacquered to acquire a semireflective sheen. But beneath the gloss lay only darkness, a black, fathomless sea.

Lakesh arranged the two smaller fragments on either side of the larger, as if he were assembling a puzzle. By turning them and shifting their position, he saw that all three pieces formed the geometric facets of an incomplete trapezohedron. According to what Balam had hinted and the information Brigid had wrung from the historical database, the Black Stone was of celestial origin and referred to in many ancient apocryphal religious texts as the Shining Trapezohedron. Always it was associated with the concept of keys.

Buddhist and Taoist legends spoke of the city of Agartha, a secret enclave beneath a mountain range on the Chinese-Tibet border from which strange gray people emerged to influence human affairs. Ancient Asian chronicles attested that within the rock galleries of Agartha rested the prime facet of the stone, known to Oriental mystics as the Chintamani Stone.

Alleged to have come from the star system of Sirius, the chronicles claimed that "When the Son of the Sun descended upon earth to teach humankind, there fell from heaven a shield which bore the power of the world."

"Aren't there some other things you ought to be looking at?"

Grant's impatient query drew Lakesh's attention away from the stones. He turned and blinked at him owlishly. "Like what?"

Grant gestured to the mat-trans chamber. The mist boiling within had thinned due to the influx of fresh air, but it had yet to completely disappear. "Like that. Have you ever seen a gateway smoke like that?"

With a sudden start of alarm, it occurred to Lakesh that he had not. The Cerberus unit was the first fully operable and completely debugged quantum interface mat-trans inducer constructed after the success of the prototype in 1989. The quantum energies released by the gateways transformed organic and inorganic matter to digital information, transmitted it along a hyperdimensional pathway and reassembled it in a receiver unit.

To accomplish this, the mat-trans units required an inestimable number of maddeningly intricate electronic procedures, all occurring within milliseconds of one another, to minimize the margins for error. The actual matter-to-energy conversion process was sequenced by an array of computers and microprocessors, with a number of separate but overlapping operational cycles.

Since Lakesh had been the overseer of Project Cerberus and had been instrumental in developing the inducers from prototype to final model, he had witnessed firsthand every permutation of its operation.

"As a point of fact," he admitted, adjusting his eyeglasses to look at the vapor, "I haven't. It doesn't appear to be the normal byproduct of the quincunx effect."

Grant had picked up enough technovernacular in the past eight months to understand that Lakesh referred to a nanosecond of time when lower dimensional space was phased into a higher one. But that's all he understood.

"Other than the smoke," he stated, "I saw something else." He held up three fingers. "I saw three other Kanes in there. Or thought I saw them."

Lakesh contemplated him without expression for a long tick of time. At length, he intoned, "Thought you saw them?"

Grant wagged his head in exasperation. "It was pretty foggy in there, with some wild energy overspills. Maybe my eyes played tricks on me."

He didn't sound as if he believed it, and Lakesh didn't believe him, either. Not only was Grant's vision uncannily acute, he wasn't prone to imagining much of anything. If he said he saw four Kanes instead of one, he more than likely was not mistaken.

"Another thing." Grant cleared his throat self-consciously, and then declared in a rush, "When I first went to touch Kane, my hand went right through him—like he was a ghost. It was almost as if the mat-trans had only locked on to his appearance, not him. When I touched him again, he was solid."

"That's impossible," Lakesh retorted.

"Then explain it," Grant challenged.

Lakesh groped for a reasonable sounding response, but before he found one, Domi piped up, "Three rocks. Three Kanes. You do math."

Both Lakesh and Grant swiveled their heads toward her, then fixed their gazes on the black stones.

Lakesh threw a nervous but gracious smile toward Domi. "They are the common factors. Thank you, darlingest girl, for not allowing me to overlook the obvious."

Grant eyed the stones suspiciously. "What do we do now?"

"We test them, see if we can isolate their interactive properties."

Grant's eyebrows rose. "Interactive?"

"Obviously the stones reacted to the quantum energies of the mat-trans inducer. We had a triple quincunx effect, simultaneously and interconnective. That might explain the volume of mist as well as the three dopplegangers of Kane."

"Why didn't it happen to Brigid?" Grant asked.

"She wasn't in close enough physical proximity to the stones."

Grant knuckled his eyes and muttered peevishly, "Let's get to the point—where did the three Kanes come from and where did they go?"

Somehow managing to sound skeptical and enthralled at the same time, Lakesh stated, "I theorize they came from three different dimensional realities, three different mirror universes. Parallel casements, to employ the term used by Balam."

Grant glared at him. "That's crazy."

Lakesh chuckled uneasily. "So are the workings of the universe at large. It will take a madman to understand them, so I suggest we get to it."

"Get to it how?" Grant demanded.

Lakesh reached out for the largest piece of stone,

but stopped short of grasping it. "Methodically, friend Grant. Methodically."

BETH-LI ROUCH slapped the flat toggle switch on the door frame, and the overhead fluorescent fixtures blazed on, flooding the armory with a white, sterile light.

The big square room was stacked nearly to the ceiling with wooden crates and boxes. Many of the crates were stenciled with the legend PROPERTY U.S. ARMY. Glass-fronted gun cases lined the four walls, containing automatic assault rifles, many makes and models of subguns and dozens of semi-automatic blasters. Heavy assault weaponry occupied the north wall, bazookas, tripod-mounted M-249 machine guns, mortars and rocket launchers.

She had been told that all of the ordnance was of predark manufacture. Caches of matériel had been laid down in hermetically sealed Continuity of Government installations before the nukecaust. Protected from the ravages of the outraged environment, nearly every piece of munitions and hardware was as pristine as the day it had rolled off the assembly line.

Rouch moved along the aisles, peering into the cases, then moving on again. Her experience with firearms was extremely limited. She had never so much as touched a blaster until she arrived at Cerberus. All of the exiles were expected to become reasonably proficient with weapons, so she had spent some time on the indoor firing range under Grant's tutelage. The lessons were restricted to the use of SA-80 subguns, lightweight autoblasters that the most firearm-challenged person could learn to handle. However, an SA-80 would not serve the purpose she had in mind.

She circled the armory, and when she caught a glimpse of two black figures standing near the rear wall, she repressed a cry of fright. With a sense of shame mingled with anger, she recognized the suits of Magistrate body armor mounted on metal frameworks. She wasn't sure which black exoskeleton belonged to Kane or Grant, so she eyed both of them with loathing.

Rouch devoted no thought to examining her hatred of Grant—he was Kane's friend and that was enough for her. Once she had contemplated seducing Grant in order to make Kane jealous, but the notion of incurring the homicidal wrath of Domi, the outlander slut, made her discard the idea. Besides, she knew Grant would spurn her, just as Kane had.

A jolt of fury seized her, and she caught a reflection of herself in the glass of a gun case. Her delicate, exotic features were contorted in a mask of rage, eyes slitted, teeth bared.

She replayed what Kane had said to her that night in the village of the savages: "Beth-Li...if you ever threaten Baptiste again, I'll fucking chill you."

She remembered how his hands clamped cruelly tight on her face, how he glared into her eyes. Once again she heard his growling voice: "I'll break your beautiful little neck."

Humiliation filled her, thickening in her chest, almost suffocating her. It was all Brigid Baptiste's fault, that barren, frigid bitch who had never known passion of any kind, but who had somehow awakened it in Kane.

Baptiste didn't know how to treat a man, certainly not a man like Kane. At least Rouch tried to convince herself of that. She had tried to convince Kane of the same thing, and he had responded with threats. She paused by a case, noting the array of small-caliber handblasters displayed inside it. Her eyes swept over them, then settled on a blue-finished Heckler & Koch P-7 M-8 with a stippled black plastic stock.

Impulsively, she opened the case door and removed the blaster, hefting it one-handed, then in both. The lightweight P-7 M-8 was only a little over six inches long and therefore fairly easy to conceal. In a cabinet drawer, she found a clip loaded with eight 9 mm Parabellum rounds. Slapping the clip into the blaster's butt, she experimented with the front-mounted squeeze cocker, strap cocking the action.

Rouch liked the feel of the weapon. Whether she had to fire it was totally up to Baptiste.

Unzipping the seal of her bodysuit's right boot sock, she inserted the blaster, tightened the tabs and left the armory, making sure to turn out the lights.

Despite the weight of the blaster, Beth-Li's step was sprightly. For the first time in weeks, she felt good about herself.

Chapter 8

The lift disk hissed to a pneumatic stop and Abrams opened the door, striding across the down ramp and into the baron's suite. His body was encased by the black polycarbonate battle armor, the helmet tucked under his left arm.

The close-fitting exoskeleton was molded to conform to the biceps, triceps, pectorals and abdomen. Even with its Kevlar undersheathing, the armor was lightweight and had the ability to redistribute kinetic shock resulting from projectile impact. A small, disk-shaped badge of office was emblazoned on the left pectoral, depicting a crimson, stylized, balanced scales of justice superimposed over a nine-spoked wheel.

The helmet under Abrams's arm was of the same color and material, except for the slightly concave, red-tinted visor. The visor provided protection for the eyes, and the electrochemical polymer was connected to a passive night sight that intensified ambient light to permit one-color night vision.

He knew he made an incongruous sight, dressed as a hard-contact Mag yet leaning on his walking stick as he strode through the foyer. The foyer was magnificent, as was every room in the suite. Glittering light cast from many crystal chandeliers flooded every corner of the entrance hall. At the far end of the foyer, flanking huge ivory-and-gold inlaid double doors, were two members of the elite Baronial Guard.

At his approach, the guards opened the doors, and the one on his right said colorlessly, "The lord baron awaits you in his private audience chamber."

The doors shut behind him, and as he expected, he saw nothing but a deep, almost primal dark. The baron's level was the only one in the Administrative Monolith without windows. Abrams walked forward, heading toward the dim glow of a single light shining over an open door. He had never visited the baron's private chamber before. As far as he knew, only Lakesh had been granted that privilege.

Baron Cobalt sat alone inside the curve of a small, horseshoe-shaped desk. Rows of buttons and toggle switches lay within easy reach of his delicate fingers. If the baron pressed one button, his guard promptly appeared. If he pushed another button, his personal staff came.

When he entered, Abrams stood stiffly at attention beside the door frame. "As per your order, I am reporting that the recce team is preparing to embark."

The baron glanced at him with dull, distracted eyes and said in a surprisingly mild voice, "Please come in, Abrams."

He did so, marching to the desk and stopping beside the one chair. Baron Cobalt waved him to it. "Sit down, my good friend. I wish to talk to you."

Abrams eased his body into it, placing the red-visored helmet on his lap. "My lord baron. How may I be of service to you?"

Baron Cobalt shifted in his chair, pursing his lips meditatively. "My good friend. That's what I called Lakesh. Several months ago he sat where are you sitting now, and I asked him for counsel. Now I ask it of you."

Abrams couldn't help but feel uneasy. Since Lakesh was abducted by Kane, Grant and Salvo, the baron had essentially quarantined himself from all one-on-one contact with members of the Trust. He had heard that isolation even extended to his personal staff. He had devoted much thought to the whys and wherefores, since they seemed fairly obvious—shame because he had been duped by Salvo, self-anger that he had not uncovered the conspiracy right under his aquiline nose until its goal was achieved.

"What do you wish of me, my lord?" Abrams asked, inclining his head toward him.

"I told Salvo I fell prey to errors of judgment, but I never made mistakes. Do you recall that?"

Abrams did indeed recall that, as vividly as if it had happened only an hour ago. Salvo, the commander of the Magistrate Division and Abrams's chief lieutenant, and a member of the Trust, had been revealed as a traitor—a conspirator involved with Kane to overthrow the barony from within.

The scheme had been complicated with a number of diversions, including the pretense of commanding the Grudge task force, which was devoted to tracking down Kane, Grant and Baptiste. Salvo had abducted Lakesh and placed the blame for the entire conspiracy on Abrams himself.

The frame job had been Salvo's fatal miscalculation, because it was too convenient for even the paranoid Baron Cobalt to easily accept.

Salvo had apparently gambled that the baron would not consult the genetic records and learn he was related to Kane. That was all the proof Baron Cobalt needed to brand him as a traitorous seditionist, in league with the Preservationists.

"I remember that very clearly, my lord," Abrams answered with a note of satisfaction in his otherwise bland voice. "He groveled at your feet, pleading with you, claiming you had misjudged him."

A deep, sad sigh issued from Baron Cobalt's lips. "And indeed I had."

It took a moment for the implications of the baron's remark to penetrate Abrams's mind. He felt his eyebrows crawl first toward his hairline, then curve down to meet at the bridge of his nose. "My lord?" he faltered. "I don't understand—"

"Neither did I," Baron Cobalt blurted, a touch of almost human desperation in his tone. "At first. I tried to deny the evidence that I had wronged him, but now I must the accept the truth."

"Truth?" Abrams echoed, not quite sure if he wanted to hear what Baron Cobalt considered truth. "What do you mean?"

"Salvo was *not* working with Kane or the Preservationists. Yes, he had his own agenda, his own ambitions, as so many members of the Trust do. He did imprison Lakesh without my knowledge and torture him. But it was to learn the whereabouts of Kane."

Abrams could only stare in stunned incredulity for a long moment. "My lord, how do you know this?"

"Salvo told me."

"Surely you did not believe him. He lied—"

Baron Cobalt raised a preemptory, long-fingered hand. "He lied about many things, but not about that. Because of his many lies, I did not believe anything he said. So I looked beneath his words. I interfaced his brain with a database and recorded his memories."

Abrams recalled how the Baronial Guard had dragged Salvo away, and he understood the baron intended to subject him to certain types of interrogation techniques, but he had never inquired about them. He feared to.

"I recorded his memories," Baron Cobalt continued, "interpreted them into subjective visual language and studied them. A schemer he definitely was, but Salvo did not betray me. His mission in life was to track down Kane, and in the process he exploited the powers I had given him to do so."

Abrams struggled to grasp the concept that both he and the baron had made a grave error. "Then why did Kane rescue him?"

Baron Cobalt shook his domed head. "What we construed as a rescue was a capture. And what we construed as Lakesh's capture was more than likely the real rescue."

"Lakesh?" Abrams echoed in astonishment. "Your most trusted adviser? He was selected by the Directorate itself to help guide the program of unification! He—"

Abrams broke off, not certain if he had revealed more knowledge of Lakesh than he should have.

"He is also a predark human being." The baron's voice dropped to a whisper. "With predark standards of ethics and morality."

"But predark human beings planned and implemented the unification," Abrams argued. "In concert with the Directorate, long before the nukecaust and skydark."

"There are some things about the Program of Unification you do not know." Baron Cobalt spoke sadly, as if he were grieving the loss of a loved one. "Would it shock you to learn there are some things even *I* don't know?"

Abrams sat silently, throat constricted. The baron's question had shocked him deeply. He could not respond.

"A number of predark scientists, all involved with aspects of the Totality Concept, were placed in cryonic stasis, sleeping through the first century following the nukecaust. At a preordained time, they were revived, resurrected as it were, to employ their specialized knowledge in furthering the plans made so long ago, to usher humanity over the threshold of a new genesis. You knew that much, didn't you?"

Abrams nodded numbly, reviewing what he knew about the Totality Concept. The initial experiments began over two centuries before, at the end of World War II. There were several subdivisions of the Concept, separate as to research areas, but all linked to a primary objective. According to what he had been told years earlier, the Totality Concept had originated with the Archon Directorate.

"What you do not know," the baron went on, "is that several of these revived predarkers resisted cooperation. They claimed they had been misled, duped, lied to. They withheld their aid. Some rebelled openly and were dealt with. Others chose a more covert path, paying lip service to their dedication to a unified humanity, but actually acting as agents provocateurs."

Abrams stirred in his chair. "My lord, you mean they were Preservationists?"

"No, I do not believe such a conveniently clearcut adversary exists. It is a fiction, it is a cunningly crafted piece of misdirection. Yes, we've had a number of convicted criminals confess to being Preservationists, but only after they were tortured to the point where they would admit to any crime."

"Are you saying Lakesh is one of these agents provocateurs?"

"I am suggesting the possibility," Baron Cobalt replied. "I do not wish to repeat the same rush to judgment I made with Salvo. I lost my objectivity with he and Lakesh. I was not bred to be so…passion driven."

"But surely you have some foundation for your suspicions."

"Several, actually." The baron began ticking off points with his fingers. Absently, Abrams noted that the middle one was nearly the length of his entire hand.

"One—Lakesh was the overseer of Project Cerberus. He was the man responsible for the initial breakthroughs in matter transfer. He was also the designer of the modular gateway units. I daresay he knows more about the mat-trans network than anyone alive.''

Baron Cobalt touched another finger. ''Two—Redoubt Bravo was the seat of project Cerberus, where the units were mass-produced. Lakesh was stationed there for a number of years prior to the nukecaust.''

He tapped a third finger. ''Three—he was also Brigid Baptiste's direct superior here in the ville's Historical Division.''

The baron hesitated before touching the fourth and final finger. ''Four—over the past three years, a small number of citizens in various villes were convicted of equally various crimes. They mysteriously vanished before their sentences could be carried out.''

Abrams's head jerked up on his neck. ''Vanished? You mean escaped?''

''I mean vanished. Without a trace.''

''I knew nothing about that.''

Baron Cobalt bestowed a small, patronizing smile on him. ''Of course you wouldn't. It would not do for any of our citizens to learn that it was possible to evade the justice of the barons.''

''Who were the criminals?'' Abrams inquired.

''Their names are unimportant, but suffice it to say almost all of them were specialists in some area—cybernetics, engineering, medicine. All of them disappeared into thin air—or into a gateway.''

Abrams pushed out a long, slow breath. ''So you suspect—''

The baron wagged an admonishing finger. "I suggest. That is all."

Nodding, Abrams rephrased his query. "So you are suggesting the possibility that Lakesh, with his intimate knowledge of Cerberus technology, might be involved in a conspiracy against you?"

"Just so. It is painful to consider, but I already allowed my emotions to misjudge Salvo. I won't make the same mistake with Lakesh, regardless of how much I value him."

Abrams scratched at his beard. "That might explain why Kane never held Lakesh up for ransom, as well as explaining how he knows enough about the operation of the gateway units to elude our pursuit."

The man's shoulders quaked in a sudden shudder. He stared at the baron with stricken eyes. "This is truly monstrous, my lord. If the criminals can't be apprehended, the Archon Directorate will intervene."

Baron Cobalt's unlined face suddenly went blank, as if he had slipped on a mask. In a very subdued, colorless voice, he intoned, "They will not intervene."

Instead of feeling reassured by the baron's declamation, Abrams had to consciously suppress another shudder. Falteringly, he asked, "Have you been in touch—I mean, have they told you they would not take action?"

"No, Abrams. I have not communicated with the Directorate nor they with me. I have never seen an Archon much less had a dialogue with one."

The statement, delivered in a flat, matter-of-fact monotone sent cold darts of shock up Abrams spine.

His mind reeled, all his thoughts scattering like a flock of panic-stricken birds. "My lord, I don't understand—you and all the barons in all the villes are the representatives of the Archon Directorate."

"That is the traditional belief." Baron Cobalt's voice whispered as if from a vast distance. "But belief and reality do not necessarily coincide. Nor should we expect them to."

Beneath the polycarbonate sheathing, Abrams's bad leg began to throb, like a warning signal. He resisted the urge to rub it.

"After all," the baron said, "everything I was led to believe about the Directorate was conveyed to me by humans."

Abrams felt trapped, but was too paralyzed by shock to do anything about it. In an instant, everything he had accepted as a given, as immutable articles of faith, was trembling, tottering, about to collapse.

Baron Cobalt seemed to sense his horror, but he displayed no compassion. "You must deal with the weight of evidence as I have been forced to do."

"With all due respect, my lord, just because you have not had direct contact with the Archons—" The rest of Abrams's words trailed off. He was unable to utter them.

The baron finished the sentence for him. "Doesn't mean they don't exist? Perhaps so, but I am not applying only my subjective point of view. Baron Sharpe was seriously wounded, apparently by Kane. Baron Ragnar was assassinated in his own chambers. Whether Kane had anything to do with that has yet to be determined. Regardless, both instances were the most blatant examples of violence against the baronies since the institution of the unification program. Where are the Archons?''

Abrams could not hazard a guess, so he elected to remain silent.

"We are links in a chain that stretches back two centuries or more," Baron Cobalt declared. "As the baronial hierarchy acts as the control mechanism for the human race, the myth of the all-seeing, all-powerful Archon Directorate acted as the control mechanism for the barons. Our belief in them curbed our individual ambitions, prevented us from warring on each other as in the old days before unification."

In an instant, everything Abrams had been taught about the world before the Program of Unification wheeled through his mind. Nearly 150 years after the nukecaust, after a century of barbarism and anarchy, humankind reorganized, rising from the ruins of the predark societal structures. Many of the most powerful, most enduring baronies evolved into city-states, walled fortresses whose influence stretched across the country for thousands of miles.

In decades past, the barons had warred against one another, each struggling for control and absolute power over territory. Then, they realized that greater rewards were possible if unity in command, purpose and organization was achieved.

Territories were redefined, treaties struck among the barons and the city-states became interconnected points in a continent-spanning network. The Program of Unification was ratified during the Council of

Front Royal, and then ruthlessly employed. The reconstructed form of government was despotic, but now it was institutionalized and shared by all the former independent baronies.

Nine baronies survived the long wars over territorial expansion and resources. Control of the continent was divided among the nine barons. The pretenders, those who were not part of the original hierarchy but who arrogantly assumed the title to carve out their own little pieces of empire, were exterminated and their territories absorbed. The hierarchical ruling system remained, and the city-states adopted the name of the titular heads of state.

Simultaneously with this forward step in social engineering came technical advances. Technology, most of it based on predark designs, appeared mysteriously and simultaneously with the beginning of the reunification program. There was much speculation at the time that many previously unknown predark Continuity of Government stockpiles were opened up and their contents distributed evenly among the barons. Although the technologies were restricted for the use of those who held the reins of power, life overall improved for the citizens in and around the villes. Manufacturing industries, totally under the control of the villes, began again.

All of that was accomplished over eighty years before, and the barons themselves had acquired a mystical, almost divine aura. Before he could stop himself, Abrams blurted in an agonized gasp, "But if you are not a hybrid of Archon and humans, then—" He clamped his jaws tight.

"Then who are the barons? What are we?" Baron Cobalt's voice was silky, sibilant. "Is it a question of identity, or are you asking what makes us fit to rule humanity?"

Abrams stammered fearfully, "My lord, I did not mean—"

"Yes, indeed you did, and it is a very legitimate question. I shall address it—what makes the barons fit to rule is simple. We hold the power to do so. At this point in our history, it is immaterial whether humans gave us that power or it was ceded to us by superior entities like the Archons. We hold the power. It is the barons who rule you, not the Archons. Whether they ever existed is irrelevant."

Baron Cobalt slitted his eyes and leaned forward slightly. "Do you understand me, Abrams? We hold the power. That is one of the reasons there has been no war in nearly two centuries. We are unified, we all speak the same tongue. It is the law of the barons.

"The people of the villes live by those laws. They are so conditioned to obey them that any opposition to a baron is unthinkable. From the day they were born, they've been indoctrinated to our universal good. So it does not matter if the Archon Directorate exists. We hold the power."

Despite his growing terror, Abrams still heard the undercurrent of menace in the baron's voice. "I understand, my lord."

"Excellent. I knew you would. That is why I revealed this particular truth to you."

Abrams did not feel blessed by being selected. He felt cursed, and an impending sense of doom seemed to settle on him like a cloak. He licked his dry lips. "Your brother barons, my lord. Are they aware of this truth?"

Baron Cobalt fluttered a dismissive hand through the air. "That, too, is irrelevant. I know it, and therefore shall conduct my affairs in accordance with it. If any of them reach the same conclusion as I, then they shall do so without any prompting from me."

The baron paused, and a thin smile ghosted over his face. "Besides, keeping this knowledge all to myself gives me something of an advantage over them."

Abrams did not know what he meant, and he wasn't inclined to find out. He was too stupefied to do anything other than sit.

"Now you know what I know," Baron Cobalt said smoothly. "It will remain just between us. You may now embark on your mission. I wish you good fortune and success."

Abrams was barely aware of pushing himself to his feet. The lightweight polycarbonate armor felt like a sheathing of the most crudely forged lead. He turned and shuffled toward the door, his cane in one hand, his helmet in the other.

The information Baron Cobalt had imparted was devastating, both emotionally and intellectually, but he found himself dwelling less on the staggering implications than why the baron seemed so pleased by it all.

Chapter 9

"How much longer?" Kane demanded.

"Not much," DeFore answered with a clinical coolness. "Only one area of your brain left."

Snapping his eyes open in alarm, he stiffened where he lay on the examination table. "What do you mean?"

"Only one area of your brain left to be recorded. Relax, or we'll have to start all over again. Try to maintain your Alpha state."

Flat on his back in a darkened examination room adjacent to the dispensary, Kane closed his eyes. Eight metal electrodes were affixed to spots on his scalp and his forehead by crossed strips of adhesive tape. Thin wires led from the electrodes to sockets in the electroencephalograph machine. The pair of slender pens moved rhythmically over the surface of the graph paper, recording the electrical impulses of his brain by etching jagged lines. The faint but insistent scratching of the pens irritated him, as did the tape on his scalp. DeFore had explained the machine recorded activity in the frontal, temporal, parietal and occipital brain areas.

Lakesh had ordered the EEG, and Kane still wasn't sure why. After a few minutes of arguing with him, Kane had relented, but for reasons of his own. First and foremost was the excruciating pain in his head, one which analgesics administered by Auerbach had done little to alleviate. A huge hollow filled with knives seemed to hold his entire skull.

Headaches were part and parcel of mat-trans jumping. Even the cleanest transit sometimes resulted in a few minutes of head pain and nausea, but the symptoms of jump sickness abated quickly. When the matter-stream carrier wave modulations could not be perfectly synchronized between gateways, a severe bout of jump sickness was the result.

The pain in his skull was nothing like that triggered by a jump, or even like those that he'd suffered from blows to the head.

This was agony, incessant and blinding, and he couldn't rely on his iron self-control to keep himself from succumbing to it. Three hours ago when he revived in the gateway chamber, he felt as if all of his internal organs had been taken out and spread over the floor. He had been aware of nothing but an inferno of nausea and pain. He felt as if his very soul had been folded into a thousand different angles.

Then there were other sensations, not exactly physical but having more to do with perception. He felt somehow detached, as if he weren't really in the Cerberus redoubt at all but in another place—or places—and only dreaming about being in Cerberus.

He had made more than a dozen gateway transits over the past eight months and never experienced a feeling like it, not even on the one to the malfunctioning unit in Russia. This feeling of disorientation shook him, frightened and bewildered him. He felt completely out of phase with the world. He tried not to dwell on the possibility of brain damage.

Splinters of memory spun through his mind, but they were not clear, more like ghostly residuals of dreams. He told himself they were not recollections of actual events, but half-remembered pieces of a jump-induced nightmare.

He knew Salvo was dead, shot and electrocuted nearly two hundred years ago on a Manhattan rooftop.

He knew he had never led a raid on anything even faintly resembling an embassy, and the creature he knew as C. W. Thrush was not an ambassador. He wasn't even a man.

True enough, he had been in space once, but by mat-trans, not on a ship. He had arrived on *Parallax Red,* a long-forgotten, predark rattletrap space station. It had been occupied by the madman Sindri and his bioengineered trolls, not something called the Ranger Division.

Despite his pain and confusion, Kane still recognized the common factor in all three of his visions— C. W. Thrush, who claimed to be a hybrid of human, Archon and machine. He didn't live, but he existed.

During the unforeseen temporal dilation effect when Lakesh's interphaser was used as a portable mat-trans, he, Brigid, Grant and Domi had been swept to four focal points in history. As disembodied spectators, all of them had witnessed Thrush's involvement in past events that affected the future and ultimately led to the nukecaust.

Brigid had described Thrush as a prototypical

MIB, a Man In Black, one those sinister figures associated with the conspiracy theories of the twentieth century, whether they dealt with UFOs or political unrest.

A faux human she had called him, a fake, and that appellation proved to be more than a guess during their final confrontation on that Newyork roof. He replayed, as best he could, what Thrush had said about himself: "Colonel Thrush is not an individual, but a program. My body is mortal, but the program will simply animate another like me."

Kane had believed him to be an Archon agent, a chrononaut dispatched by the Directorate to prevent their machinations in time from being undone. In retrospect, Thrush had never actually admitted to working for the Archons, and it hadn't occurred to Kane to ask Balam about his true nature and purpose. He doubted he would have received a solid answer to even the most specific questions.

He remembered Thrush's parting words to him. "Another time."

A sudden click startled him into opening his eyes. DeFore had turned off the EEG machine, and the scratching of the pens ceased. Looping the graph paper over an arm, she announced, "That's it, Kane."

He reached up and started carefully peeling the tape from his forehead. DeFore pushed his hand away, saying crossly, "That's not the way to do it."

Ruthlessly, she ripped away the adhesive strips, plucking more than a few hairs out by their roots. Kane barely noticed the pain. It was nothing compared to the sleet storm throbbing within the walls of his skull.

Wincing, he pushed himself to a sitting position. "Do you have anything stronger than those pills you gave me?"

DeFore eyed him critically. "Your head still hurts?"

"You have no idea."

She glanced down at the triple row of jagged lines on the paper. "I haven't interpreted the results yet, but the EEG doesn't show any spikes indicating head trauma."

Kane didn't move from the table. "I don't give a shit," he rasped hoarsely. "I'm hurting and I'm hurting bad. Now will you get me something, or will I have to find it myself?"

DeFore gave him another appraising stare, unease flickering momentarily in her dark eyes. Kane met her stare through narrowed eyes. DeFore had never disguised her dislike of him—or rather, her dislike of what he represented. In her eyes, as a former Magistrate, he embodied the strutting arrogance of ville law enforcement, glorying in his baron-sanctioned power to deal death indiscriminately.

She also believed that because of his Magistrate conditioning, he was unable to reconcile his past with his present, and the psychological conflict had him teetering on the brink of nervous collapse. Therefore, she didn't believe he could be trusted.

Still, she had treated Kane for a number of injuries since his arrival at Cerberus, from broken bones to burns, and through the worst of it he had never uttered so much as an "Ouch."

Stepping to a cabinet, DeFore removed a syringe and a glass ampule of clear fluid. As she filled the hypodermic she said curtly, "I'm giving you a solution of a predark analgesic known as Percocet, a class-A narcotic. If it doesn't clear up the pain, or if it returns in the same intensity, we'll have to come up with another approach."

Kane rolled up the right sleeve of his bodysuit and she injected the contents of the syringe into his brachial vein. The sting of the needle was remote.

"Sit there for a minute," she instructed him. "We'll see if it works."

Kane nodded. "Thanks."

DeFore only grunted and busied herself gathering up the graph paper.

Brigid appeared in the doorway. Her white bodysuit, the duty uniform of Cerberus personnel, clung in the all the right places to her tall, willowy figure. Her thick mane of red-gold hair was tied back, and Kane noted the small filmlike patch of liquid bandage shining dully high on her forehead.

"How are you doing?" she asked.

Kane forced a smile, indicating DeFore with a nod. "Ask her. She's the expert."

DeFore faced him. "You really must be out of your head, Kane, to make that admission."

She turned to Brigid. "The EEG is complete, but I haven't done the workup. It'll be several hours. He's still complaining about a severe headache, so I gave him a few cc's of diluted Percocet. We'll see if it reduces the pain.''

Kane realized that the agony was slowly receding. ''It is,'' he said in relief.

''Good. Go to your quarters and stay off your feet for a while. Try to sleep. Even diluted, that stuff will make you woozy.''

He edged off the table, then grabbed it as the floor seemed to tilt beneath his feet. ''So I see.''

The surge of dizziness passed and he moved toward the doorway, slowly at first, then with growing confidence. Brigid walked beside him.

''I don't need a valet, Baptiste,'' he told her.

''No, but if you fall down and break your head, you might need somebody to mop up the mess.''

''Call Banks. He's out of a job.''

She acknowledged his comment with a smile. Banks had served as Balam's warder and keeper for the past three-plus years. He was chosen for the duty by Lakesh because he could tune out Balam's telepathic touch. Over the course of the creature's captivity, the young man had developed a bond, even a fondness for him. All of them had been surprised to learn that not only had Balam understood Banks's feelings, he actually appreciated him.

''Both he and Lakesh are disappointed Balam didn't return with us,'' she said, ''but Lakesh has other things to occupy him.''

''Like what?''

''Like wiring up the pieces of the stone and running them through a spectroanalysis. That sort of thing. Lakesh-type-stuff.''

As they turned a corner in the corridor, Kane commented, "It's going to take some getting used to."

She gave him a wry half smile. "Not having an enemy on which to focus your hatred is almost more upsetting than having one."

She spoke truly, and Kane could not debate her. Over the past eight months, ever since he had learned about the existence of the Archon Directorate and how they had orchestrated the nukecaust, he had grown comfortable with hating Balam and his people. He had lived in a world of hate from morning to night. He woke up hating Archons, and he went to bed hating Archons. Now it was all gone.

He had been told that the entirety of human history was intertwined with the activities of the entities called Archons, though they had been referred to by many names over many centuries—angels, demons, visitors, ET's, saucer people, grays.

Balam stated that his people did not call themselves Archons. It was a term first applied to them in the twentieth century, and referred to an ancient force that acted as spiritual jailers, imprisoning the spark of the divine within human souls.

Their involvement with humanity stretched back at least twenty thousand years, and perhaps further. Beginning at the dawn of history, the Archons subtly— and sometimes not so subtly—influenced human affairs.

In order to survive, Balam's people conspired with willing human pawns to control man through political chaos, staged wars, famines, plagues and natural disasters.

Their standard operating procedure was to establish a privileged ruling class dependent upon them, which in turn controlled the masses for them. The Archons' manipulation of governments and religions was all-pervasive. Allegedly, they had allied themselves with Nazi Germany and switched their allegiance when the Allies were victorious. However, as time progressed, the world and humankind changed too much for their plenipotentiaries to rule with any degree of effectiveness.

But their goal remained the same—the unification of the world under their control, with all nonessential and nonproductive humans eliminated. Now, nearly two hundred years after the nukecaust, the population was far easier to manipulate.

But it was all a ruse, bits of truth mixed in with outrageous fiction. The Archon Directorate did not exist except as a vast cover story, created two centuries ago and grown larger with each succeeding generation. There was only one so-called Archon on Earth and that was Balam, the last of an extinct race.

Balam claimed that the Archon Directorate was an appellation created by the predark governments. Lakesh referred to it as the Oz Effect, wherein a single vulnerable entity created the illusion of being the representative of an all-powerful body.

Even more shocking than that revelation was Balam's assertion that he and his folk were humans, not alien but alienated. Kane still didn't know how much to believe. But in if nothing else, he no longer subscribed to the fatalistic belief that the human race had had its day and only extinction lay ahead. Balam had indicated that was not true, only another control mechanism.

Brigid picked up on his thoughts and murmured, "The bigger the lie, the more people will believe it."

Startled, Kane swung his head toward her, despite the hot flare of pain the swift movement caused. "That's familiar. Who said it?"

"Adolf Hitler."

The memory of the granite, mustached face carved on Mount Rushmore drifted through his mind. Once again he told himself it wasn't an actual memory, only the residual of a jump dream. He had seen pix of Mount Rushmore, and it held faces of four predark American Presidents. According to Lakesh, all of them but Lincoln's had been obliterated by bomb-triggered earthquakes.

"Lakesh will want a full report from both of us when you're feeling better," Brigid said as they approached the door to his quarters. "We're dealing with a completely different set of circumstances now."

"That must make Lakesh happy," Kane replied, not concealing his sarcasm. "Now he can come up with a whole different set of strategies and plots to get us chilled. I'm sure he can't wait to get started."

They stopped at his door and he pushed it open. The room beyond was dark. He quirked an eyebrow at Brigid. The overhead track lighting system was programmed to come on when the open door intersected with a floor-mounted photoelectric beam.

"Damn thing must've shorted out," he muttered peevishly. "The place is going to hell."

"You were just going to catch some sleep anyhow," Brigid pointed out.

"Yeah," he replied, stepping over the threshold, "but I'd like to be able to find the bed. Hold the door open while I turn on the light in the head."

Brigid obliged, leaning her weight against the door as Kane made his way through the murk. As he approached the bathroom, his point man's sixth sense rang with a distant alarm, but it was too feeble to penetrate the drug haze blurring the edges of his awareness.

Reaching the bathroom, he groped along the wall for a moment, found the switch and flicked it up. As the overhead light flashed on, he heard the door snick shut behind him. He turned, and peering into the semigloom, it took him a couple of seconds to identify the small, indistinct figure standing partially behind Brigid.

The white-clad figure shifted soundlessly to Baptiste's right side, and he glimpsed the dark handblaster jammed against Brigid's head.

"Stay where you are, Kane," Beth-Li said calmly. "It's Baptiste I want."

Chapter 10

Bry pushed himself away from the eyepieces of the spectroscope and said, "At least we know a few things the stone isn't—it's not a tektite or a rare earth or any kind of ore the spectrograph recognizes."

He turned to look at Lakesh. "My experience with minerals is limited, but I know those black striations in the rock are very unusual. The spectrometer can't seem to get a fix on them. It's almost like they aren't there. I don't detect any electromagnetic radiation or atomic bond lines, no matter how many diffraction grating values I use."

Lakesh, Bry and Banks sat at low trestle table in the workroom adjacent to the armory. Rows of drafting tables lined one wall, and various chassis of electronic equipment lined the other.

Running a frustrated hand through his copper-colored curls, Bry asked, "Balam called the stone a conductor?"

"Technically," Lakesh replied, nodding to the thin young black man perched on a stool, "Banks did."

Because of his long association with Balam and his latent telepathic abilities, Banks had empathically melded with the creature to facilitate a verbal dialogue between warder and prisoner.

"Do you remember anything about the exact nature of the stone that Balam transferred to you?" Lakesh asked him. "Something implanted in your memory, yet you might not have spoken of?"

Banks frowned in concentration for a long moment, then dolefully shook his head. "I can only remember what he directed to me say. 'It is a creation, pure matter crafted from scientific principles understood millennia ago, then forgotten. Through it the pulse flows of thought energy converge. Through it the flux lines of possibility, of probability, of eternity, of *alternity* meet.'"

Lakesh nodded thoughtfully. "He—you—also said the stone was a key to doors that were sealed ages ago, and that time and reality are elastic, but in delicate balance."

"'When the balance is altered, then changes will come—terrible and permanent,'" Banks quoted.

Bry's eyes flicked nervously back and forth between Banks and Lakesh. "I hope that esoteric babble means something to you, because it sure as hell doesn't to me," he said flatly.

Lakesh regarded him with a slightly mocking smile. Bry served more or less as his apprentice, and although brilliant, he was largely self-taught. His mentor's frequent flights into metaphysics confused and irritated him.

Reaching over, he removed the primary facet of the stone from the spectrograph and turned it over in his hands, eyeing it keenly. "Our tests on this have revealed very little. In fact it reacts as if only part of it exists within our scientific concept of matter. As if it were not matter at all, but antimatter…antimatter forced partially into our space-time.

"Perhaps we can't analyze it because our temporal and spatial values can't be applied to it. It might have rules of its own that seem only madness to us, but are quite as ordered in relationship to it as ours are to us."

Bry frowned at him skeptically. "How can it be antimatter? Wouldn't we have a mutual annihilation?"

"Not if the stone's negatively charged nuclei were shielded by some kind of undetectable field or aura."

Bry stopped short of snorting in derision, but he did say, "Sheer speculation."

With an edge in his voice, Lakesh replied, "Long ago, scientists speculated that an electromagnetic field surrounds all things, that all life is connected to the pattern of the universe itself. On a subatomic level everything that exists is in vibration. That same magnetic principle that causes gravitation, chemical affinities in macrocosm and microcosm, controls our dimension and those beyond it."

Before Bry could respond, Lakesh plunged on. "We already know that Balam's people mastered space and hyperdimensional travel aeons ago, using the quantum-pathway technology left by their forebears. That same technology formed the basis of the mat-trans units. It's obvious that Balam's people utilized scientific principles that went beyond mere nuts and bolts and subprocessors."

Bry couldn't deny that, but he looked as if he fervently wished he could. With a resigned shake of his head, he declared, "Well, something happened to the gateway when Kane and Baptiste materialized. The effect was very similar to the time when they used your interphaser to make a transit."

"Similar, but not identical, I take it?"

An expression of discomfort crossed Bry's face. "I ran a system wide diagnostic through all the shared data links, the target coordinate locks and imaging autosequencers. I found some—" he paused, groping for the proper word "—anomalies."

"Like what?"

"To make a point A to point B jump, the matter stream is channeled linearly from the transit origin point along the quantum pathway to the destination unit. Of course, I'm not telling you anything you don't know."

"I didn't know it," Banks said with a grin. "But then I've just been a nursemaid for the past three and a half years."

Lakesh chuckled. "I'm gratified that Mr. Bry at least acknowledges I know a little something about the system I designed. Go on, please."

Bry flushed in embarrassment but continued. "According to the molecular imaging scanners, the matter stream began linearly enough from the gateway in Tibet. Then, just for an instant, it appeared to branch off."

The smile vanished from Lakesh's face, and he stared at the slightly built man over the rims of his spectacles. "Branch off? Explain."

Bry held up three fingers. "Ancillary branches, three of them from the primary stream. Like I said, the effect lasted only for a microsecond, but I've never seen anything like it. Have you?''

A note of challenge underscored Bry's query. Lakesh pursed his lips. "I must admit, no. Never. Completely without precedent."

"When you built the interphaser, didn't you design it to activate the side arteries branching off between the primary entrance and exit points of the quantum pathways?" Bry inquired.

"Yes, but it was programmed to activate and interact with naturally occurring quantum vortices, not the Cerberus system. I asked Balam if the Trapezohedron is a point of power, a nontechnological hyperdimensional quantum vortex, but he didn't answer me."

"Then how do you explain it?"

Smiling ruefully, Lakesh intoned faintly, "'Three rocks. Three Kanes. You do math.'"

Bry's eyebrows knitted. "What?"

Forcing a laugh, Lakesh slid off the stool. "Just quoting an obscure yet gifted physicist. I think the conclusion is fairly obvious. The stones in Kane's possession triggered the branching-off effect."

"Maybe," Bry said doubtfully. "But branching off in what directions?"

Lakesh shrugged. "We don't know all the directions in which our own universe moves. It might, for all we know, have a sideways movement through the dimensions at an angle different from all others."

"To accept that, you have to take an awful lot for granted."

"Before the nukecaust," Lakesh replied, "scientists did extensive research into the multiverse theory. They were pretty convinced it could be proven by quantum physics.''

"Life and the universe are getting too complicated for me," Banks said.

Lakesh laughed shortly. "One thing's clear, gentlemen—the Black Stone has a lot of mysteries to be solved, and a lot of new ones will start when we begin our research."

"Research into what?" Bry demanded a little acidly. "The rock or the mat-trans glitch?"

"Good question." Lakesh stepped toward the wall trans-comm unit. "And that's one question only Kane can answer, so I suppose we had better put it to him."

"BAPTISTE HAS A LOT to answer for," Beth-Li said, digging the barrel of the H&K into the side of Brigid's head.

Kane looked at Brigid. She was composed, apparently not frightened, but he knew she had gone to great lengths as an archivist to perfect a poker face.

"Let me answer for it, Beth-Li," Kane said. "Put the blaster down."

Rouch smiled triumphantly. "That's not part of the program, Kane."

"Do you mind telling me what is, then?"

"Baptiste and I are going to take a little trip. We're going to Cobaltville. I know she's memorized the codes for the baron's private gateway."

Kane felt his facial muscles going slack, then contorting. After a moment, he said thoughtfully, "I suppose you'll get around to telling me why?"

In a voice trembling with barely suppressed fury, Rouch said, "I'm escaping this prison. There's nothing for me here."

Brigid spoke for the first time, in a calm, level voice. "There's less for you in Cobaltville."

"Not if I bring you as a prize," she snapped. "A criminal, a seditionist, the assassin of Baron Ragnar."

"You know I had nothing to do with that," Brigid replied.

"But Baron Cobalt doesn't know that, does he? Even if you deny it, do you think he'll believe you? And even if he did, so the fuck what? You skipped out on a death sentence, remember?"

Kane struggled against the effects of the drug, fighting to keep alert. "Do you really believe Baron Cobalt will reward you for bringing in Baptiste, that you won't share her death sentence?"

Uncertainty flickered for a moment in Rouch's dark eyes, then was washed away by flinty resolve. "Why wouldn't he? I have a lot a valuable information to barter with. And so does she."

"You'll betray Cerberus," Brigid stated.

"Why shouldn't I?" Beth-Li's voice hit a high note of fury. "What do I owe this place, or any of you? I had no choice about coming here. Lakesh set me up in Sharpeville. If I stayed there, I was dead."

Forcing a reasonable, sympathetic note into his voice, Kane said, "We're all the same here, Beth-Li. Exiles. That can't be undone."

"That remains to be seen."

"If you and Baptiste show up in Cobaltville," Kane declared flatly, "you'll both be chilled. Maybe you'll live a little longer than Baptiste, but you'll end up just as dead."

Rouch edged backward toward the door, the blaster still on a direct line with Brigid's temple. "We'll take our chances."

Kane took a cautious half step forward, cursing the weakness in his legs. He spoke tersely, doing his utmost to pack every word with an unshakable, persuasive conviction. "I was a Mag, Beth-Li. I know what they'll do to you. You won't be rewarded—you'll be tortured. No matter how much information you give them, they'll think you have more you're *not* giving them."

Glistening tears sprang to Beth Li's eyes. In a fierce whisper, she hissed, "That torture can't be any worse than what I'm suffering here—the mockery, the laughter—"

"Nobody's laughing at you," Brigid interrupted.

Beth-Li jabbed her hard with the barrel of the pistol, making her jerk her head and wince in pain. "Shut up! You're the worst one! You started it. You wouldn't step aside when I asked you. I told you if you fought me, you'd lose because I don't fight fair! You didn't believe me, did you?"

Grabbing a handful of Brigid's tied-back hair, Beth-Li pulled on it savagely, shrilling, "Do you believe me now?"

Swallowing his anger, Kane said, "Even if you're

allowed to jump out of here and make it to Cobaltville, I'll come after you.''

"Come for me?" she spit derisively. "Or for Baptiste? To save her and to chill me? You already told
me you'd do that if I threatened her again.''

Surprise glinted in the swift glance Brigid threw
toward Kane, but she said nothing.

Beth-Li laughed, a high, quavery note of hysteria
in it. She prodded Brigid with the H&K again. "Does
this qualify as a threat? I think it does, so even if I
let her go, you'll just chill me like you promised.
Another reason not to stay here, right?''

Kane made a semiexaggerated show of relaxing,
letting the tension ease out of his posture. The situation was uncomfortably similar to the time when
Salvo held Lakesh hostage at blasterpoint, but at least
then he had been armed with his Sin Eater.

"I won't chill you,'' he said calmly, quietly. "I
shouldn't have told you that. I didn't mean it, and
I'm sorry I said it. Tell me what you want, Beth-Li.
I'll do whatever you ask of me.''

Rouch bared her teeth in a silent snarl. "Until I
had this bitch at the point of a blaster, you wouldn't
do *anything* I asked, you son of a bitch. You couldn't
even give me respect! Who do you think you are,
treating me like you did? You've got no right—
you're nothing but a killer, a murderer of outlanders
and people who couldn't fight back! How dare you
act like I'm beneath your notice?''

Rouch's words stung him. She was a spurned,
scorned woman, and her ego would not allow her to
tolerate the humiliation, the insult to her pride. But

mixed in with her words of rage were the cutting blades of truth.

Beth-Li furiously blinked back the tears of shame. Lakesh's reedy voice suddenly blared from the wall trans-comm. "Kane, are you up and about?"

Reflexively, Rouch swung her head in the direction the unit. In that instant, Brigid and Kane moved simultaneously.

In one swift motion, Brigid stepped backward, stamping down hard with her foot on Rouch's instep, pivoting on it with all her weight, her hand sweeping back to chop at the blaster.

At the same time Kane lunged forward, but his body felt as if it were draped in heavy chains. He seemed to drift, as slow as a broken-legged tortoise. The H&K went off with a sharp, hand-clapping bang. Something hard and hot drove into Kane's left side, pushing him backward to sprawl in a loose-limbed heap on the floor.

Beth-Li uttered a half-scream, struggling to pull her foot free from beneath Brigid's heel and bring the blaster to bear. She tried to align her captive's body with its muzzle. She squeezed the trigger just as Brigid leaned to one side.

Brigid felt the thundering shock wave and the bullet splashed hot air across her cheek. She hooked her left fist into Rouch's body. Starting from the hip, the punch hinged the woman in the middle, and her mouth and eyes flew wide. Latching on to her right forearm with both hands, Brigid snapped up a knee as if her adversary's arm were a stick of kindling she intended to break in two.

Beth-Li uttered a gagging shriek, and the pistol fell to the carpet. Brigid shifted her hold, trying to get her into a hammerlock and force her facedown on the floor.

"Kane?" Lakesh's voice filtered out of the trans-comm, sounding puzzled and a little alarmed. The trans-comms were voice activated, so Beth-Li's inarticulate cry had been transmitted to him.

Brigid gritted her teeth and applied more pressure to Beth-Li's arm. She had received a few lessons in rough and tumble from both Grant and Kane, and she assumed it wouldn't require much effort to lay the woman out.

Her adversary surprised her, first by wriggling out of her grip, then by headbutting her in the lower belly with such force she felt bile leap up her throat.

Rouch's hands lashed out, sharp fingernails seeking her eyes. Brigid slapped them aside and found herself battling less of a woman than a crazed animal. She opened her mouth to call out to Lakesh, but Rouch's hands lashed out, clutching her around the throat.

Prying on the woman's wrists, she tried to break Beth-Li's mercilessly choking grip. But the woman headbutted her in the breasts and unrelentingly held on, her momentum shoving Brigid backward.

Brigid chopped a karate blow at the base of Rouch's neck, like Kane had demonstrated, but the woman saw it coming and twisted away. The edge of her hand bounced off Beth-Li's shoulder. Both of them voiced short cries of pain, but she released her stranglehold.

As Brigid tried to drag enough oxygen into her lungs to call for Lakesh, Rouch swung her small, knotted fist in an arc that caught Brigid a glancing blow on the chin. She returned the punch with a fast, hard jab, landing it solidly and splitting Beth-Li's sensuous lower lip. She staggered, spitting blood.

Rouch feinted to the left, then leaped to the right, pivoted and swung her left leg up and around in a pretty fair crescent kick.

Brigid surged forward in the opposite direction. Rouch's boot grazed her head, but she slammed against her, grabbing a handful of silky black hair. Both women fell heavily.

Rouch struggled, heaving and gouging savagely at Brigid's eyes. She grasped her adversary beneath the chin, her long nails raking at her face. Brigid sank her teeth into Beth-Li's thumb, and she shrieked in pained fury.

Batting aside the woman's hands, Brigid dashed a straight right into the snarling face under her and started a flow of blood from Rouch's nostrils.

With a twist and sidewise wrench of her whole body, Beth-Li managed to shove Brigid to one side. She rolled and came swiftly to her feet, planting a boot on the side of Brigid's neck as she tried to rise.

Brigid went with the force of kick, back-somersaulted to her feet and rushed her. Rouch rammed the crown of her head forward, trying to butt her face into the back of her skull.

Dodging, Brigid kicked out with one long leg, clipping Beth-Li at ankle level. The woman fell, caught herself on the flats of her hands and swiveled, kicking

Brigid's already tender midsection. As she stumbled, Rouch sprang to her feet and launched a left hook.

Brigid shunted the blow aside with a right arm sweep, then brought her left fist up fast, connecting with the underside of Rouch's jaw.

The uppercut snapped the woman's head back. Arms windmilling, she toppled off her feet and crashed into the door. The rear of her head struck the stainless-steel doorknob, and she crumpled to the floor in a senseless heap.

Breathing raggedly, not knowing whether to rub her belly or her stinging knuckles, Brigid turned toward Kane. She estimated that the struggle with Beth-Li had comprised less than twenty seconds.

In those twenty seconds, a pool of blood, almost black in the dim light, had spread out around Kane's body. He had not stirred from where he had fallen.

Her cry of horror echoed in the room and activated the wall-comm.

"What's happening?" Lakesh demanded stridently. "Answer!"

"Send a medical and security detail!" Brigid shouted hoarsely as she fell to her knees beside Kane. "Stat!"

The blood-saturated carpet squished beneath her. She saw the ragged rent on the left side of Kane of bodysuit, with a wide crimson stain blooming around it. His eyes were closed, his respiration shallow and labored.

"Brigid?" came Lakesh's anxious voice. "What's going on?"

Biting her lip, she unzipped the front of his garment. The bullet from the H&K had ripped a deep gutter perhaps five inches long across Kane's left side, tearing the flesh and exposing a gleam of hipbone. Blood literally poured out of it.

"Kane's been shot," she replied, "by Rouch. It looks bad. Hurry!"

Getting to her feet, she raced to the bathroom, grabbed a towel and returned to Kane, pressing it against the wound, holding it there, applying steady pressure with one hand. She checked the pulse at his throat with the other. It beat thready and fast.

"You were trying to save me, Kane," she grated between clenched teeth. "I'm not going to watch you die again. I'm not going to watch you die!"

She spoke without thinking, and when she did think about her words, they frightened her. As she slapped Kane's cheek, trying to evoke any kind of response, the vivid memories of her vision during the gateway transition to Russia exploded full blown into her mind.

Brigid saw herself lashed to the stirrup of a saddle, lying in the muddy track of a road. Men in chainmail armor laughed and jeered above her, and long black tongues of whips licked out with hisses and cracks. Callused hands fondled her breasts, forced themselves between her legs.

Then she saw a man rushing from a hedgerow lining the road. He was thin and hollow-cheeked, perhaps nineteen or twenty years old. His gray-blue eyes burned with rage. She knew him, she called out to him, shouting for him to go back, go back—

He knocked men aside to reach her, and a spiked

mace rose above his head, poised there for a breathless second, then dropped straight down.

Her lips formed one word, a breathy rustle. "Kane…"

Holding him by the shoulders, she shook him, only vaguely aware of tears sliding hotly down her cheeks. The reasoning part of her mind coolly told her that the wound, although unsightly, was not mortal. Kane was unconscious due to the double effects of shock and the pain medication.

But that reasonable inner voice was drowned out by a clamor of visceral terror that *this* time she would watch him die. In a panic, she cuffed his face again. As she prepared to slap him again, his hand came up and grasped her around the wrist.

Eyelids fluttering, Kane said in a groaning whisper, "Goddammit, knock it off, Baptiste."

Her heart lurched with joy, and she scooted around to cradle his upper body, still holding the towel in place with one hand. "Medics are on their way," she said hoarsely. "Stay quiet."

He tentatively touched his reddening face where she had struck him and winced. "I will if you will."

Kane squinted up at her, lines of pain deep around his eyes. Lifting a hand, he gently fingered the wetness on her cheek. "What's this for? Not for me."

"Stay quiet," she repeated gruffly. Her voice broke, and she began weeping in earnest, ashamed of herself but not able to stop.

Kane moved his hand up, placing it on the back of her neck. "It's all right," he said. "You won't ever watch me die. As long as you're around to back me up, you won't have to watch me die.''

He pulled her head down to his, and her tears spilled onto his face.

Neither of them noticed Beth-Li regaining consciousness. She glared around, dazedly and painfully, then pushed herself to a sitting position. She stretched out a hand for the H&K on the floor.

Kane's lips had just touched Brigid's when the door burst open, propelled by Grant's 220 pounds of muscle. The doorknob cracked loudly against the back of Rouch's skull, knocking her forward and unconscious.

Behind Grant came Auerbach, DeFore, Domi, Banks and Lakesh. There was a wild, confusing babble of questions and demands. It took only a minute to revive Beth-Li, and she stood between Domi and Lakesh, her arms pinned behind her. Curtly, Brigid told them what happened.

When DeFore removed the blood-soaked towel to examine Kane's wound, Rouch said, ''Tough luck, Kane. I didn't mean to shoot you, but I see a couple of inches over would have made a good difference.''

Snarling, Domi backhanded the woman's mouth.

''A deep graze,'' DeFore said. ''The bullet tore through the epidermal and muscle tissues.''

Brigid swallowed a sigh a relief. What she had interpreted as exposed bone in the wound was only a scrap of Kane's white bodysuit.

''I don't think you have anything to worry about as long as you don't get into knife fights for a couple of days.''

"What's the chance of that?" Grant snorted.

"Let's get you back to the dispensary," DeFore stated crisply. A faint smile touched her full lips. "I might as well put a bed under permanent reserve for you."

Kane looked like he might argue but subsided when Brigid said, "Do as she says. While you're there, I'll have a cleanup crew brought in."

Auerbach and Banks slid their arms under Kane's body, clasped each other's forearms and lifted him up. As they carried him out, Brigid noted how Auerbach tried to make eye contact with Beth-Li, but she aloofly refused to look in his direction.

"Would you two mind escorting Beth-Li to the detention level?" Lakesh said to Grant and Domi.

Grant reached out toward the woman, but Brigid said matter-of-factly, "No. Not yet."

She fixed an emerald hard stare on a surprised Lakesh. "There are a few things that need to be cleared up first."

"Security protocols," Lakesh protested, then he closed his mouth.

"Grant, Domi, could you two wait outside?" Brigid asked. "Close the door."

Although she had made a request, her tone made it clear she wouldn't allow them to refuse. After a second or two of hesitation, they did as she asked.

When it was just the three of them, Brigid picked up the H&K from the floor, removed the magazine and tossed the blaster onto the bed.

"Really, dearest one," Lakesh said. "This is not the time or place for an interrogation of a prisoner."

"What makes you think she's a prisoner?" Brigid asked him coldly.

Both Lakesh and Beth-Li stared at her, startled.

"What do you mean?" Lakesh demanded angrily.

"Be quiet. I'm asking the questions here, and you've got more to answer for than Rouch."

Beth-Li swiped a sleeve over the blood trickling from her nostrils and lips and looked at Brigid with a combination of apprehension and curiosity.

Eyes boring into Lakesh's own, Brigid announced, "She claimed you set her up in Sharpeville so she had no choice but to leave and come here. I don't see any reason why she should lie about that. All I want from you is a direct confirmation or a direct denial—not a five-minute dissertation on whys and wherefores."

Lakesh bristled, trying to act as if he were deeply offended. "You've no right to question me. After all, without me—"

"Without you," she broke in, "I'd still be an archivist in Cobaltville without a termination warrant hanging over my head."

Lakesh did not react, not even with an eyeblink.

"You were in the process of setting me up with that bit of theater of the Preservationists recruiting me."

"Kane got involved," Lakesh objected. "That changed everything."

"By your own words," she said, "all he did was bump up your timetable. I quote 'If Kane hadn't involved you in his own personal crusade, you would have been brought here eventually…your case was already decided.'"

Lakesh knew it was futile to argue with her eidetic memory, so he elected to remain silent.

"Therefore," Brigid continued, "if you decided my case, and you decided Beth-Li's in a similar fashion, it's logical to conclude you decided everyone else's here in Cerberus, too."

She nodded toward Rouch. "Except you didn't make allowances for ever making a bad choice. It's not her fault, it's yours. And rather than take responsibility, you want to trundle her off to detention…so Cerberus can have another resident prisoner to make up for Balam's absence."

Lakesh and Beth-Li reacted with discomfited surprise to Brigid's accusations. Lakesh made a helpless gesture with his hands. "What else is there to do?" he bleated. "We can't release her, she knows too much. She intended to betray us to Baron Cobalt, she tried to kill Kane—"

"That was an accident," Brigid bit out. "What you did to her, maybe to all of us here, was deliberate. Perhaps not with malice aforethought, but you still used us as pawns in your chess game with the barons."

Genuine anger sparked in Lakesh's eyes behind the lenses of his spectacles. "And what were you in the villes?" he challenged.

"Safe," Rouch said.

Lakesh ignored the comment. "You were worse than pawns…you were drones, worker ants, dray animals from cradle to grave—or rather, from cradle to the processing plant. I gave you an opportunity to govern your own destinies, to reclaim the humanity that had been stolen from you.''

''As long as we abided by your personal definition of humanity,'' Brigid retorted, an icy edge in her voice. ''And you've yet to address the issue—did you frame Beth-Li for a crime she didn't commit?''

Lakesh exhaled a weary breath. ''Yes. But you must understand, the circumstances were such that I couldn't offer her or you an up-front choice about joining me.''

''You decided what was best for us,'' Brigid replied. ''Just like the barons.''

Lakesh shifted his feet, then glanced down at them.

Brigid turned to Rouch. ''I don't know what to do with you, Beth-Li. You should be Lakesh's responsibility, but he's obviously at a loss about what to do with you. So am I.''

''Then let me take responsibility for myself.''

''That would be nice,'' Brigid said dryly, ''in a perfect world. But you can't be allowed to go back to the villes. This is the dilemma Lakesh intentionally constructed—none of us can go back to our old lives even if we want to. What Kane said they'd do to you was true…you'd be kept alive only so they could torture information out of you. Lakesh can attest to that. And regardless of how you feel about Cerberus right now, it's still the only sanctuary you have.''

Beth-Li silently contemplated Brigid's words. Then she asked, ''What will you do to me?''

''I think we should leave that up to Kane.''

Lakesh jerked his head up, eyebrows curved high

over the rims of his spectacles. "She attacked you, she attacked Kane. We might have few rules here, but violence among the personnel and the intent to betray the redoubt cannot be countenanced!"

"Extenuating circumstances," Brigid intoned. "You invoke them whenever it suits you. I can do the same."

Lakesh gaped at her in stunned outrage. His lips contorted for several seconds before he sputtered, "You're not in charge here!"

"I don't recall anyone officially putting you in charge, either."

"But you can't—"

"Why not?" Brigid snapped, her voice trembling with barely repressed fury. "Didn't you give us the opportunity to govern our own destinies? Or do you really mean that you'll govern our destinies for us?"

She inhaled a calming breath. "I'm willing to overlook this, Beth-Li. But the final decision about what to do with you will be up to Kane. And until he makes it, I want your promise you'll confine yourself to quarters."

Beth-Li quirked an eyebrow. "And not try to leave the redoubt?"

"As far as I'm concerned, you're free to go. As long as you do it overland and on foot. Just so you'll know, I'll be locking out the autosequencer on the gateway, personally encrypting the codes so not even Bry can operate it."

Beth-Li's face remained expressionless, but Brigid knew she was visualizing the long, dangerous trek down the mountain road—and to the flatlands inhabited by the Lakota and the Cheyenne. They had no particular reason to love her, either.

"If I give you my word, make that promise, you'll believe me?" she asked.

"Until you give me a reason not to, yes."

Beth-Li nodded. "I give you my word."

She turned toward the door. Before opening it, she paused to say quietly, "I'm sorry, Baptiste."

Brigid's lips twitched in a rueful half smile. "I've been held hostage before."

Beth-Li shook her head. "No, not about that. I'm sorry I was so blind."

Brigid looked at her quizzically. "Blind?"

"I didn't know how deeply Kane loves you."

Brigid almost said, "Neither did I," but she let the observation pass without comment.

After Beth-Li closed the door behind her, Lakesh said sourly, "Even if Kane is as forgiving as you, we still have to figure out what to do with her."

Brigid looked at him dispassionately. "She can wait. The most immediate problem is to figure out what to do with you."

Chapter 11

Kane's wound was treated and dressed within the hour. As DeFore had diagnosed, it was superficial and required little more than disinfectant and a pressure bandage. She refused to administer any more painkillers, and Kane didn't argue with her.

DeFore also refused to administer medical advice. She knew that he would pay as much heed to her recommendation to stay quiet for a few days as Grant had regarding his own injuries.

She had not completed the interpretation of Kane's EEG and sourly pointed out that she never would if the interruptions continued.

Brigid and Grant ushered Kane out of the dispensary. To their questions about how he felt, he responded gruffly, "At least it takes my mind off my headache."

Brigid didn't smile. "Lakesh is waiting for us in his office. He's got some explaining to do."

Kane nodded grimly. "That he does. And so does Rouch. Did you lock her up?"

"No," she answered. "She's in her quarters. I'm leaving the decision of what to do with her up to you."

He glanced at her in surprise. "Up to me? *You're* leaving it? What's Lakesh's take on this?"

"Until we get some things straightened out, he's not going to be calling all the shots around here," Grant rumbled.

Kane squinted in his direction. "What are you planning? An insurrection?"

He spoke in jest, but his tone indicated he found the prospect pleasing.

Brigid pinched the air between thumb and forefinger. "A little one, for the time being at least."

Kane quickened his stiff-legged stride down the corridor. "Count me in."

Lakesh sat behind his desk in his small, sparsely furnished office. Besides the desk and four chairs, the only other piece of furniture was a small computer console. On the desk rested the primary facet of the Trapezohedron.

As the three people sat down, Lakesh said without preamble, "Let me remind you that although Cerberus was once a military installation, we are not bound by their laws and regulations."

"If by that you mean we can't bring you up on formal charges," Kane said with studied nonchalance, "we haven't really thought about it."

Lakesh's blue eyes flickered with momentary apprehension, but he said firmly, "I offered everyone here an alternative to a lifetime of serfdom in the baronies. If that is a crime, then go ahead and judge me guilty so we can get on with the real work here."

"That's the main question now, isn't it?" Brigid inquired. "What *is* our real work now, since we've learned the Archon Directorate doesn't exist?"

"The population of hybrids still swells," Lakesh

bit out. "The barons still rule. Our work is the same."

"But the way we approach it has to be different from now on," Grant stated. "With no Directorate guiding the barons—"

"We have only Balam's word for that," Lakesh broke in.

Kane uttered a scornful laugh. "You were the one who figured out that the only so-called Archon was Balam. What did you call it—the Oz effect?"

Lakesh nodded in reluctant agreement. The twentieth century exobiologists had postulated that all Archons were anchored to one another through hyperspatial filaments of psionic energy, much like the hive mind of certain insect species. Lakesh had always assumed the mind link was passive, and therefore Balam could not clearly communicate to his brethren of his three-year-long captivity.

Lakesh had also contemplated the possibility that Balam no longer had brethren with which to communicate. And if Balam was indeed the last of his kind, then there was no Archon Directorate, just as there were no Preservationists.

"You've been more than willing to accept everything else that Balam told us," Brigid declared. "Why doubt this, when there's actually hard evidence he was telling the truth?"

"Balam's people have deceived and tricked humanity since time immemorial, always constructing a web of diversions and cover stories. Balam's tale of his race, as compelling as it was, cannot be taken completely at face value."

"What a coincidence," Grant said snidely. "Neither can you anymore."

Lakesh removed his glasses and wearily massaged his eyes. "Do you have any idea of how tiring it is to have the fate of humanity on your shoulders? True enough, I chose the burden when I could have just as easily lived out my second life as one of the baron's elite.

"But when I chose that burden, I also had no choice but to employ the rule of what is best for the greatest number. Withal, I know that sooner or later...somewhere, somehow, I must settle with the world and make payment for what I have done."

"That time could be now," Kane said harshly. "If what Beth-Li said is true, you've done a lot of things you need to pay for. And it's not just her you owe a debt—its everyone in the redoubt."

Lakesh dropped his hands from his face and blinked at them. He looked exhausted. Not for the first time, Kane received the impression of a great, soul-deep pain, in equal measure to his great age. He had carried two centuries' worth of guilt in his stoop-shouldered frame.

Only a few days before Kane had accused him of being less concerned about the fate of humanity than erasing the remorse from his psyche.

"Perhaps everything I've done over the last fifty years is straw-grasping," Lakesh said haltingly. "Ingratiating myself with Baron Cobalt, trying to create a superior breed of human to build a resistance movement—maybe it was all a grand, utopian delusion. But I couldn't adopt your fatalistic attitude, Kane.

Not when there was the most microscopic chance that humankind could overcome the tyranny of the barons. Even if it was only one chance in a million—*ten* million—I couldn't overlook it.

"All of my schemes, my plans, and yes, I admit it, my conniving, might not amount to much right now. But it's the future that obsesses me. I've come to terms with the fact that the past can't be undone, so I must focus on the future."

"And what about the present?" Brigid demanded. "You can't ignore it or shrug it off, saying it doesn't matter."

"Let's get to the crux of the present situation, then," Lakesh shot back. "Do you wish me to stand down? Should we have a vote among our personnel about who is the most qualified to make decisions?"

"Why not?" Kane drawled. "You didn't give them the option to vote on whether they wanted to be forced into exile."

"The situation is not quite as cut and dried as Beth-Li implied," Lakesh replied. "And even if it was and you tell everyone here I set them up, framed them for crimes, do you honestly think they'll vote me out of office?"

"No," Grant stated darkly, "I think they'll lynch you."

"Ah, I see. Do you want that to happen or do you want to prevent it?"

The three people did not respond for a long moment. Lakesh surveyed them silently, one by one. When no answer was forthcoming, he said, "If I had not done what I did, followed a course of action determined by circumstances, the resources represented by the people here would be in service to the barons, directed against humankind, to insure they were kept in heavy harness. What do you think would have happened to you three if I hadn't interfered in your lives?"

He pointed a gnarled finger at Kane. "You would be a member of the Cobaltville Trust, completely subservient to Salvo. Didn't you say he told you he recruited you into the Trust so he could assign you every filthy, soul-breaking job imaginable? More than likely you would be quite mad by now, a raving psychotic. Or dead."

The finger moved to Grant. "And you, sir—it's even easier to extrapolate your fate. Due to your close association with friend Kane, you would not have received your administrative transfer. You would be months dead by now…and if Kane wasn't ordered to pull the trigger himself, he would be ordered to stand aside while the deed was done."

Lakesh shifted his attention and finger to Brigid. "And you, dearest one…if you hadn't been convicted of a crime, you'd certainly be under suspicion by now. Your intellect is too active, too probing, your devotion to the truth would not have permitted you to live out the rest of your life inputting false history. As with the fabled cat, your curiosity would have gotten you killed."

"Are you trying to convince us you did us a favor?" Kane asked bleakly.

Lakesh spread his hands in a take-your-pick gesture. "Whether I performed a service for you is strictly subjective. All choices, no matter how trivial, might have enormous consequences, not just for the individuals involved, but for all of history. Tiny changes in probability can trigger events so long-range and far-reaching that our minds can't comprehend them.''

Kane forced a smirk. ''You sound like Balam with his bullshit about parallel casements.''

He reached out to pick up the primary facet of the Trapezohedron. ''Why don't you consult this like his people did—''

He felt his thoughts and body tense up in shock. A sudden riot of images exploded in his mind. They were only wheeling pieces, splinters of fire and blood and the gulfs of deep space. He felt a crazed tumble of emotions, all different, but all simultaneous—anger, stark terror and a grief so deep it seemed his heart would shrivel.

As if from an unimaginably vast distance, he heard Lakesh shrill, ''Drop it! *Now!*''

Kane tried, but he couldn't open his hand and release the rock. The stone seemed to have become a part of him, splitting then propelling his awareness, his very identity into hundreds of directions. An awful chill seemed to settle in his body, numbing his nerve endings and paralyzing his will.

The swirling kaleidoscope of chaos formed a funnel, and Kane felt an insistent probing deep inside his mind. He felt the presence of the galaxy, spreading inward from his own point of perceptions, layer upon layer of it, time piled upon time.

He sensed something that did not fit, something

that was more than alien or extraterrestrial. It was not nonhuman, it was *antihuman*. With that sensing came a knowledge of what it was, and the chill spread from his body, seeming to seep into his soul. He had been psionically probed before—there was the blind doomie, Morrigan, the crazed psi-mutie Crawler and of course Balam. But this touch felt different in texture. During the prior experiences, he had been aware of a tincture of humanity behind the mental energies.

But this was different, as though he were being examined by the embodiment of total evil, of utter hatred. A white something appeared at one end of the funnel, and in piecemeal fashion it acquired a face— a familiar one.

The high-boned face was very pale, with sharp cheekbones and a jutting chin. His ears were very small and delicately shaped, nestled close to the hairless skull. His inhumanly large, curved eyes had no pupils, only obsidian irises with a bare hint of white at the corners. The eyes were less organs of vision than apertures leading to the fathomless ends of the universe.

The chalk-colored, sensually shaped lips didn't move, but a thready nonvoice insinuated itself into Kane's mind. The intensity of the emotion behind the voice was savage.

You. I know you. On how many casements must we contend with each other before you bow down to the inevitable?

The first time Kane had seen the man—the creature—calling himself Colonel Thrush, he had been overwhelmed with a hate-fueled mad rage to strangle what passed for life out of him. That intense emotion returned, flooding him, blotting out all reason.

The image of Thrush seemed to smile, coldly and mockingly. Behind the smile Kane sensed a dreadful hunger, an equally strong hatred for what it needed to consume—its opposite, human life, human aspirations, human dreams. The human spirit.

You know so little, whispered the voice, *about why things are, even if you profess an understanding of the how. Long ago the race you call the Archons learned how to conquer sidereal space. For millennia, all their efforts were devoted to this task. Instead of building spaceships, they discovered how to manipulate space itself.*

Your own scientists regarded sidereal space as a negative universe. To them, it was only a theory. The race you called Archons made it a fact.

Kane writhed and twisted, trying to break the contact, straining to free his limbs and mind.

They could occupy Earth not only in the present but in all past and future ages. Do you know what this means, not just for your Earth, but all of those lying parallel to it?

Images flooded Kane's mind, one after another, coming so fast they melded together to form a reeling tapestry of horror that stretched to infinity. The images weren't depictions of actual events, they were primarily symbolic, but he understood their meaning all the same. He felt a sickening sensation as all stability and sanity crumbled, then he careened through scenes of carnage, of blood and fire.

Monstrous pillars of flame roared above the skyline of cities. Men, women and children fled, howling like souls in hell.

No more human race, except as slaves or dumb brutes. Where the Archons failed on one casement, they have succeeded on others. I saw to it, and I will continue to see to it.

Kane saw rows of red things strapped to tables, living human beings in the process of dissection. He glimpsed white bones and blood and strips of flesh laid back for the inspection and removal of internal organs.

He stared at a world, at many worlds in torment, of skies across which curtains of black smoke scudded, of blistering shock waves wrenching mountains from their beds, flattening cities, monuments and all the works of man.

There is no use in fighting.

Terror drove out the rage and hatred in Kane. This was not a war like most wars. It did not hinge on economics, conflicting ideologies or even the survival of a threatened species.

I penetrate all the barriers between casements, going back into the past, infiltrating the highest corridors of power so that when the proper historical moment arrives to strike, the world changes. Forever.

Kane struggled, fought and wept in furious frustration.

War burns across all the casements. The war that was fought and lost on your own world still wages across many others. You continue to fight it, as you do here. And as here, you continue to be defeated.

You must learn to accept the fate we have in store for you, for it is my fate to bring it forth into reality.

Kane screamed, trying to blot out all the implications of the fate Thrush visited upon humankind.

You need not take any action. You will know my presence in your own casement soon enough. By then, I hope you will have resigned yourself to what cannot be changed. Do not fight anymore. There is no use in it.

Chapter 12

A tiny constellation of sparks flashed within the stone, visible between Kane's fingers. Thread-thin electric discharges played up and down its length.

"Drop it!" Lakesh shrilled. *"Now!"*

Kane stared at the stone fixedly, his hair weaving slightly as though he were standing in the face of a breeze. The crackling display from the stone built in intensity inside of a second.

Grant moved first. His big brown hand slapped the chunk of black rock out of Kane's hand. It went spinning and bouncing across the floor, clattering into a far corner.

Gasping, Kane fell back in his chair. Shivering violently, he hugged himself, his pale eyes bright and crazed. An anguished, hoarse whisper came from his lips. "No, you bastard—"

Lakesh and Brigid stared in wonderment, first at Kane, then toward the facet of the stone. Putting his eyeglasses back on, Lakesh arose from the desk and approached it gingerly, nudging it with a foot. Nothing happened. It just lay in the corner like a harmless chunk of inert mineral.

"What the hell happened?" Grant demanded, trying to cover his fear with a veneer of anger. "As soon as he touched it..." His words trailed off.

"Just speculating off the top of my head," Lakesh said in his reedy voice, "because I'm too amazed at the moment for rational thought, I submit that Kane and the Trapezohedron share some sort of hyperdimensional bond—most likely due to him making a gateway transit with the pieces in physical proximity."

"You might have mentioned that to me," Kane grated, dabbing at the beads of perspiration pebbling his forehead.

"I had no idea you were going to grab it and use it like a Magic Eight Ball," Lakesh shot back.

Nobody knew what a Magic Eight Ball might be, and nobody asked about it. Brigid cast her eyes nervously toward Kane. His breathing was less labored, but fear still shone in his eyes. "Zakat made two mattrans jumps with at least one fragment of the stone in his possession," she said. "He didn't mention anything about a phenomena like this."

She paused and asked Kane, "Did he?"

Kane pulled in a deep breath and said, "No, at the end there we didn't have a whole lot to say to each other. But forget him—I had a communication."

Grant's eyebrows knitted in skepticism. "When?"

"Just now."

"You weren't holding the rock for more than five seconds, if that."

Shaking his head, Kane said, "I don't care. Thrush talked to me."

Lakesh swung his head sharply toward him, his blue eyes alight with excitement. "Through the stone?"

"Guess so."

Brigid regarded him with a troubled gaze. "You had a vision of him when you touched the stone in Agartha, too. It can't be a coincidence."

"It's not," Kane replied in a grim, flat tone. "He—"

Lakesh cut him off with a gesture. "You've yet to fully brief me on everything that happened in Tibet. Do so now."

Grant cleared his throat with a rude sound. "Hold on. We've other matters to settle."

Bending, Lakesh poked at the dark stone with a finger, then picked up it, holding it as if it were incredibly fragile. He returned to his chair behind the desk. "Those are secondary, administrative matters. I submit the topic of the Shining Trapezohedron takes precedence."

His lips twitched in an impish smile. "However, if that doesn't meet your democratic impulses, we can put it to a vote."

Kane and Brigid eyed the facet of the Trapezohedron. The anticipatory tingle of nerves that a challenge always stimulated began to push away the fear clouding Kane's mind. "The stone."

He exchanged a quizzical look with Brigid, and after a thoughtful moment, she intoned, "The stone."

Grant hissed out *"Shit,"* then grunted, "The stone."

THE DEBRIEFING TOOK so long that Grant regretted not casting a dissenting vote. Lakesh questioned nearly every statement made by Kane and Brigid, particularly Kane. Their experiences in Agartha bordered on the fantastic, but what they had undergone and witnessed were no less believable than some of the other ops they had been on.

Grant was less interested in the nature of the Trapezohedron than Kane's statement that Balam's assertion of the nonexistence of the Archon Directorate appeared to be substantially true.

Breaking into Kane's report, Grant declared, "That's a little hard to swallow. The Archon Directive was the predark governing body overseeing the development of the Totality Concept projects, right? After the nukecaust, it became the Directorate. Surely somebody in power knew it was all a shuck."

"Never underestimate the capacity of the human mind to embrace an illusion," Lakesh gently admonished him. "Particularly if that illusion is beneficial in a material sense."

Brigid nodded. "For power-mad bureaucrats and military men, the belief in the Directorate provided them with everything they ever dreamed of having. If any of them ever wondered why Balam seemed to be the only representative of this superior race, they kept it to themselves."

Lakesh smiled dourly. "I'm certain there were a few of Balam's people still alive back in the 1940s and early fifties when the covert agreement was drafted. Even if there were only a handful of so-called Archons, human greed and imagination multiplied the number by a factor of ten. One of their aircraft became a fleet, one of their infrasound weapons became a vast armory.

"In any event, I'm sure by the mid-1980s, Balam's human allies—or pawns—were pretty much running the whole show."

Wearily, Kane said, "He as much as said so, but that still doesn't let him off the hook. He set the whole goddamn doomsday scenario into motion from the time he was dug out of the tundra in Russia and traded to the American military."

Lakesh favored him with a reproachful gaze. "You miss him as a focus for your hate, don't you?"

Kane met that gaze with a glare, but he did not acknowledge the query. "To me, the main question is whether the barons know or ever knew there was no such thing as an Archon Directorate. Barch in Ragnarville didn't believe in them."

"But he wasn't a baron," Brigid pointed out. "Not a hybrid. If Balam was psychically linked, even passively, to the hybrids since their nonhuman genes derived from him, might they not still be linked to him in some fashion? The barons may still have the impression they're connected to the Directorate."

Lakesh pursed his lips. "Possibly. But they're not idiots. A few of them have probably been asking the same question Barch asked—with all that's happened in the past few months, why have the Archons not interceded?"

Grant smiled humorlessly. "Like the predark bastards who bought into the Archon Directorate, it's in their best interest not to have that question answered."

"Exactly!" Lakesh exclaimed with surprising heat. "And since only we know the answer, we've given a powerful weapon to unseat the barons—the truth.''

Kane uttered a derisive chuckle. "I think blasters will be of more use in the long run.''

Lakesh grinned. "I must disagree, friend Kane. I think rocks—or one rock—will beat out firearms.''

He tapped the Black Stone on the desk. "Keys to doorways, Balam called the Trapezohedron, but I believe he was speaking metaphorically. The human brain is the actual key, in its electromagnetic interaction with the energies pent-up in the stone.''

He beamed at Kane as if he were his child who had just completed toilet training. "*Your* brain.''

Narrowing his eyes, Kane mulled over Lakesh's pronouncement for a handful of seconds. "Is that why you had DeFore give me an electro-whatever-the-hell?''

"One reason," Lakesh confirmed. "There was the genuine concern for your well-being, too, you know.''

"No, I didn't. If you're interested, my headache is pretty much gone.''

"Good.''

"But only because where Beth-Li shot me hurts worse at the moment.''

Lakesh's eyes flashed in annoyance by the digression to an earlier topic. "You weren't aware of it, but some highly unusual phenomena occurred when you materialized in the jump chamber.''

"Like what?" Brigid asked.

Lakesh inclined his head toward Grant. "Tell them.''

Grant did so, not enjoying the expressions of incredulity crossing Kane's face. When he spoke of Kane's apparent noncorporeality of form, even Brigid's normally stoic face registered astonishment.

"So much for friend Grant's perspective," Lakesh said, eyeing Kane keenly. "What about yours?"

"What makes you think I have one?"

"Intuition—and what happened when you touched the stone a few minutes ago."

Gusting out a sigh, Kane said, "Back in Agartha, when I first touched the main piece of the stone, I had a vision or a hallucination or something. I saw myself dying on a street somewhere. I'd been gut shot by Colonel Thrush. During the gateway transit, I had three more visions."

He licked his lips. "Not visions, really. More like experiences. It was like I was in other places, all at the same time."

"Tell us," Lakesh urged.

Haltingly, Kane did so.

"The first experience seemed to be the same place as my vision in Agartha," he concluded. "And though the others were different, Colonel Thrush was involved in each one. And so was war."

He rubbed his forehead, face drawn in a grimace. "I don't remember all the details. They're getting hazier by the minute."

"Jump dreams," Grant suggested uneasily. "Caused by a bad transit feed line to the unit in Tibet. It's happened before."

"That might have a little something to do with it,"

Lakesh conceded. "But not in the way you might think. Brigid, did you have jump dreams?"

"No, and if I had, I would've remembered them since they're usually so vivid."

Grant threw up his big hands in frustration. "Can we just get to the point here?"

"That's the trick," Lakesh stated smoothly. "There isn't just one point, but an infinite series of them."

Grant groaned, squeezing his eyes shut. "Here we go."

Lakesh ignored him. "According to the Many Worlds interpretation of quantum mechanics, all choices lead to a new universe splitting off."

"A branching probability universe?" Brigid inquired.

"Just so. At a fundamental level, this includes every quantum event, even on a subatomic scale. We're talking probability wave functions, which were in effect when we utilized the Omega Path program a few months back."

"That dealt with time travel," Kane said. "Trying to achieve what Operation Chronos had done without duplicating their efforts."

Lakesh shrugged. "If you take for granted that time is cyclic in accordance with the other known laws of the universe—although, as you well know, the Omega Path seemed to prove that there is more than one particular time flow operating in our own universe—if you take that for granted, we can describe the rest by the means of lines."

Brigid cocked her head toward him. "Lines?"

Making elaborate hand gestures, Lakesh replied, "Imagine that we have a finite number of space-time continua, each with some mutually shared laws. They're all, like us, traveling this way. There is no contact between us, but we exist side by side without being aware of each other's presence, all stretching out in different sets of dimensions. Imagine that the normal continuum, as we understand the word normal, lies horizontally, as it were."

"Parallel casements," Kane murmured.

Lakesh nodded. "Imagine these other parallel casements lying vertical to it. "

Brigid tentatively reached out to touch the stone, thought better of it and withdrew her hand. "Balam mentioned sidereal space, where there are many tangential points lying adjacent to one another."

"Exactly. Theories such as these are among the most intellectually challenging in science, but I remind you that Balam's people successfully reconciled quantum and relativity physics ages ago. The primary subdivisions of the Totality Concept were built on their discoveries."

Addressing Kane, he asked, "When you were in mind-meld with Balam, didn't you glimpse his people's method of using the Trapezohedron?"

Kane nodded slowly, trying to dredge up the chaotic memories of the images Balam had imparted, and make sense of them. The survivors of the ages-old cataclysm that had decimated Balam's people consulted the Shining Trapezohedron, desperate to find a solution to their tragedy within its black facets. It had showed them how to build thresholds to parallel casements. Kane remembered seeing what seemed to be a glimmering archway over the stone.

Hesitantly, he said, "In ages past, the root races of Balam's people, the Annunnkai and the Tuatha Da Danaan, used such interdimensional thresholds created by the stone, because Earth was the end of a parallel axis of a casements."

"Hmm," Lakesh said. "Obviously, the basic principles of the mat-trans units were in use, although expanded far beyond linear travel from place to place."

"This is all very not interesting," Grant said sarcastically. "Just tell me—is the stone really a rock or a machine disguised to look like one?"

Lakesh threw him a forced smile. "The tests we performed on the stone were inconclusive. In fact there were no results, period. I suggest that the artifact is a complex probability-wave packet, a mathematical equation in physical form. It is an interface between our universe and others. Balam described it as a piece of 'pure' matter, which does not necessarily mean it's *our* universe's matter."

Kane rubbed his temples. "My headache is coming back."

"And I'm getting one," Grant rumbled.

"There's no reason why the human mind shouldn't question everything," Lakesh said reasonably.

Kane shook his head in angry frustration. "Except you, I guess."

Lakesh's shoulders stiffened at the gibe, but he did not respond to it.

"Just what does all this mean, exactly?" Kane demanded.

Spreading his hands palm up, Lakesh answered, "I'm not really sure. When you touched the primary piece of the Trapezohedron in Agartha, a connection between you and it was formed. When exposed to the quantum energies of the gateway, that connection became an actual conduit, shunting your perceptions, your mind as it were, to these parallel casements, to your dopplegangers in the other universes.

"Why Colonel Thrush figured so prominently is still something of a mystery, but I surmise it's the same reason all three of you—and Domi—encountered him during your interphaser-induced time travel. The quantum mechanics in use are essentially the same."

Kane's eyes and voice were cold when he said, "It's not a mystery why Colonel Thrush was the central figure in all of those casements."

Lakesh looked at him in surprise. "It isn't? Why?"

"Thrush intends to conquer them all, all the lost Earths, one by one until humanity is either enslaved or extinct. And I don't think he plans to overlook this particular casement, either."

"How do you know this?" Grant challenged.

Kane gave him a level stare. "He told me."

Chapter 13

Grant, Kane and Brigid all retained exceptionally unpleasant memories of their first meetings with Colonel C. W. Thrush. Even Domi had her own tale to tell of how she saw Thrush execute Adolf Hitler on April 30, 1945.

Brigid had watched Thrush issue the orders to cover up the Roswell Incident in 1947.

Kane had witnessed Thrush's involvement in the assassination of President John F. Kennedy in 1963.

On January 19, 2001, Grant observed Thrush personally setting the timer on the nuclear warhead concealed within the Russian embassy. The warhead detonated twenty-four hours later, triggering the global apocalypse known to later generations as the nukecaust.

In each time period, Colonel Thrush had sensed their disembodied presence, and he had even told Grant his name was derived from a poem by T. S. Elliot, a verse that asked: Should the deception of the thrush be followed into our first world?

When Kane and Brigid finally confronted him, face-to-face in the past of an alternate temporal plane, Thrush claimed versions of him existed in all times to prevent the interference in human history from being undone.

According to Lakesh, he had seen him in the Overproject Whisper testing facility, back in the 1990s, where he claimed to be a colonel in the Air Force.

Swiftly and grimly, Kane related what he had seen and been told during his brief communication with Thrush when he held the Black Stone.

Lakesh paled, but he tried to keep his voice steady when he said, "It's possible—indeed probable—that all of the alternate worlds, the lost Earths, came about due to Thrush's actions throughout time."

"Makes a certain amount of sense," Kane said. "A version of Thrush exists in all of those parallel casements."

"And more than likely so do analogues of all of us," Lakesh stated. "You most certainly."

"And apparently," Brigid ventured, "all of those versions of you are in conflict with all of the versions of him and his agenda."

"But Thrush was an Archon agent," Grant objected. "His agenda is the Directorate's agenda."

"He never actually admitted to working for the Directorate," Brigid replied. "He said, 'do you think the Archons would entrust one of you creatures with my responsibilities?' He made an oblique reference to his employers, but he never identified them."

Everyone knew better than to dispute Brigid's perfect and total recall, but Kane declared, "The Archon Directorate still had something to do with him."

Brigid cast him an irritated, impatient glance. "Don't state the obvious, Kane. Of course he was involved with the Archon Directorate."

"*An* Archon Directorate," Lakesh interjected.

"Not necessarily 'the.' Perhaps a Directorate on parallel casements where they went about their conquest and subjugation of humanity differently than here."

His lips compressed contemplatively and after a silent second of pondering, he said, "On our Earth, the Archons allied themselves with the Third Reich, but the Nazis lost the war. Perhaps on the casement you visited, Kane, they were victorious and therefore there was no need to rig a global nuclear holocaust.

"On another casement, perhaps they established more overt contact, using diplomacy to get what they wanted.

"On the other, an all-out open state of war exists between Earth and the Directorate, a conflict that extended to space itself, where perhaps they had established beachheads on some of the planets in the solar system.

"It seems likely in retrospect that Thrush was more than a chrononaut, guarding the temporal streams. When you visited the past, it was that of an alternate Earth, a branching probability universe created by an alternate Archon Directorate."

Kane was only half listening, his thoughts leaping ahead. "I figured that out myself. But if the visions I saw of three alternate Earths were true, I wasn't just witnessing them, I participated in them."

"Which might explain," Lakesh replied, "the three ghostly afterimages of you friend Grant saw in the jump chamber."

He poked at intercom button on his desk. "DeFore?"

After a moment, the woman's slightly waspish voice filtered from the speak. "Yes?"

"Have you interpreted Kane's electroencephalogram yet?"

"Almost. I'm—" Her voice trailed off, as if she had walked out of range of the trans-comm. The silence lasted so long Lakesh called her name again.

She responded with a terse, "Is Kane there with you?"

"He is."

"Have him meet me in the cafeteria in about five minutes."

DeFore closed the connection. Lakesh regarded Kane gravely. "I think it's safe to assume the good doctor found some abnormalities in your brain-wave patterns."

Apprehension rose up in Kane, forming a hard lump in his throat that made swallowing difficult.

Noticing his anxiety, Lakesh said reassuringly, "I doubt it's anything serious. DeFore wouldn't have chosen a public place like the cafeteria to discuss anything life-threatening with you."

Stiffly, Kane pushed himself out of the chair, wincing at the pain lancing through his left hip. "Let's all find out what *she* found out."

The four people made their way along the softly gleaming corridors and down a elevator to the cafeteria. Most of the briefings were held there, even though there was a formal briefing theater on the third level.

DeFore was already seated at a corner table. Farrell and Cotta, two more Cerberus personnel, sat on the far side of the room, and they nodded to them as they entered.

DeFore had her left elbow propped on a folded sheaf of graph paper. With her right hand she poured a cup of coffee. One of the few advantages of being an exile in Cerberus was unrestricted access to genuine coffee, not the bitter synthetic gruel that had become the common, sub-par substitute since skydark. Literally tons of freeze-dried packets of the real article were cached in the redoubt's storage areas. There was enough coffee to last the exiles several lifetimes.

DeFore glanced up at their approach, and if she was nettled by the presence of Grant, Lakesh and Brigid, she didn't show it. More than likely she had expected them. Grant fetched cups at a serving table, and when all of them were seated, DeFore declared, "My training in brain anatomy and function is limited, largely self-taught since I came here. Cerebral activity is very complex, encompassing organic and electrical processes. So, it's possible—but not probable—I didn't perform the EEG correctly. Or I misinterpreted some of the data."

Kane took a careful sip of coffee to cover his surprise that DeFore, even in a backhanded fashion, was admitting her medical knowledge might be flawed.

"What did you find?" Lakesh inquired.

Stretching out a strip of graph paper, DeFore pointed to the rows of squiggly, jagged lines inscribed by the recording pen. "We've got the expected large magnitude alpha waves occurring at a frequency of eight to twelve cycles per second. Fairly normal.''

She pointed to another line, which dipped dramatically and jumped and dipped again. ''Here we have the spiking associated with epileptic seizures.''

She indicated another line that appeared identical to the first. ''Alpha waves again. Below that, we have the spikes again. The entire EEG alternates those wave forms.''

Grant frowned at her. ''And?''

''And the EEG wave forms shouldn't change very much during different kinds of sensory input or stimuli. But they did—almost as if the machine read several neural patterns produced by Kane's brain…all occurring simultaneously.''

She gazed at the people around the table expectantly, waiting for a response. When none was forthcoming, she announced a bit acidly, ''I guess I'll have to spell it out for you—I recorded at least three types of brain activity when there should have only been one. It was as if Kane were at rest, performing a verbal or spatial task, and undergoing a synaptic seizure, all at the same time.''

Brigid's eyes widened, then narrowed. ''Verbal and spatial tasks are controlled by different hemispheres of the brain, right?''

''Right.'' DeFore sounded slightly relieved that someone finally understood the reason for her confusion. ''However, toward the end of the test, the electrophysical signs of differences in activity between the hemispheres tapered off, almost as if they were integrating.''

Putting down his cup, Kane gazed at the woman levelly. "What does that mean?"

Folding her arms over her ample chest DeFore answered dogmatically, "I have no idea. You're either suffering the most extreme case of multiple-personality disorder on record—and the record goes back hundreds of years—or you're a mutie. But at least I know why you had such a severe headache. With readings like that, I'm a little surprised you didn't have a stroke."

Kane resisted the impulse to add, "And probably a little disappointed, too." Instead, he turned to Lakesh.

"Theories? Hypotheses? Speculation? My market is open."

Lakesh chuckled uneasily. "Very well, but keep in mind, you *did* ask. When you were caught in the altered quincunx effect, like the time you used the interphaser to jump from England to here, the amplified electromagnetic energy of your mind broke free of the synaptic organic structure of the brain. It breached the barrier between dimensions, and you were drawn to three parallel casements and three parallel versions of yourself. A kind of simultaneous sideways movement.

"You, the physical you sitting in that chair, were not there. Your molecular pattern was caught in the quincunx effect, trapped in a pocket of nonexistence while your mind melded with those of your extradimensional dopplegangers."

Lakesh paused to draw in a breath, not meeting DeFore's incredulous stare. He continued in a rush.

"In a time period so short it could never be measured, you knew what they knew, saw through their eyes, had access to their memories. If the meld had lasted longer, perhaps your own personality and thought patterns would have fully integrated with theirs. As it was, when the gateway materialization cycled to completion, you returned with hyperdimensional echoes of your alternate selves. Just traces of them—of you, rather. That's why your memories of what you witnessed are fading."

"Why wasn't he solid until I grabbed him?" Grant demanded, his dark face a hard mask of disbelief.

"Your question is its own answer," Lakesh retorted. "Kane was hovering at the interphase juncture, the hyperdimensional crossroads between the relativistic here and there. When you touched him, you provided a three-dimensional channel for his pattern to follow from the interphase point."

Grant rolled his eyes ceilingward. "You really don't know any more than the rest of us. You can just spout the jargon and make this bullshit sound reasonable."

Lakesh regarded him resentfully. "I can do more than that, friend Grant. I can realign the gateway's autosequencers and phase-transition coils and prolong the quincunx effect and duplicate what happened accidentally...as long as the pieces of the Trapezohedron are used as transitional-tap conduits."

"Rocks as conduits?" Grant growled.

"Remember what Balam called them? Conductors. Obviously, he meant conductors of quantum energy flows. Therefore—"

"Why would you want to duplicate this?" DeFore interrupted in surprise. She was more than a little at sea about the topic, but it was obvious she hadn't cared for what she had heard so far.

Lakesh didn't appear peeved by her interruption. "Perhaps duplication is an inaccurate term. Who knows, the intensely vivid jump dreams reported by the *Wyeth Codex* might not have been products of the imagination at all, but glimpses into other realities and other times."

Brigid's lips pursed in a thoughtful moue. "You said that those adverse effects were due to the modulation frequencies of the carrier wave not perfectly interfacing with individual metabolisms."

Lakesh nodded. "True enough, as far as it goes. But that does not preclude what I just postulated. In fact it supports it. Because the carrier wave wasn't perfectly in sync between the origin and destination gateway units, the dimensional barriers could have been weakened just enough to permit stimuli from other realities to leak in, to impinge upon the human mind while it was in the matrix of interphase."

Brigid and Kane did not respond to Lakesh's declarations, but they pondered the implications, drawing on their memories of high strangeness during gateway transits.

During the jump to Russia, both of them had shared the same vision of past incarnations. A short while later, while transiting to England, Kane had experienced a telepathic communication from the mad but psionically gifted Sister Fand. During that communication, he had glimpsed vignettes from what appeared to be a past life as the legendary Celtic warrior, Cuchulainn.

Comparing their own experiences with Lakesh's hypothesis, as incredible as it sounded, it did not seem out of the realm of possibility.

Kane shook his head grimly. He could accept the idea of one infinite universe if not understand it, but his mind could not quite contain the concepts of many universes. "I'm not able to grasp any of your theories about sidereal space, multiverses and shifting through dimensions. But if Thrush intends to do here what he's done on those other Earths, then he has to be stopped."

Brigid ran her hands through her thick hair in exasperation. "The mystique of theoretical science," she murmured. "At once a monster and a salvation."

Gazing directly at Kane, she asked, "Stop Thrush from doing what, exactly? He already interfered in our time line, remember? He rigged history so it would lead to the nukecaust. For all intents and purposes, he accomplished what he set out to do."

"Don't tell me I'm stating the obvious again," he replied sarcastically.

Lakesh lifted an admonishing finger. "Did he? Humankind still survives. There is opposition to the barons. And we know the Archon Directorate doesn't exist."

"Do you think he knows that we know?" Brigid asked.

Lakesh tugged absently at his nose. "I think we can't take that chance. We don't know the depth of his communication with friend Kane, whether he riffled through his thoughts and knowledge. Apparently, he has in his possession a version of the Trapezohedron, and when Kane achieved a link with it, he achieved a link with Thrush, as well.''

Grant set down his coffee cup with such force that liquid sloshed out of it. In a harsh, aggressive tone, he snapped, ''What are we supposed to do about it?''

No one responded for a long moment. Slowly, deliberately, Lakesh lifted his cup to his lips, blew on the coffee, took a sip and placed it gently on the table, in direct counterpoint to Grant's anger.

Calmly, he extended a finger and pointed one by to one to Kane, Brigid and Grant. ''Three rocks, three of you,'' he intoned. ''You do math.''

Chapter 14

The star-speckled indigo tapestry of the sky lit up with a series of dazzling explosions. Fanciful purple fire-flowers bloomed, spreading their sparkling petals in all directions. Iridescent streamers showered to the ground, and the booming echoes of the cannonade over the city shook walls and rattled windows in their frames.

Kane paid no attention to either the colorful display of pyrotechnics or the thunder of the explosions. He concentrated on Beth-Li's lithe little body as she plunged herself down on him. Her wordless cry as he filled her was smothered by another detonation of fireworks.

The bursting flare briefly illuminated her perfectly sculpted figure, gleaming on her flat belly and her face, twisted now in passion. She breathed heavily, arching her back, her long hair spilling down to her narrow waist like a flow of India ink.

Reaching up, Kane cupped her pear-shaped breasts, enjoying the feel of the stiff nipples poking against the palms of his hands like wooden pegs. Beth-Li moaned, digging her long nails into the smooth, muscled contours of his chest. She bucked and writhed atop him, pelvis rocking in a steady motion.

Rotating her hips, she leaned forward, bringing her breasts down to his lips. She cried out and shuddered as he tongued them. "I've waited so long for this," she half gasped.

Beth-Li had already borne him one child, and the Purity Control Foundation had been so pleased with their offspring—Kane wasn't sure, but he thought Beth-Li had told him the baby had been a boy—they had ordered him to impregnate her a second time. Inasmuch as he was a Level Four Breed, the elite of the elite, and Beth-Li was a Level Four breeder, a second pairing was inevitable.

She had enjoyed the seeding the first time, but there had been several breeders since their initial coupling, and all of them claimed to have enjoyed it. Whether they or Beth-Li had been sincere or simply pretending from fear, Kane neither knew or cared.

Another burst of fireworks shook the walls, and Kane's concentration faltered. Although it was the standard Unification Day celebration, observed every January 20 for the past one hundred and ninety-nine years, the bombardment always put him in mind of the time he had been pinned down by Canadian artillery fire.

Beth-Li didn't notice his distraction. She was completely absorbed with riding him, uttering grunts and groans, bouncing up and down.

Kane realized he'd had enough of her. The novelty abruptly wore off, and he wanted it finished.

Closing his hands around her firm buttocks, he rolled over and positioned himself atop her. He thrust and plunged deep into Beth-Li, hard and fast. Her hips matched his pistoning, savage rhythm.

Beth-Li's gasps blurred into a broken, aspirated scream as her body locked in a spasming contraction of release. As another rocket burst into multicolored flame, Kane imitated the explosion with one of his own. He clenched his teeth, not allowing any sound to escape as he poured his seed into her.

Beth-Li was unwilling to release him, moaning and wriggling, holding him close. Finally, with a small sigh of disappointment, her legs fell away from him and Kane withdrew.

Sitting on the edge of the bed, Kane waited for the weakness in his legs to abate and get his breathing under control. Beth-Li stroked his sweat-filmed back and murmured, ''I won't be happy with just this one night.''

Kane felt a surge of annoyance, almost a revulsion. ''It's not up to you,'' he said slowly.

She was silent for a moment, then asked, ''What if it was up to you?''

The truth of the matter was that he was tired of Beth-Li, in fact tired of all the simpering women the Eugenics General paired him with.

He arose from the bed, suddenly desperate to take a bath, to wash the scent and feel of Beth-Li from his body. She called after him tremulously as he stalked to the bathroom and stepped into the shower stall. He stayed beneath the cold spray for a long time, scrubbing with soap and brush.

When he felt as clean as he could possibly get with only soap and water, he returned to the bedroom, and to his irritation, Beth-Li was still there. He reached for his uniform, hanging in the closet. "I've got to go."

Beth-Li propped her head up on one hand. "Go where? It's a holiday, Unification Day."

"I've got intel reports to review," he replied brusquely, tugging on his black, flared jodhpurs. "There's Roamer activity out in the Dakotas."

He knew how lame his excuse sounded. Even if the reports of a Roamer band were true, such matters were the province of the regional Provost Marshals, not the Rapier Legion.

Beth-Li did not question him further. She watched him don the wide-collared uniform tunic with the silver piping running in a tight line along the shoulder and chest. The insignia patch on the sleeve, three black inverted triangles against a triangular red background, looked like a splotch of blood in the semi-darkness.

He pulled on a pair of high black boots and strapped a pouched leather belt around his trim waist, making sure his Sin Eater was snugged securely its spring-powered holster.

Settling the peaked, leather-visored black cap upon his head, he checked his image in the bureau's mirror, through force of habit.

Another bomb burst momentarily flooded the room with yellow light, and he saw a stranger gazing back at him from the mirror. No, not a stranger exactly— the reflection looked like him, but insanely, somehow didn't feel like him.

The high-planed face with the faint scar on the left

cheek was certainly his face, as was the pair of pale eyes staring out from the shadows cast by the visor. But for an instant, he saw another reflection, superimposed over his own, a ghostly twin with hair much longer than his own short, regulation length, and wearing an accusatory expression.

Grant and Baptiste. They're here somewhere. I've got to find them!

He didn't hear the whispery voice, but he recognized it as his own.

Find them!

The flare faded and as it did, Kane's bedroom tilted around him. A blade of excruciating pain stabbed through his head, feeling as if it pierced his brain from front to back, then was sadistically twisted.

He felt himself staggering, but as swiftly as the agony had lanced into him, it vanished. Kane swayed for a moment, teeth bared, feeling beads of perspiration forming at his hairline. He heard himself murmur, "Grant and Baptiste…"

Pushing herself up from the bed, Beth-Li asked in alarm, "Kane? Are you all right?"

Slowly, he turned to face her. A genuine expression of concern crossed her lovely Asian features. But the expression melted and another one formed, like a translucent mask. That expression was one of rage, the fury of a woman scorned. He heard her say, "You've got no right—you're nothing but a killer, a murderer of outlanders and people who couldn't fight back! How dare you act like I'm beneath your notice?"

He felt rage fountain up within him and took a step forward, hand raised to strike her.

"Kane!" Beth-Li shrank against the headboard, clutching sheets to her body. Her voice held a sharp note of fear and confusion. "What did I say?"

Kane caught himself, realizing the woman had not spoken those words. He forced a smile to his face to cover his bewilderment. "Nothing. A little headache. All that foolishness—" He gestured out the window, toward the fireworks blazing in the night sky.

Beth-Li frowned at him. "Foolishness?" she echoed, sounding slightly scandalized. "It's Unification Day."

Kane dredged up an imperious tone and attitude. "I don't need to be reminded of what fucking day it is."

Fear returned to Beth-Li's dark eyes. "I'm sorry, I didn't mean to anger you, Kane—"

"Major," he snapped. "When I'm uniform, you address me by my rank."

He reached for the plaited leather crop hanging by a hook on the wall. "Maybe you need to be reminded not to be so overly familiar."

Beth-Li's eyes followed the motion of his hand with something akin to dreadful fascination—and then anticipation.

A jolt of nausea surged through Kane's belly, and it turned a cold flip-flop of disgust. The sudden, eager gleam in Beth-Li's eyes revolted him.

With a visible effort, he shook off the impulse to flog her and turned toward the door. Without looking at her, he said, "Be gone when I get back."

Closing the door behind him, he stood on the dark landing and bit back a startled curse when another fireworks charge detonated overhead. He knew Unification Day was the only real holiday observed by the Reich, but the excesses in the festivities irritated him.

Although he would have never admitted it to anyone, he found celebrating the nuclear destruction of Washington, D.C., on January 20, 1945, more than a little morbid. As he walked down the stairwell, he reflected that despite the Third Reich's victory on that day so long ago, there had been plenty of other wars between then and now that were never celebrated.

Then again, when Nazi sympathizers within the U.S. Army Air Corps dropped the twenty-kiloton U-235 bomb, it set in motion the unification of the world, and such an accomplishment was definitely to be celebrated.

"As beasts of burden are unified by a whip."

Kane made a surprised intake of air, realizing with horror that not only had he simply thought those words of treachery, they had passed his lips in a sarcastic whisper.

He cast his gaze around swiftly, eyes darting for an eavesdropper, even though he knew the stairwell was private, leading only to his quarters. And even if anyone had been lurking, the explosions would have drowned out his voice. Besides, had there been a lurker, Kane would have been well within his right to shoot him dead on the spot.

He wasn't worried about the spy-eye vid lens

bolted to the ceiling. It hadn't functioned in years, and Kane was in no hurry to report it.

Crowds surged in the streets of Dulce, once called New Mexico, but known as New Thule for the past two centuries, since the Program of Unification had divided up America into Balkanized states. The night air was quite comfortable, even so late in January.

In the distance, several miles from the village proper, the Archuleta Mesa pushed up from the desert floor, its deeply fissured bulk washed by streaks of color. The fireworks were being launched from its flat top.

Pushing his way through the dancing, cheering throng, Kane had to bat aside miniature flags waved in his face, all of them duplicates of the insignia patch on his uniform sleeve.

The entire population of Dulce, numbered at less than four thousand, appeared to be out on the cobblestoned streets. Of course, by law the citizens had to be, except for the very young or the very infirm. Black armored and helmeted Zone Troopers stood on elevated platforms erected at every intersection, box-fed machine guns cradled in their polycarbonate shod arms.

Kane was annoyed by the crowd, but he didn't allow his emotion to show on his face. Clusters of people stepped aside for him, once they got a good look at his uniform and the silver major's bars glinting on his collar.

He shouldered aside those people who didn't get out of his path fast enough, once pushing a one-legged veteran of the Calgary campaign into the gutter. It would have been faster to use side streets and alleys to reach the Chancellery Building, but a knighted officer of the Rapier Legion did not step aside for the lesser breeds.

I'm such an asshole.

The voice didn't whisper in his ear, but within his mind and it frightened him. He kept walking, increasing the length of his stride and quickening his pace, worried about delayed effects from old head injuries assailing him.

Not too long ago, he had suffered a concussion. A gossamer wisp of memory floated by. He dimly recalled Lord Strongbow's vicious attack, his fists battering him mercilessly about the head and face.

Kane swallowed a curse, his gait faltering, and wondered who the hell Lord Strongbow was.

He paused at the cross-braced base of a watchtower, leaning against a support post, his throat constricted. A razor-edged cleaver of pain chopped into his skull, splitting his brain in two. The agony was so sudden, so intense and blinding, he could not suppress a cry of pain. His surroundings grayed out, seemed to implode into nothingness, then billow out again. He saw and heard himself in a place he had never visited, roaring words he would have never dreamed of uttering. "Like *hell* we don't! Order out of chaos, law from anarchy, peace with honor and every other bit of self-serving dogma ever puked up by fascists who don't have the guts to admit they're fascists!"

He felt his knees buckling, then a hand touched his shoulder. Kane jerked his head up, almost dislodging his cap. He stumbled and would have fallen if the Zone Trooper hadn't steadied him.

"Are you ill, Major?" The trooper's voice was neutrally solicitous, as if he suspected the major was really drunk and he employed the least offensive euphemism. Kane couldn't read his eyes, masked as they were by a blue-tinted visor.

That's not right. It should be red.

"Major?" the trooper inquired, his tone acquiring a harder edge. "Do you wish me to call a medic? Or perhaps your brother?"

"My brother?" Kane echoed dazedly.

"Yes, sir. Lieutenant Colonel Salvo lives nearby, doesn't he?"

Kane dragged in a deep breath and pulled away from the trooper's hand. He recognized his blunt jawline. "Not necessary, Corporal Pollard. I have a bit of a headache. It's better now."

Pollard nodded formally and respectfully. "Sir."

Kane touched a finger to the visor of his cap and moved on, temples throbbing, seeming in cadence with his heartbeat. He considered briefly taking a detour and stopping by the officers' dispensary, but he knew DeFore wouldn't be on duty. She was the only medic in the Health and Welfare Division he trusted.

By the time the Chancellery came into view, the pain had abated until it was no more than a distraction. The stone facade of the sprawling building rose five dignified stories above a lambent green lawn. In the center of it stood a marble statue of Goebbels and Himmler, dressed in medieval plate armor.

Kane strode up the short flight of wide stone steps,

returning the stiff-armed salute of the trooper stationed beside the brass-bound door. A banner hung from a pole above it, depicting in black on a red background inverted triangles within a larger triangle motif.

The entrance hall was brilliantly lighted, and people hustled around him, most of them wearing the black-and-silver uniform of the Reich. He headed straight for the Intelligence Division.

The spacious room held a dozen people, half of them sitting before banks of computers with flashing readouts and indicators. Kane strode over to Morales at the outer field station. "What's the most recent report about the Roamer movements around Mount Rushmore?"

Morales looked up from his computer work station, his swart face impassive. "One came in a few minutes ago, but it's being decrypted."

"Who has it?"

"I do, Major," a throaty, female voice said from behind him.

Kane turned and saw a woman standing in the doorway of an adjacent room, a sheaf of printouts in her hand. She gazed at him with a hesitant, slightly challenging smile on her lips, and Kane felt the rise of the short hairs at his nape.

She wore the same black-and-silver uniform as he did, the tunic slightly longer than his, reaching the tops of her thighs. Her tall, willowy figure filled out the uniform in a manner he had never noticed before. A wide belt spanned what appeared to be about a twenty-two-inch waist. Snugged into a holster above her right hip was a compact Walther TPM automatic pistol.

Her long tawny hair was swept up on top of her head and fastened there in a sort of braided bun. It framed a well molded face with big, slightly tip-tilted eyes the color of cold emeralds.

Kane stepped toward her, hand outstretched. "I'll take that, Captain Baptiste."

Chapter 15

Their fingers brushed momentarily, her touch a soft, yet electric caress. Kane felt his heart suddenly flutter wildly within his chest, like the wings of a captured bird.

Surprise, quickly veiled, flickered in Baptiste's eyes. It was so brief Kane nearly didn't catch it. His reaction to the woman startled and mystified him. He knew she had come to work as a decrypter in the Chancellery some eight months earlier, and Kane doubted he had exchanged more than three perfunctory nods with her. Baptiste was certainly attractive, but she had struck him as no different than any other intel officers he had met: guarded, shallow and devoted to their duty.

He cleared his throat. "You've decoded the transmission?"

"Using Key 12." Her lips pursed in disapproval. "That code key is in danger of being deciphered. It's at least a year old."

"In that case, work on developing Key 13 should take priority."

Baptiste nodded. "I advised that in my last report. So far, Field Marshal Thrush hasn't responded."

At the sound of the name, Kane felt his jaw muscles bunching reflexively. Captain Baptiste noticed and crooked a curious eyebrow. Kane did his best to smooth his features.

"Where is he?" Kane asked, striving for a casual tone.

Her eyebrow acquired a steeper angle. "I really couldn't say, Major. I don't keep tabs on him." An undercurrent of suspicion ran through the woman's tone. "I've only spoken to him once, the first day I was posted here."

Kane didn't know why he had acted on the impulse to ask about Thrush's whereabouts, or what had prompted the impulse. He covered his confusion by pretending to study the decoded printout. He saw the words without comprehending them.

Intelligence Division, Reich Chancellery/Dulce/ New Thule

Re: Mt. Rushmore. A number of Roamer bands are congregating within the territory. Though their numbers appear to be less than five hundred, they appear to be well-armed (see report #01039, looting of Bismarck munitions depot) and it appears the monument itself is their intended target of terrorism. Surveillance continues, will advise of further movements.

He read the report over again, struggling to remember what he knew about Mount Rushmore. A long time ago, it had housed an ambitious Continuity of Government facility known as the Anthill, so named because of its similarity in layout to an anthill. He remembered Lakesh telling him that—

No! his mind snarled. *Lakesh never told you anything about it. Mount Rushmore is a national treasure, dedicated to the five greatest leaders of America—Washington, Jefferson, Lincoln, Roosevelt and Hitler.*

"Major?"

Kane looked up from the paper, meeting Baptiste's quizzical, slightly ironic gaze. He realized his hand trembled. "Yes?"

"Is there something wrong with the report?"

"No, it's—" He groped for something reasonable to say. "It's disturbing news, that's all."

"It is?" A hint of mockery lurked in the back of Baptiste's question. "I wouldn't think that a knight in the Rapier Legion and the hero of the Calgary Front would find a bunch of ragbag Roamers and brushwooders very disturbing."

The woman's attitude came very close to insubordination, but after the first jolt of anger passed, Kane felt a distant wonder that his overriding emotional reaction was akin to comfort, as if it were all too familiar.

He tried to suppress the amused smile he felt tugging at the corners of his mouth. "Really? What would you say I find disturbing, Captain?"

"Paperwork," a lionlike voice rumbled.

Kane glanced swiftly around and with an irrational surge of relief he saw a uniformed, clean-shaven black man swaggering into the room. Major's bars glittered on his tunic collar.

"Good thing you're here," Grant continued, hooking a thumb over his shoulder. "There was an intruder alert at the Foundation. Field Marshal Thrush is already out there and he's requested our presence. They have a suspect in custody."

Kane started to hand the printout back to Baptiste, then hesitated, giving her an appraising look. "Care to join us, Captain?"

He appreciated the flicker of surprise in the green depths of her eyes. She hadn't expected the invitation. "I don't have the security clearance for the facility."

"It's about time you received one. Come with us."

Grant frowned uncertainly but said nothing. Kane marched toward the door and after a moment, Captain Baptiste fell into step beside him, first grabbing her cap from a wall hook.

Kane, Grant and Brigid strode down the corridor, and for the first time since the onset of the head pain, he did not feel out of sync with his surroundings. Bracketed by the big black man and the green-eyed woman, he had the sense that the world was now the way it was supposed to be, the three of them marching purposefully toward an unknown, always together.

As soon as the notion registered, he tried to banish it from his mind. He and Grant were fellow officers, holding the same rank, and had often worked together, but they were not close. Within the Legion, competition for promotion was fierce, and framing rival officers for crimes both high and low was not uncommon. Outright assassination of competitors was not rare, either.

For some reason, Kane found it exceedingly difficult to erect his guard in the company of these two people. He felt irrationally comfortable in their presence.

As they walked toward the rear entrance and the vehicle compound, Grant inquired quietly, "What's that old term for feeling like you've done something before?"

Baptiste immediately replied, "Déjà vu, a French term literally meaning 'already seen.' It refers to a strong sense of familiarity with an experience one believes one has never had before."

Kane smiled crookedly. "That's the problem with having a photographic memory—worthless facts and important items come out in equal measure."

Baptiste swiveled her head to stare at him. "How did you know I have a photographic memory?"

Kane had no idea how he knew and rather than say that, he said, "I must have seen in it your personnel file or something."

Hoping to change the subject, Kane asked Grant, "Are you having déjà vu now?"

Grant shrugged. "I don't know. I've been having severe headaches off and on for the last hour. Maybe that has something to do with it."

Kane massaged his forehead. "Yeah, me too. They come and go."

Baptiste eyed them both curiously. "I've been suffering from the same thing. Must be a bug. If that's the case, it might not be a good idea for all us to go to the facility—''

Her words turned into a muffled gasp of pain. Squeezing her eyes shut, she stumbled to a halt. Alarmed, Kane reached out for her.

''Headache again,'' she said tightly, tears oozing from the corners of her eyes. ''Give me a second—''

Bowing her head, Baptiste took several deep breaths. After a few moments, she murmured. ''Better now, I think—oh, hell!''

Kane saw her patting her left cheek. Perplexed, he asked, ''What is it?''

''My contact came out. Goddammit—'' Then she uttered a relieved exclamation. ''Here it is, right on my face.''

As she replaced it in her eye, Grant commented, ''I thought you wore glasses.''

Baptiste blinked her big eyes rapidly. ''What makes you think that?''

Grant opened his mouth, closed it and heaved the wide yoke of his shoulders in a shrug. ''I don't know. I just pictured you with glasses—old-fashioned things with wire frames and square—no, rectangular lenses.''

''I do have a pair like that.'' She scowled at him. ''But I only wear them when I'm off duty, in my quarters. The only way you'd know that is if you were spying on me.''

She surveyed Kane coldly. ''Just like you knew I had a photographic memory. It's not in my personnel records. I never told anyone. Am I under surveillance for some reason, Majors?''

Grant did not reply, so Kane, in a tone matching hers for frostiness, said, "Not that I'm aware of, Captain. Is there some reason you should suspect that you are?"

Tension born of lifetimes of looking over their shoulders sprang up around the three people, as electric as a storm cloud. Suddenly, Baptiste smiled, and it transformed her face. "Paranoia is such a subtle yet devastating weapon, isn't it?"

"You're not paranoid if they really are after you, Baptiste," Kane shot back automatically.

"What the hell are you two carrying on about?" Grant demanded gruffly.

The smile vanished from the woman's face, replaced instantly by an expression of fearful bewilderment. Kane knew his own face mirrored her expression.

Hoarsely, Baptiste said, "I don't know. It's like we had that conversation before…but that couldn't be. Could it?"

An electroplasmic vision wafted through Kane's memory. He glimpsed a man wearing black body armor, head concealed by a helmet and red-tinted visor. He faced a disheveled woman wearing a baggy yellow coverall. The two people stood in a stark and bare corridor, and he realized the man and woman were himself and Baptiste.

"No," he said at length. "It couldn't be."

The three people gazed at one another in silent surmise, then continued on their way to the compound.

WORLD WAR II ended rather abruptly for such a costly conflict that had dragged on for years across several continents. The Allied Forces had been driven back from Europe after the disastrous Normandy invasion. They engaged in a slow, stubborn retreat, their weapons no match for those of the German war machine.

"Foo Fighters," the term given to the Third Reich's remote-controlled drones, decimated the American Air Corps and the RAF. Microwave emitters broadcast frequencies that shorted out the electrical systems of tanks, personnel carriers, supply trucks of the entire Allied infantry. The Russian-German Nonaggression Pact held firm, and there was no aid forthcoming from the Soviet Union.

Repeated deep strikes made by V-4 rockets with incendiary warheads destroyed Allied bases all over Europe, the North Atlantic and eventually the Pacific. But still the Allies fought on, the British and French armies driven from their homelands.

It all came to an end at twelve noon on January 20, 1945, when a mile-high mushroom cloud billowed up from Washington, D.C., the capital of the world's last bastion of human freedom.

The bomb, code-named *Liebchen,* was simple in design, but it destroyed more than buildings, monuments and lives. It obliterated the fighting spirit of the American people.

Faced with the threat of more A-bombs dropped by the Reich's invincible fleet of flying fortresses, for the first time in its relatively short history, the United States formally surrendered to a foreign aggressor.

Within two months, proud tanks bearing swastikas rumbled swiftly down Manhattan's Fifth Avenue. Smiling troopers, heavily armed, marched through the streets lined by weeping crowds.

The Nazis knew well the uses of propaganda, the winning of a war by conquering the spirits of the enemy. The victory parade and the announcement of world unification were more effective than a dozen cities consumed by nuclear fire.

Thunderous *Seig Heils* shook New York City's skyline and the brown-uniformed Hitler made a speech at the base of the Statute of Liberty. He was the conqueror of Europe, of America, of Asia and now the leader of the entire world. He was the epitome of the destiny of the superman, who could afford to be magnanimous. The world was at long last united, with no more national borders or disputes over territory or religion. It all belonged to the Third Reich now.

They used everything they knew—or had been taught—to establish a global empire; assassination, myth, treachery, superior armed might and a ruthless campaign of terror that brought about the deaths of millions.

And then there were the others, hidden away, secret, shadowy, their existence only hinted at in ancient manuscripts and legends, who knew the Third Reich's victory had only been the first phase of a plan conceived millennia ago.

THE SMOOTHLY SURFACED blacktop road cut through board-flat desert. The armored Mercedes they had requisitioned was several years old and needed a new coat of paint, and the triangle symbol of unification decal was peeling at the edges, but the diesel engine purred smoothly.

The fireworks display was long over by the time Grant braked at the first of three security checkpoints. In the near distance, the gigantic dark bulk of the Archuleta Mesa blotted out a huge portion of the star-speckled night sky.

After a quick inspection, the guard waved the car through, and Grant steered past the sentry kiosk and the machine-gun emplacements. Kane secretly considered that such security precautions were a bit extreme. There had not been a truly major conflict since the pacification of the Russian-Japanese Federation in 1960. Even the last spot of bother, the border uprising in Canada, had been little more than a series of skirmishes, barely qualifying as a bush war.

If Roamer rebels or saboteurs wanted to breach the defenses of the Purity Control Foundation, buried deep beneath the mesa, they wouldn't come in force, through the checkpoints. They'd sneak in overland, through the miles of uninhabited desert and mesquite. And if they managed to make it past the motion and heat sensors that ringed the perimeter and actually got inside the place, they would require a vast knowledge of the complex security measures and protocols that not even Kane had.

The car passed through gates in three twenty-foot-high cyclone fences, each one topped by curls of razor wire. Armored guards on foot and astride motorcycles constantly patrolled between the fenced perimeters. Brilliant halogen floodlights left no square foot of ground unilluminated.

After Grant drove through the third and final gate, the Arculeta Mesa loomed above them like the tombstone of a Teutonic god. The top of it glowed with lights, like a crown of stars.

A sentry motioned them to drive onto a great rimmed disk of gray metal. Grant guided the Mercedes to the center of it, parked and turned off the ignition. Brigid, sitting between Grant and Kane, looked around wide-eyed. In a strangely hushed voice, she asked, "Now what?"

With a grinding rumble, the disk began to descend, the metal rim forming the lip of a vertical tunnel. They sank into utter blackness, then the shaft walls began to shine, casting the interior of the vehicle in a soft light.

Kane had visited the facility several times, twice in the company of Grant, but he still found the method of entering it impressive and a little intimidating.

With a protracted hiss of compressed air, the lift disk jolted to a stop. A lighted observation platform stood before them. A tall, lean man stood at the railing. He was more than just gaunt, he was cadaverous. His erect figure wore the funeral-black uniform of the Reich military, his high-boned face starkly pale above the dark clothing. A high-peaked cap sat at a jaunty angle on his hairless skull, his eyes invisible behind the dark lenses of sunglasses. An array of silver insignia pins twinkled all over his tunic.

As Grant, Kane and Brigid disembarked from the

car, the man looked vaguely surprised, even a little unsettled, to see Baptiste. The three of them snapped off stiff-armed salutes, and the cadaverous officer on the platform returned them rather laconically.

"Captain Baptiste," Field Marshal Thrush said in an uninflected, well-modulated voice. "I didn't expect you, although in retrospect, perhaps I should have."

Chapter 16

The cryptic remark did not confuse Kane as much as enrage him. The underlying vibrations in Thrush's flat, oily voice made his hand reflexively move toward his holstered Sin Eater. With a conscious effort, he checked the movement, frightened by what felt like an instinctive, visceral reaction. The field marshal was his commandant, and though Kane feared him, he had never felt hatred for a moment.

Thrush turned away from the railing, making a sharp, autocratic gesture. "This way."

The three officers moved off the metal platform, their boots striking chiming echoes from it. The air smelled clean and fresh, but it held a faint, tart chemical scent, too. Kane glanced up at the small circle of starlit sky above. He felt as if he were standing at the bottom of a gargantuan drainpipe.

A short flight of stairs on the far side of the observation platform led down into a wide, white corridor, lighted by very bright neon strips inset into the ceiling. Men and women in white and pale blue Reich uniforms strolled along it. A number of them were small and compact of figure, with delicately featured faces that seemed to be all brow, cheekbone and chin. The craniums were large, but not inhumanly so. Their heads bore wisps of thin, fine hair.

The eyes beneath delicately arched supraorbital ridges were big and slanted, but white could be detected around the irises. Their steps were graceful, almost mincing, their hands long and slender. Several of the men wore plastic tube-shaped holsters strapped to their thighs.

Kane was assailed by an instant of irrational dread when he saw the holsters. One part of his mind knew the infrasound batons converted electrical current to sound waves by a maser and were very precise weapons—a necessity in a facility with so much fragile equipment—but they were very limited in range.

He had only witnessed demonstrations of the wands and never been on the receiving end of their ultrasonic kick. But now he had the distinct and uneasy impression that he had been, but he couldn't lay his mental hands on the vaporous trace of memory to examine it closely.

Increasing the length of his stride, he caught up with Thrush. "I was told there was a security breach."

"You were told correctly," Thrush replied smoothly. "We have the intruder in custody. Lieutenant Colonel Salvo is administering the first application of interrogation. Thus far, no useful information has been forthcoming, and your brother suggested you and Major Grant might have some ideas."

Thrush gave him a swift sideways look that held no particular expression. "I understand you two are very good at this sort of thing."

Tension coiled in the pit of Kane's belly, like a length of heavy rope.

Thrush turned to the right, pushing open a pair of glass-and-chrome doors. A tiny female, pretty and crisp in her whites despite her large cranium and oversized eyes, sat behind a solid oak reception desk. Her huge blue eyes were startlingly clear and calm.

"How is the patient?" Thrush asked.

"No change," the woman answered blandly. "You may go in."

Baptiste hung back uncertainly. "Perhaps I should wait out here."

Thrush regarded her with amusement. "Nonsense, Captain. Since Major Kane saw fit to bring you here, there's no reason why your movements should be restricted. You'll come with us."

Although his tone was flat, it was apparent the field marshal was not making a request.

Crossing the room, Thrush pushed open a metal-sheathed door with the word Examination stenciled in red upon it. The room was fairly spacious and bare-walled. Light spilling from an overhead fixture blazed down on a stainless-steel table in the center of the room.

Wide bands of canvas bound a slight, white form to the surface of the table. The straps ran across the naked girl's waist and ankles, her slender arms pinned to her sides. Her skin was white, as was her ragged mop of close-cropped hair. The only color about her was a pair of glaring eyes, as red as a cutting torch flame—and the numerous blue-black bruises marring the pearly perfection of her sleek, petite figure.

Salvo stood next to her head, stroking the girl's sweat-soaked hair and crooning to her. In his left hand he held a humming infrasound wand. He grinned when he saw Kane, but it didn't reach his mud-colored eyes.

"Brother mine," he said by way of a greeting. "Figured you might have some ideas on how to loosen this slut's tongue. She's stubborn like all her kind."

He hefted the wand, its silvery length made hazy with vibration. "She's running out of bones to break. I've given her a choice about the next ones. She hasn't made up her mind yet."

It was more than a struggle to keep the riot of conflicting emotions from showing on Kane's face— it was a knock-down-drag-out internal brawl. Salvo's flat, sallow face was all too familiar, as was his very short, gray-threaded dark hair. He was a couple of inches shorter than Kane, a few years older and considerably heavier.

Anger, remorse and a craving for revenge all warred for dominance within Kane's heart and mind. At the outer fringes of his awareness, he noticed an absence of a physical characteristic—where there should have been a wealed scar seaming his broad forehead, cutting down to the corner of his left eye, there was only unblemished flesh. Another vague echo of a memory drifted incompletely through his mind—he saw himself slashing the barrel of a Sin

Eater across the side of Salvo's scalp, splitting open the scalp in a gush of blood.

Coinciding with the image, like a sympathetic pain, a drill bit seemed to bore into his skull. He barely managed to turn a startled cry into a disinterested grunt before it passed.

Grant's voice, sounding strangely unsteady asked, "Who is she?"

Kane tossed a quick look over his shoulder. Perspiration glistened on Grant's dark face despite the cool air, and his jaw muscles bunched in knots. He was either in pain—or angry—and doing his damnedest not to show it.

Another surreptitious glance showed him Baptiste's pale and stricken face, emerald eyes disturbingly bright. As soon as she felt Kane's gaze, her expression smoothed itself into a clinical, impersonal mask.

"Says her name is Domi," Salvo replied with a cheerful insouciance. "That's all she's admitted to, but we know what she did and tried to do."

"Which is?" Baptiste inquired, as if she were scarcely interested and just asking to be polite.

Thrush answered the question, curtly and quickly. The girl had killed a careless sentry on the far outer perimeter. She used a long knife with a serrated blade, expertly cutting his throat.

She had hooked electronic circuits to the alarm system on the fence, which bypassed their transmitters. A compact acetylene torch burned through the links of the fence.

Pointing to shapeless black mass of a semiglossy

fabric on the floor, Thrush said, "A Stealth cloak, blocking body-heat signatures and wired with reflective circuitry, which scrambled the motion detectors."

Domi then made her way to the third fence, but she got overconfident. She overlooked that at the third perimeter, all alarms were equipped with redundancies. She was discovered and captured.

"What did she have on her?" Kane asked, not wanting to look at the girl on the table. She seemed familiar to him, even though he knew he had never seen her before.

"Other than the knife, the electronic components and a grenade—probably intended to knock out the power generators—only this," Thrush answered.

From a belt pouch he removed a small cylindrical vial made of metal. Revolving it between thumb and forefinger, the overhead light struck dull highlights on it.

"And that is what?" Grant asked. "Plastique or something?"

"It's a hundred times more lethal. It contains a microorganism, a genetically tailored virus designed to attack the immune systems of our Battle Class breed. I suspect if she could have gotten in here to the incubation chambers and added this to the amniotic fluid cyclers, an entire generation would have been lost."

Replacing the vial in his belt, Thrush added, "It's patently obvious an inferior creature of her limited intellect did not conceive of this plan independently. She had inside help."

The notion, mentioned so casually, was at once stunning and frightening.

"A traitor?" Kane demanded. "Who can that be?"

"That's why you and Major Grant were summoned," came Thrush's mild reply. "You two enjoy a certain reputation for wringing information out of recalcitrant tongues, as if you were squeezing out wet towels."

Kane looked at the girl and she looked up at him, hatred seething in her ruby eyes in an almost palpable wave. A cold sickness crept over him, a dim realization that he had earned that hate, that scorn.

"Domi, is there a chance you'll behave reasonably?" he asked quietly. "This is the only time I'll ask. If you don't answer me now, it'll be too late."

Domi looked at him questioningly, surprise engulfing the fury in her eyes. Her lips parted.

Salvo gently stroked her rib cage with the tip of the wand. The girl shrieked, arching her back, straining against the canvas restraints. The wand popped as the fragile, fibrous cartilage between her ribs ruptured.

Grant lunged around the table, moving with amazing swiftness for a man of his size. Closing one big hand around Salvo's wrist, he jerked his arm up violently. Salvo cried out in angry surprise as the wand flew from his hand and clattered to the floor, where it lay humming.

Face contorted in a bare-toothed grimace, Grant cocked back his arm for a punch.

"Major!" Field Marshal Thrush's voice carried as sharp as a whip crack in the room.

Grant caught himself, trembling arm and fist poised. The flames of rage in his dark eyes dimmed, but they did not gutter out completely. He released his grip, and Salvo took a clumsy half step backward, rubbing his wrist and glowering. "What the fuck is with you, Grant?"

Grant groped for a reply, looking almost as bewildered as Salvo.

On impulse, Kane said, "It's a new technique of interrogation Grant and I developed. The officers beat the hell out of each other while the prisoner goes to pieces from the agony of watching."

Both Salvo and Grant frowned in his direction, but Thrush threw him a fleeting, appreciative smile. "Very whimsical, Major Kane. I never knew you had a sense of humor."

His dark lensed eyes slowly scanned Kane, Baptiste and Grant. "Perhaps there are depths to the three of you that hitherto escaped my notice. For instance, Major Grant's *very* uncharacteristic display of compassion."

Grant's scowl deepened and he fearlessly met Thrush's masked gaze. "Compassion had nothing to do with it. It was possible this piece of outlander trash was going to cooperate. Salvo screwed it up."

Thrush nodded contemplatively. "Nice save, Major. I will accept that as a reason for your outburst—at least for the nonce."

He turned his attention to Domi. "You may answer the major's question now."

Breath coming in harsh, ragged gasps, her small breasts rising and falling spasmodically, Domi tried to speak. Sweat pebbled her face. Outlined in blue and red against the porcelain whiteness of her skin, a road map pattern of broken blood vessels and capillaries extended across her upper torso.

"Make deal," she said in a husky, aspirated whisper. "Let me sit up. Can't bear being tied down. All I ask. Let me sit up and I tell you everything. My word, I give you my word."

Salvo snorted in contempt. "When is the word of outlander shit worth anything?"

The term "outlander" rang a faint chime of recognition in the dark recesses of Kane's memory, but he dismissed it.

It means the same thing here as it does at home.

Thrush glanced expectantly from Grant to Kane. "Majors? Your call."

The two men exchanged looks, and Kane caught himself just as he was turning to solicit Baptiste's opinion, as if it were the most natural thing in the world.

Kane nodded curtly to Grant. "Do it."

Grant reached down and began unbuckling the straps, his expression stony and impassive. Domi allowed him to help her sit up on the edge of the steel table. Kane couldn't help but notice his surprisingly gentle touch.

She sighed in relief, grimaced in pain, holding her left arm at an unnatural angle. Kane guessed the elbow joint had been broken, and judging by the discolored, swollen condition of her right foot, all the fragile bones there had been pulverized.

"Now," said Grant sternly, "keep your word. Talk."

Domi nodded. "Sure, sure I tell you everything." She sank her teeth into her full underlip and hung her head as if in resignation.

Then, like a white wraith, she hurled herself from the examination in a burst of blurring speed. She stiff-armed Salvo out of the way as Kane reflexively lunged to block her way to the exit.

But the albino girl's objective wasn't the door. As soon as she hit the floor, her right leg collapsed beneath her with a mushy crackle of splintered bones grinding against crushed tendons.

Domi bottled up the scream and slid across the slick floor on her naked belly, right arm clawing for the infrasound wand. She snatched it, whipping it up and around as everyone went for their holstered side arms.

Flipping the silver rod, Domi inserted the tapered tip into her right ear. There was a muffled pop, as if of a wet paper bag bursting. A slurry of blood and liquefied brain matter geysered from her left ear, spraying the wall and floor. Scarlet spewed from both nostrils as a convulsion shook her slim frame. She fell limply in a half-sitting position against the wall. The wand rolled from her lifeless fingers.

For a heavy, hushed moment dead silence reigned in the room, broken only by Thrush's announcement. "And that, as they say, is that."

Grant passed a hand over his sweat damp face, muttering, "Fucking fireblast."

Thrush jerked his head toward him. "A unique expletive, Major. I don't believe I've ever heard you utter it before. Or anyone else, for that matter."

Salvo hammered a fist in frustration on the steel table. "Goddammit, our only lead. Grant, you stupid bastard—"

Thrush cut off Salvo's profane tirade with a gesture. "Enough, Lieutenant Colonel. Everyone is entitled to an error in judgment. You, for example, should have taken the outlander's high tolerance for pain into account and done more to incapacitate her."

Kane averted his gaze from the bloodied rag doll Domi had become, trying not to be too obvious about it. He caught a glimpse of Captain Baptiste, her eyes glittering as she fought back tears.

"Now what?" Kane asked calmly.

Thrush lifted a narrow shoulder in a negligent shrug. "Nothing left to do now but to report to the administrator. He asked me to keep him apprised of the progress of the interrogation."

Stepping toward the door, he said, "Majors Grant and Kane, Captain Baptiste, come with me, please. I'm sure the administrator will be interested in your views on this unfortunate event. Lieutenant Colonel Salvo, you will oversee the cleanup. Remove the body to the processing level. She'll serve a use in a death that she never had in life."

Thrush led the way through the reception area and along the corridor. Grant, Baptiste and Kane followed him to a junction that jogged left. It ended at a heavy steel door framed within a recessed niche. It bore the red triangle and vertical lines symbol. Kane did not speak to either Grant or Baptiste or so much as catch their eye.

Thrush tapped in a three-digit code on the keypad on the frame and with a hiss of pneumatics, the portal slid into its slots between the double frame. He stepped into a long, low-ceilinged passageway. The trio followed him. Cool air fanned their faces from the far end, and they heard a rhythmic drone of turbines and generators. A faint chemical odor entered their nostrils.

The mechanical throb grew louder the farther they went. The passageway was blocked by a turnstile checkpoint. A slender, dome-craniumed man wearing a pale blue uniform peered at them from a glassed-in booth on the other side of it and threw a lever. Thrush pushed the steel prongs aside and one by one, the three people followed him.

The passageway took on a downward slope, the floor changing from tiles to metal grillework. After a dozen yards, they reached a railed balcony. Thirty feet below lay a broad mezzanine, illuminated by crackling red light that played along the lines and ceramic pylons of a voltage converter system.

In the center of the mezzanine, thick power cables sprouted from sockets in the concrete floor and snaked toward a strangely shaped generator. It was at least twelve feet tall, and looked like a pair of solid black cubes, the smaller balanced atop the larger. The top cube rotated slowly, producing the steady drone of sound. An odd smell, like ozone blended with antiseptic, pervaded the air.

Beyond the cubes stretched a complex of glass-walled cubicles, each no more than three by three. Within each, hanging from ceiling racks, were transparent sacs filled with a semiliquid amber gel. Small figures, curled in fetal positions, floated within the gelid contents. The large craniums were pinkish-gray in color, spotted here and there with wispy strands of hair. The noses were pairs of tiny nares. Their upslanting eyes were dull and fathomless. The limbs were disproportionate, far too long for the torso.

A man was seated at the rail, his thin emaciated body hunched over in a wheelchair. Thrush said quietly, "Administrator, I bring news."

The man grasped the wheels of his chair with clawlike hands and turned it. He was old, the oldest man any of them had ever seen.

His blue-veined head trembled slightly on a wattled neck. What little hair he had was no more than snarled white tufts. His yellowish brown face was withered and crisscrossed with a network of wrinkles, seams and lines, but his eyes burned as hot and as blue as the sky high above the desert. Transparent plastic tubes were attached to shunts in both liver-spotted arms. A small oxygen tank rested in a pocket on the side of his chair and from this stretched a respirator mask. A blanket draped him from hips to ankles.

In a wheezing, reedy rasp of complaint, Lakesh said, "It's about time. What did the bitch have to say?"

Chapter 17

Field Marshal Thrush bestowed a small, patronizing smile on the old man. "Very little of use, I fear, beyond her name. She committed suicide before she made any revelations of who supplied her with the means to break into the facility and contaminate the gene pool."

Lakesh looked at Kane with a ferocity that was almost a homicidal anger. "Don't you find that suspicious?" he brayed.

"Convenient might be more applicable." Thrush removed the metal vial from the compartment on his belt and extended it toward Lakesh. The old man hesitated, then reached out palsied fingers to take it.

"A viral mixture like that could not have been cooked up in an outlander's cellar." Thrush's voice held no particular emotion or tone. "It required not only a deep understanding of how to breed microorganisms, but also the proper equipment. Then, of course, there is the sophisticated nature of the devices employed by the girl to breach our defenses. She had exactly what she needed."

Lakesh clapped the respiration mask over his nose and mouth, staring first at Thrush, then Kane, then Grant and back to Thrush with his bright blue eyes. He inhaled deeply for a few moments before removing it. "If you're working yourself up to make a point, Field Marshal, I suggest you get to it. You might have the all the time in the world, but mine is strictly rationed."

"As you wish." Hooking his thumbs into his belt, Thrush allowed a faint but mocking smile to play over his lips. "I suspect the rebel activity around Mount Rushmore is nothing more than a feint, to focus military attention there instead of what is going on right under our noses...metaphorically speaking of course."

"Of course," Lakesh echoed sarcastically. "And what might be going on right under our noses?"

The smile on Thrush's face suddenly broadened. He turned his head and stared directly at Kane. "Another time, Administrator," he said deliberately. "Another time."

He continued to gaze at Kane as if to gauge his reaction to his words. They meant nothing to him.

Yet, whispered the inner voice that had plagued him for the last hour.

Lakesh cackled. "I don't have much time left."

Thrush returned his attention to the man in the wheelchair. "You don't appear to find that prospect disturbing."

"On the contrary. I find it quite liberating."

Thrush nodded to him perfunctorily and addressed Kane. "Major, tomorrow you will accompany a troop to pacify the Roamers encamped in the vicinity of Mount Rushmore."

Kane's eyes widened in surprise and disquiet.

"You're dispatching the Rapier Legion to scatter a group of outlander scum?"

"I made no mention of the Legion," Thrush retorted coldly. "No, Lieutenant Colonel Salvo will command a troop of the Battle Class genotype. Look at it as a training exercise. You will go with him as his executive officer. Allow the troopers to do all the fighting, if there is any. You and Salvo are there primarily as observers, but don't let any of the enemy escape."

Kane's nape hairs prickled with suspicion. "Isn't such an action usually assigned to the regional provost marshals?" He forced himself to add hastily, "Sir."

Thrush regarded him speculatively. "First a sense of humor, then an attitude bordering on insubordination. You're displaying a wide range of new behaviors tonight, Major. Intriguing how you've kept them hidden from me during the fifteen years you served in my command."

Kane shifted his feet uncomfortably. "I apologize, sir. I didn't intend to be insubordinate. I was merely curious."

"Which is another characteristic you've managed to keep in check—until tonight. I suggest you revert to old habits."

Thrush pivoted on the ball of his right foot and marched away, past Lakesh, down the passageway. Kane stared after him, loathing him and wondering why. The field marshal's orders had irritated him a few times in the past, but he had always respected his superior officer.

Lakesh laughed, a harsh bitter sound. "What's the problem, Major Kane? Having an attack of independent thought? I've tried and tried to breed it out of your particular genotype, but it keeps cropping back up, like the measles."

Lakesh turned his wobbling head toward Brigid. "I don't believe I've met this lovely lady before."

She nodded to him deferentially. "Captain Baptiste. However, I think we might have met somewhere. I just can't recall it."

"I'd recall meeting a woman like you." Lakesh cackled again, and it turned into a coughing fit.

He fit the oxygen mask over his face, breathed deeply, took it away and asked, "Major Grant, what exactly happened to the prisoner?"

"She committed suicide," he replied brusquely, "with a wand."

Lakesh winced and he murmured, "Poor child. I had hoped—" He stopped speaking, clamping his lips tight over his toothless mouth.

"Hoped what?" Grant demanded.

Putting on the respirator again, Lakesh gestured impatiently, back toward the way they had come. They hesitated, then walked in the direction of his arm waves.

Gusting out a weary sigh, Grant said, "Thanks for covering for me back there, Kane."

"You would have done the same for me," Kane replied distractedly.

Grant eyed him in disbelief. "I don't know what would have given you that idea."

With a sinking sensation in the pit of his stomach, Kane realized he didn't know either.

The three of them marched back along the passageway, and once more Kane was assailed with the sensation they had done this before, in the very same place—but they hadn't been walking, they'd been running for their lives.

Back in the main corridor, they met Salvo, who stared sourly at a pair of attendants dragging a body bag along the floor.

"Just carry it," he snapped at them. "The little whore couldn't weigh more than a hundred pounds."

One of the attendants replied sulkily, "A living hundred pounds is different than a dead hundred pounds, sir."

Salvo's sallow complexion reddened and put his hand on the butt of his Sin Eater. "Let's test that, why don't we? I'll lift you when you're alive, then after I blow your inferior brains out. If you're heavier dead than alive, I won't piss on your grave."

The attendant quickly tried to heave the body bag over his shoulder, but he wasn't braced correctly and it slipped through his arms, striking the floor with a loud thud. Kane heard a faint growling noise. He glanced surreptitiously at Grant. The man's unblinking stare was fixed on the body bag. The sound of primal anger emanated unconsciously from his compressed lips.

Catching sight of the three of them, Salvo called out, "You and me tomorrow, Brother. Just like the old days. Slaughter and smoke, smoke and slaughter." His eyes were alight with anticipation.

"Yeah," Kane muttered noncommittally as he stepped around him. "Slaughter and smoke."

KANE, GRANT and Brigid spoke very little on the drive back to the Chancellery. Once there, they went their separate ways, although Kane was reluctant to part from them.

He walked back through the streets of Dulce, past the sanitation workers who were busy picking up the litter left in the wake of the celebration. There seemed to be a lot of the little flags going into the trash bags, and Kane thought derisively that the flag meant nothing to them.

Why the hell should it? It's the symbol of an invader, an oppressor.

He ignored the voice this time, even refusing to acknowledge the lancing pain that always accompanied it. He focused his mind on other matters, like the flag of the Reich.

The pyramid enclosing the three elongated reversed triangles had replaced the swastika nearly a century earlier. It was supposed to represent a pseudomystical trinity functioning within a greater, all-embracing body, but he suspected it symbolized something else—that the Nazis, all the trappings of the Reich from the eagles to the death's-heads had been props, nothing but theater. The German war machine had been used, manipulated to achieve a goal, and once it had been reached there was no longer a need to continue with the melodramatic pageant of Aryan superiority.

As he climbed the stairs to his flat, he recalled a

comment Lakesh had once made: "World War II was not just the defeat of the Third Reich, but a defeat of the Archons, as well. Unfortunately, they took measures to make sure they would never be beaten again. If the Archon Directorate had a written constitution, that would be its first article."

"The Archons?" he murmured aloud, hand on the knob of the door. "Who the hell are the—"

A sun of white pain went nova behind his eyes, far worse than before. He sank his teeth into his lower lip, tasting blood. Shouldering open the door, he stumbled over to the bed. He didn't know or care if Beth-Li was still in it. He collapsed onto it, hands gripping the sides of his head to keep his cranium from flying apart. He was only dimly aware of thrashing to and fro.

The onslaught of agony was far more intense and protracted than before, as if his skull contained a little pocket of boiling hellfire. Through the roaring flame storm in his head, he heard his voice saying savagely, *Stop fighting me! Let me in and the pain will stop! Go to Baptiste, she'll help you, help us both!*

Within his staggering mind, a series of separate geometric shapes appeared, then rushed together, interlocking to form first a polyhedron, then a trapezohedron.

The torture stopped as quickly and abruptly as it had come over him. Kane lay on the bed, gasping and drenched in sweat. Slowly, he cracked open his eyelids, half expecting and fearing he would see another place. He was only a little comforted by the sight of his shabby, utilitarian quarters—and that Beth-Li had made the bed before departing.

Slowly, he pushed himself to a sitting position, elbows propped on his knees, hands cradling his throbbing head. He knew that more than one officer in the Reich's military had lost his mind. Sometimes it was that very insanity that had helped them to achieve great things and high rank.

As a knight, Kane was privy to certain tidbits of unconfirmed data, and it was an unofficial historical fact that Hitler had been insane and several of his inner circle went stark, raving mad.

Reportedly, Hitler had suffered from more than disembodied voices. He was prone to horrific episodes of paranoia, screaming at some entity that influenced his mind. The entity's name, according to legend, was Balam.

But Kane knew if he lost his own grip on reality, he could not expect a promotion. More likely, there would be experimental brain surgery to find out why one of the Reich's elite genotypes had lost his sanity. Euthanasia would almost certainly follow. Regardless of what happened, one thing he would not receive was an upgrade in rank.

He took a steadying breath. If he was indeed going mad, it was a peculiarly structured kind of dementia. Although the worst of the pain had passed, the compulsion to seek out Baptiste remained just as insistent.

Reaching down, he picked up his cap from the floor, automatically brushing a few specks of dust from the peak and visor. Absently, he thought it would have been nice if Beth-Li had swept up as well as making the bed before she departed.

He glanced at the pyramid-triangle insignia on the front of the cap and experienced a queasy, uneasy feeling that it carried more symbolic significance than simply as a replacement for the swastika. For some reason, it now made him think of a sword, but not just any sword, but a special one, an enchanted one. His lips formed the word "Excalibur."

Squeezing his eyes shut, he made a fierce effort to drive away the cobwebs of confusion draping his mind and tried to dredge up the "damned data" he had heard in regards to the true agenda of Hitler and the Nazis.

One of the tenets of Nazi Germany was the creation of a superior breed of human, the New Man. The Reich's breeding farms had only so many successes in the conventional way of birthing a pure master or ruling class. And no matter how many were born, there were a dozen inferior breeds for every New Man.

Although World War II had severely depopulated the planet of its inferior races, and after unification global sterilization programs were put into effect, such measures were not practical economically. Too many precious man-hours were wasted on rounding up undesirables. The ideal solution to achieve a united world and thus a perfect one lay in the creation of the ideal humans whose numbers grew exponentially. Then the final depopulation of the inferior type of man could be realistically and profitably accomplished on a timetable.

Nazi geneticists like Josef Mengele argued convincingly that even the most advanced bioengineering methods could go only so far. After a certain degree of success, it was reduced to mere tinkering and genetic fine-tuning. The only solution was a form of neomutagenics, the hybridizing of other genetic material with that of humans.

Kane had heard only rumors of where this other genetic material was derived—from the same mysterious allies who'd provided the Nazi war machine with all the superior technological tools to subjugate the world.

They were called the Secret Chiefs, and according to word-of-mouth legend that had filtered down through the generations, the Chiefs were from somewhere else and they had guided humankind since the dawn of time. The main Secret Chief was called Balam.

The legend had become myth by the time it reached the ears of a young Corporal Kane, attached to the Rapier Legion. He had devoted little thought to the veracity of the tale. After all, Hitler had died over a century and a half earlier, despite the best medical efforts to prolong his life even further.

But his dream of breeding the New Man, the superman, lived on.

Getting to his feet, he looked around at his utilitarian, shabby quarters with a sudden loathing. They scarcely seemed to be the proper home for a superior human. They held almost nothing of a personal nature, and even though he had lived in them for nearly five years, since he was knighted, they still exuded an air of temporary occupancy. There was a sound reason for that, of course. If he was killed or simply vanished, a new tenant could be smoothly moved into place within an hour.

He glanced at the wall clock, a particle-board replica of the elaborate ones crafted in Switzerland before the war, and saw the hands were close to midnight. He shifted his gaze to the black telephone on the bedside table and immediately decided not to dial Baptiste. All calls were routinely monitored and recorded through the main switchboard.

Putting on his cap, he left his apartment, not allowing doubts about what he was doing and why to rise to the forefront of his mind. Even if he roused Baptiste from a deep sleep, she would have to let him in. As a junior officer, she had no choice.

Chapter 18

Dulce, like all villages in the province of New Thule, was divided into districts, and the residents of each were compelled to monitor one another as part of their civic duty and report any infractions. Because of its proximity to the Mesa, scrutiny was very intense, the rewards for informing greater. Being on the streets after the midnight curfew was not a high crime, necessarily, but it wasn't just a misdemeanor, either.

Since the quarters for the lower-ranking officers were several blocks away, Kane didn't use the main thoroughfares to reach them. To avoid being spotted by the watch posts, he threaded his way through side lanes and back alleys. He was more concerned about staying out of sight of only one Zone Trooper, and that was Pollard. He knew, without knowing how he knew, that if Pollard spied him, he'd report his movements directly to Salvo. And even though Salvo was his brother, one of his own genotype, he didn't trust him.

Kane climbed fences, duckwalked in shadows and squeezed through narrow openings between buildings. After about half an hour, the facade of the junior officers' quarters came into view. It was identical to his own. Only one window, on the second floor, showed light, a tiny slit peeping between drawn curtains. He was certain that window was Captain Baptiste's.

He stood in the gloom of an alley for a minute, making a careful visual recon of the area. Other than the faint scream of a Panavia Tornado fighter jet taking off from the air base on the outskirts of Dulce, he heard nothing.

He saw no movement, so he swiftly crossed the cobblestoned street. He could do nothing about the spy-eye sec camera bolted above the door, so he simply walked brazenly beneath it. If he was recognized, days would pass before any internal sec officers screwed up enough courage to question him.

The interior of the building was utterly silent, no murmur of voices, no music from radios or phonographs. Television sets were restricted to the officers' wardrooms, common areas in the cellars of the buildings. The one channel broadcasts were primarily educational or propaganda oriented. Once a week, the *Triumph of the Will* was aired, as well as some ancient Three Stooges shorts made in the 1930s. They served as object lessons, not only as the decadent kind of entertainment enjoyed by preunified America, but of the kind of cretinous breeds that once brought chaos to the country. Documentaries showing the animalistic squalor in which outlanders and Roamers lived were also staple broadcasts.

Still and all, the extreme kind of racism as practiced by the Nazis in Europe hadn't been part of the Reich for a long time, a century or more. Those early excesses were explained away as an overreaction to a legitimate problem. Of course, that problem had been solved by unification.

Kane went up the stairs on the balls of his feet, grimacing when a floorboard creaked beneath his weight. He rapped lightly on the door, hoping his guess about the apartment was correct. When there was no response, he knocked again, but he feared to make too much noise and thus draw attention from the other tenants.

Turning the knob, he wasn't surprised when the door opened. Since every possession was more or less just on loan from the state, there was little point in citizens stealing from one another.

Baptiste's flat was almost identical to his own. He heard the shower running and saw her uniform hanging in the open closet. On her bedside table, next to the telephone was a pair of eyeglasses, wire-framed with rectangular lenses, just as Grant had described. A small lamp near the closed window provided a feeble illumination.

As he closed the door quietly behind him, the sound of flowing water ceased, replaced by the faint jingling of hooks as the shower curtain was pushed aside.

He opened his mouth to call out her name when she strolled out of the bathroom, toweling her hair and completely naked. Kane's voice clogged in his throat.

She was maverick beautiful, with her tousled mane falling artlessly over her bare shoulders. Her body was slender but rounded, long in the leg, the breasts deep, yet taut, her belly hard and flat above a soft, honey-blond triangle at the juncture of her thighs. The air around her was electric.

Baptiste caught sight of him and uttered an outcry, quickly muffled. She clutched the towel to her body and squinted toward him. Her "Major Kane?" was an apprehensive whisper.

He realized that without her contacts she couldn't see him clearly in the dim light of the room.

"Yes," he said, imitating her low tone. "I need to talk to you."

Baptiste took a long step to the closet and pulled a robe from a hanger, turning her back to him as she shrugged into it. "You might've phoned."

"Yes, I might have. But I wanted this to be a private chat."

He admired the way she maintained her pose, not allowing the fear that had to be racing through her to register on her face.

"Don't be frightened, Captain," he said striving to sound reassuring and businesslike at the same time.

"You don't frighten me, Major."

Her retort took him aback. "I don't? I mean— good, there's no reason to be." He paused, then asked, "Why don't I?"

She tossed a strand of damp hair away from her high forehead. "I don't know. I should be. Any other officer, yes. I'd be terrified. But for some reason I trust you."

Kane's heartbeat sped up and respiration became difficult. Crisply, Baptiste asked, "What do you want to chat about, Major?"

He struggled to find the right words. "About us—"

Her eyebrows arched questioningly.

"And Grant, too. I find it more than a coincidence that all three of us have been experiencing headaches. A little while ago, just before I came here, I was in such pain I was incapacitated."

He surprised himself that he made such an admission. It was tantamount to confessing he wasn't as superior as he was supposed to be.

"And there's something else," he continued in a rush. "Memories that aren't really memories. Thoughts that are my own, but aren't. Words, visions, things I can't make any sense of."

As he spoke, he saw Baptiste's eyes narrowing in interest, then widening in understanding. "What kind of words?"

"Archons for one. That came to me right before I had the last headache. The Archon Directorate."

When recognition flooded her face and glittered in her eyes, he took a step forward. "That means something to you, doesn't it? The Archon Directorate?"

She stepped away from him, stopping when she bumped against the bed. Dropping her voice to a rustle of agitation, she replied, "That's something you're not supposed to know about."

Genuine fright was stamped on her face and bearing, and he stopped walking toward her. "Or you either, Captain?"

She nodded, her face pale and grimly drawn. "Anyone. It's the secret of all secrets. It's how the Third Reich won the war, won the world. Only the elite know of it, and I doubt they know the whole story.''

He eyed her suspiciously, a little nettled that a mere captain had access to information barred from him. ''And you know it?''

She shivered, hugging herself. ''Only the beginning of it, what I read in an old file transferred here from Berlin, waiting in storage for two centuries to be input into the database. It had been overlooked by the wartime censors. It wasn't supposed to be there, so I destroyed it.''

''And,'' Kane ventured, ''because of your photographic memory, you've never been able to forget a single word.''

Her fists tightened on her elbows, knuckles standing out like ivory knobs. ''How did you know I have an eidetic memory? I never mentioned it to anyone. I went to great lengths to hide it.''

Kane tried to dredge up a reasonable sounding response and ended by shaking his head in frustration. ''I don't know. I guess it's the same way Grant knew you wore those.'' He gestured to the eyeglasses on the bedside table.

In a faint, hoarse voice, Baptiste said, ''And I guess it's the same way I know I can trust you. That you'd give your life for me…like you've done before.''

The comment shocked Kane into speechlessness. He stepped closer to her, and this time she didn't retreat or flinch. She tilted her head back and gazed directly into his face, as if searching it for something she would not recognize until she found it.

He returned her stare, searching her eyes and saw no duplicity in their green depths, only a flicker of an awakening passion tinged with apprehension.

Before he knew it, Kane pulled Baptiste to him, pressing his mouth against hers. She resisted only a second before her lips parted. She uttered a tiny sigh as his tongue tentatively touched hers.

They were in a wild embrace, kissing and gasping. Kane felt his knees trembling. He felt a sense of distant wonder at the sudden intensity of his desire. He allowed it to sweep him up. It was as if he were finally allowing the embers of a long-banked passion to burst into full flame.

Baptiste appeared to be consumed by that same fire, caught up in the same madness. She shucked out of her robe and Kane lifted her up, swung her in a semicircle and placed her on the bed. They clung to each other as he shed his clothes as quickly as possible. Arousal had already spread through his loins and made worming out of his jodhpurs difficult. Eyes bright, Baptiste helped him tug off his boots.

They rolled across the bed, mouths kissing, hands stroking, fondling and cupping. Twice Baptiste cried out, her body trembling, rising on orgasmic wings.

Kane positioned himself over her and slid in slowly, her moist warmth tightly clutching him. He thrust carefully at first but Baptiste's hips lifted, upward and forward.

He moved harder and faster, and she moved with him, gasping, her arms encircling his neck and pulling his head down to her breasts. They surged, strained and twisted against each other, Kane answering Brigid's wordless calls with his own.

Then her emerald eyes flew wide and she stared at him for a long moment. She began thrashing wildly beneath him, a piercing cry of release reverberating against the walls of the room.

Kane echoed that cry as he exploded within her. At the same instant, a bomb seemed to go off, not only in his loins but in his head. A flash of dazzling light completely filled his field of vision, and an excruciating pain sent his consciousness skittering into the blaze.

Mercifully, it lasted only a second. He lay limp and panting, temples throbbing, eyes tightly shut, seeing and knowing nothing. Beneath him, Baptiste gulped in air and he felt her hands on his sweat filmed back. Then they flew away, and he felt her body go as tense and as taut as a bowstring. She inhaled sharply.

Kane pushed himself to his elbows and opened his eyes. She blinked up at him, dazed, confused and troubled. "Kane?" Her voice held a high, trembly note of consternation.

Realization came to Kane in an ice-cold torrent. "Baptiste?"

She raised her head, craning her neck, looking around frantically. "What's going on?"

Kane closed his eyes again, bowing his head. "And you accuse *me* of always stating the obvious."

Chapter 19

The digital chronometer on the wall shifted glowing numbers to 030.00.

"At the halfway point," Bry called, raising his voice to be heard over the rhythmic throb. "Field cohesion holding steady. T-minus 30 to cycle reversal."

Lakesh didn't need Bry's report regarding field cohesion—he saw it for himself on the readout screens linked to the dedicated control console. Sine and cosine waves stretched and rotated across them. The instrument panel at which he sat had been built and installed a few months before to oversee the temporal dilation of the Omega Path program.

Its design did not conform to the symmetry of the rest of the control consoles in the complex. Dark, long and bulky, like an old-fashioned dining table canted at a thirty-degree angle, it bristled with thousands of tiny electrodes and a complex pattern of naked circuitry. A switchboard at Lakesh's elbow contained relays and the readout screens.

He glanced up, peering through the open door of the anteroom to the mat-trans chamber beyond. The phase transition coils produced the steady, high-pitched drone, an electronic synthesis between the device's hurricane howl and down-cycling hum.

Because of the translucent quality of the brown-tinted armaglass shielding, he could see nothing within it except vague, shifting shapes without form or apparent solidity.

He knew the chamber was full of the plasma bleed off, the ionized wave-forms that resembled mist. So far, all was as it had been in the tests and preliminary experiments. As had been done with the Omega Path, the mainframe computers were reprogrammed with the logarithmic data recorded during Brigid's and Kane's transit from Tibet with the three pieces of the Trapezohedron. The new program prolonged the quincunx effect produced by dematerialization, stretching it out in perfect balance between the phase and interphase inducers. To maintain the effect, the power drain on the energy resources of the redoubt was enormous. Several nonessential systems had to be taken off-line.

Lakesh wasn't too concerned, since he had the utmost faith in Wegmann, the installation's engineer, mechanic and all around maintenance man. He was down in the generator room, monitoring the curve of energy consumption and would activate the reserves if necessary. Thus far, there had been no substantial change from the initial tests.

The only difference from the tests was that Kane, Brigid and Grant were being subjected to the new process instead of inanimate objects. Each had a piece of the stone in their possession.

The margin for error had been minimalized but whether their individual consciousness could be sent into sidereal space to link with their analogues on a parallel casement would not be known for another half an hour.

Certainly without the introduction of the facets of the Trapezohedron into the quantum energy matrix, nothing would happen. Brigid, Kane and Grant would simply be incorporeal molecular patterns for an hour.

Matter transfer worked on the principle that everything organic and inorganic could be reduced to encoded information. The primary stumbling block to actually moving the principle from the theoretical to the practical was the sheer quantity of information that had to be transmitted, received and reconstituted without any making errors in the decoding.

The string of information required to program a computer with every bit and byte of data pertaining to the transmitted subject, particularly the reconstruction of a complex biochemical organism out of a digitized carrier wave ran to the trillions of binary digits.

Matter transfer had been found to be absolutely impossible to achieve by the employment of Einsteinian physics. Only quantum physics, coupled with quantum mechanics had made it work. And only Balam's people had made the discovery, which they shared in piecemeal fashion with the scientists of the Totality Concept.

That was not quite right, Lakesh silently corrected himself. Not Balam's people, but their forebears.

When Lakesh had attempted to solve the mystery of the so-called Archon Directorate and its agenda by delving into the dark corners of human history, the morass of complex and broad legends, more often than not contradictory, made him give up in despair.

The little he had learned, the intelligence Kane, Grant and Brigid had gathered, was still the most shallow, imperceptible scratch on the surface of a vast tapestry of secrecy.

At the dawn of humankind, a reptilian race of beings known in ancient Sumerian texts as the Annunkai arrived on Earth. They inhabited much of the land masses, exploiting the natural resources and even tinkering with the indigenous life-forms to create a labor force, which eventually, and perhaps mistakenly, became *homo sapiens*.

The Annunkai gradually reduced their involvement and mining colonies on Earth and triggered the global cataclysm known in all cultures as the Great Flood.

After a thousand years or more, an expeditionary force of Annunkai returned and found another advanced race had established a foothold, the humanoid but not human Tuatha Da Danaan

The two races warred for centuries, the conflict extending even to the outer planets of the solar system. Finally, with both the Danaan and the Annunkai at the brink of extinction, they struck a pact whereby not only their cultures would mingle, but their genetic stock and bloodlines as well.

From this union was born the progenitors of the race that would eventually be called the Archons. What was left of the Annunkai and the Danaan withdrew from Earth, leaving behind a wellspring of confusing myths about wars in heaven, serpent kings, demons and angels. But the root races, as Balam referred to them, left their knowledge behind, in the care of their offspring.

Balam's folk initially did not hide from humanity, they coexisted with them as advisers to mighty princes, friends and high counselors of kings.

But a catastrophe rocked the world, most likely a pole shift that might have caused the sinking of Atlantis and the blotting out of entire nations, whole civilizations.

Humanity was hurled back into a state of savagery, and Balam's people fared little better, not escaping the common ruin that shattered the face of the Earth. Only the Black Stone, the Shining Trapezohedron, remained as their link with their former stage of civilization.

Lakesh recollected Balam's description of the stone: "It is more than an artifact. It is a key to doors that were sealed aeons ago. They were sealed for a good purpose. Now they may be thrown wide and all the works of man and nonman will be undone."

Intriguing as it sounded, his definition of the Trapezohedron was still vague. Balam had hinted, implied and filled in some blank spots but by no means all of them.

Lakesh couldn't help but wonder if Balam had chosen to remain a prisoner in Cerberus for over three years because he had foreknowledge of the events leading up to this attempt to breach the barriers between the parallel casements.

If not for Balam, the existence of the Black Stone and its properties would have most certainly never been discovered, at least not by the personnel at Cerberus. God only knew what would have come of Grigori Zakat's manipulation of it. But perhaps, the stone was manipulating Zakat.

Lakesh felt his flesh crawl at the thought. Not too long before, in a sour mood, he had toyed with the concept that Balam might be a pawn, manipulated by vast, dark intelligences. He had dismissed the idea simply because it could not be proved empirically. But then, almost none of the information Balam had conveyed could be proved.

His people's knowledge of hyperdimensional physics was proved out at least insofar as the mattrans units were concerned. But they had not shared their knowledge that the gateways could accomplish far more than linear travel from point to point along a quantum channel.

Project Cerberus, Operation Chronos and sidereal space were all aspects of the same mechanism. Only the applications of the principle differed. Perhaps that was why the entire undertaking had been code-named the Totality Concept because it encompassed the totality of everything, the entire workings of the universe.

The venal humans involved in the endeavor were too fixated on reaching short-term goals, making quota and earning bonuses to devote much thought as to why it was called the Totality Concept. Lakesh included himself in this number, although he hadn't been so much venal as naive to the point of imbecility.

Of course, Grant had called them imbeciles when Lakesh voiced his proposition to use the facets of the Trapezohedron in conjunction with the gateway to travel sidereal space. Actually, imbeciles was the least offensive of the terms he had chosen to direct at Lakesh, Brigid, Kane and ultimately himself, for agreeing to participate.

He had declared, "If you're bound for hell, I'm bound to go with you."

Bry's voice drew Lakesh back to the present. He called out, "Virtual focus conformals marginal."

"Acknowledged," Lakesh replied. He was still surprised that Bry had not voiced a blizzard of objections to the undertaking. His cooperative, eager attitude was a complete turnaround from the one he had displayed toward the Omega Path plan.

Lakesh glanced again at the readout screens, saw the wave-forms holding steady and when he turned back around, Domi was there.

He didn't need to look into her drawn-tight, tense face to know she was exceptionally nervous. Her crimson eyes fixed on the slabs of armaglass surrounding the jump chamber.

"Everything's fine, darlingest one," he said encouragingly.

Her head nod was a jerk. "Grant's hurt. Doesn't need to go through this."

"I've explained that to you," he responded as patiently as he could manage. "Only Grant's consciousness—his mind, all of their minds—are being transported, not their bodies. You experienced something similar not long ago."

Again came the head jerk. "Saw a very bad man chill another very bad man. Happened a long time ago."

"Yes, over two hundred and fifty years ago. Your physical body wasn't there, just your perceptions."

She shook her head in annoyance. "I was like ghost. Scared me big time."

Under stress, her abbreviated outlander mode of speech became more pronounced. Lakesh consulted the wall chron. "Only twenty-eight more minutes and they should be back here, safe and sound."

Her brow wrinkled in a frown. "An hour not much time for them do a lot."

Lakesh adjusted his spectacles, looking at her over their rims. "As I said two days ago, the passage of time between two casements may not be exact. What's an hour here might be a month there—wherever that is—and vice versa."

"How you so sure they all end up in same place?"

"I can't be," he admitted. "That's why we limited the transition time to an hour. But if Kane's mind is the key, attuned to the energies of the stone, Grant and Brigid should be swept along the same channel with him."

He added, a touch acidly, "We'll know in twenty-seven and a half minutes."

Domi leaned a hip against the control console, oblivious to Lakesh's disapproving glare. "Long time to wait."

"Yes, a long time. I only hope it's long enough."

"I'VE BEEN WAITING a long time," Wegmann said waspishly.

Beth-Li closed the door behind her and leaned

against it. "I had to wait until everyone was occupied and I was sure nobody was watching me."

Her teeth glistened in the timid smile she threw him. Hesitantly, Wegmann returned it.

Despite the throbbing resonance of the nuclear generators, they spoke in subdued tones. Wegmann perched his slight, skinny frame atop a stool. A man in his midthirties, he was no more than five and half feet tall, weighing maybe 140 pounds. His hair, swept back from a receding line, was tied in a ponytail at the back of his head.

Behind him, within a huge wire enclosure, were three ovoid, vanadium-shelled generators. If the central complex two levels above was the brain of Cerberus, the subterranean room was its heart, pumping life and power to it. Opposite the cage sprawled a long operations-and-monitoring station. Liquid crystal displays glowed, needle gauges wavered and rheostats clicked.

Wegmann nodded his balding head toward the console. "Nobody can watch anybody right now. I had to divert power from the sec system. All the vid cams, inside and outside, are off. If somebody was going to stage an attack on the redoubt, this would be the best time. We wouldn't know they were there until they knocked on the door."

Beth-Li moved toward him with a silent, feline grace, tossing her long black hair over her shoulders. "You read my note?"

Wegmann patted a flapped pouch on the thigh of his bodysuit. "Twice."

He made no move to slide off the stool and meet

the woman halfway. She stepped close to him, gently sidling her body between his knees. "You don't seem very upset by it."

"Why should I be?" he retorted. "You didn't tell me anything I hadn't already guessed. Just because I'm stuck down here twelve hours out of twenty-four doesn't make me stupid."

Beth-Li leaned into him, looking up into his face. She breathed, "You're not angry?"

"I didn't have much a life in Snakefish."

"You don't have much of a life here. Stuck here in the basement, wiping down machines, mopping up oil, tuning up the wags."

She put her hands on his waist and tugged. Wegmann didn't climb off the stool. He liked the novelty of being able to look down on someone.

"Even if Lakesh framed me," he said, "there's not much I can do about it, two years later. I didn't leave anything behind worth pining over."

"But you have something now."

"You?" Wegmann asked bluntly.

Beth-Li's smile became shy, coy. "Could be. What I meant is that you have a great deal of power in your hands here. You control the redoubt."

He looked startled as if the thought had never occurred to him before. "I guess that's right," he admitted. "I'm the only one who really knows how to maintain and operate everything down here—the air-conditioning and heating system, the lights, the water."

Placing a hand on his chest, over his heart, Beth-Li whispered, "You're the most powerful man here, but you're treated like a trained monkey. I know about you, how you to yearn to play music, to have your talents and not just your skills recognized."

"Like I said," Wegmann commented dryly, "I'm not stupid. What do you want of me?"

She leaned in closer, parted lips only a tantalizing inch from his. "I want an ally, I want a partner, I want a lover."

"Big order. What about Auerbach? You ran off with him awhile back, didn't you?"

She made a dismissive, derisive spitting sound. "He ran off with me. Like everybody else here, Auerbach is under the thumb of Lakesh and his blasterman, Kane. You're not afraid of Kane, are you?"

Testily, Wegmann shot back, "Hell, yes, I'm afraid of him. How many times do I have to tell you I'm not stupid?"

Beth-Li almost drew away, but she slid her hands over Wegmann's belly. When she felt his muscles tense, she said softly, conspiratorially, "But you're not intimidated by him, are you?"

"No," Wegmann responded. "And I don't hate him, either. He's always treated me fairly."

"But he's still a Mag and he thinks you're his inferior. He only treats you well because he knows the redoubt can't get along without you."

"Let's get to the point," Wegmann said impatiently. "You want an ally, you want a partner, you want a lover. What do I have to do to be all of those things?"

"Nothing, right now."

Beth-Li's hand dropped lower, fingertips just a teasing fractional margin above the juncture of his thighs. "I just want to know if I can rely on you when the time is right."

Wegmann took her by the shoulders and tried to pull her closer, but she resisted, her smile broadening. "When the time is right for what?" he asked.

"We'll discuss that later...after you show me around down here and give me a good working idea of what can and can't be done with these machines."

Her long-nailed fingers tickled lower. "And after that, you can give me a working idea of what you can and can't do."

Chapter 20

"Get a grip, Baptiste," Kane snapped. "It's not like we haven't done this before."

"Not with each other we haven't."

Kane and Brigid sat on opposite sides of the bed, their backs to each other, both of them draped in sheets.

Dry-scrubbing his face in exasperation, Kane said, "It's not really us."

She snorted in derision. "It is now."

"But it wasn't—not until we..." He let his words trail off.

"Until our brains underwent biochemical and electrical changes," she finished in a musing tone. "The release of endorphins and the firing of neurons in the cortical and subcortical portions of our brains finally triggered the breakthrough."

"You're as much a romantic here as you are back home," Kane said.

As a sudden notion occurred to him, he swiveled his head swiftly toward her. "If this is what it takes to complete the mind-body fusion, Grant is on his own."

Brigid surprised him by laughing. "I don't think the sex act is the prerequisite stimulus. It's the stimulation of areas in the brain."

Standing up, but keeping the sheet wrapped toga-like around her, she said, "I apologize if I sounded like I was accusing you of taking advantage of me. I was in a state of shock, disoriented."

He gave her a small smile. "And at least we know what it's like."

She nodded gravely. "On this casement, anyway. How are your memories?"

"Of what? Of where we're from, of how we got here, of the last ten minutes?"

Sounding aggrieved, she said, "No, of this Earth's Kane."

He frowned slightly, pondering, recollecting. After a few moments he said, "Pretty bloody and brutal. A single-minded fixation on advancement by any means necessary." He did a poor job of disguising a look of disgust. "I'm a ruthless, stone-cold bastard, far worse than I ever was in Cobaltville. I'm a murderer, a backstabber, a liar, a rapist and I'm the most arrogant son of a bitch I ever met. What about you?"

Her eyes went distant and vague. "Fairly mediocre. I'm having an affair with a married colonel. I don't like him, but I hope he can get me promoted. He likes to hurt me. I'm very paranoid and depressed much of the time."

"I can't imagine why. So much for personal history. What about world history?"

They compared notes, matching their analogues' memories with each other. The year was the same, 2199 A.D. by the old calendar, but that wasn't much of a revelation. Their conscious minds, their identities were not moving up or down along the hyperdimensions but sideways.

Not surprisingly, Brigid's font of knowledge was deeper than Kane's. His information was primarily doctrine and dogma. Any of the mysteries or contradictions of the world, his parallel self tended to discount as not relevant to the priorities of his life.

Roamers and outlanders were essentially the same disenfranchised groups as on their own world. These versions were descendants of the generation who witnessed the Nazi invasion and occupation of America. They retreated from the cities, the villages, the urban areas.

They struck a truce among the Indian tribes on reservations and thus began a long, sporadic guerrilla war. It wasn't an active resistance. The warriors were too spread out, too poorly armed to do more than stage ambushes and acts of terrorism every now and then.

When the city-state of Calgary declared its independence from the Reich six years before and executed the viceroy, a horde of Roamers massed on the Canadian border to help repel the inevitable invasion force from America.

Whether the Reich had been victorious or not was still an open question. After a dozen skirmishes and two halfway major engagements, the rebel armies simply drifted away, melting into the wilderness, allowing the Reich to reclaim Calgary, which was a classic Pyrrhic victory, since the city had been burned to the ground.

"Before we—" Kane cleared his throat self-consciously. "Earlier you said something about the Archon Directorate."

Brigid nodded, pacing the small room, face intent. "It's about the only halfway interesting memory I—she has."

She stopped pacing, took a breath and declared, "It's not much different than what Lakesh initially told us months ago, back when we first arrived at Cerberus. Secret societies that flourished in Germany after World War I, like the Vril and the Thule, were in contact with the Archons—their liaison was an entity called Balam."

"Why am I not surprised," Kane put in dourly.

"These societies struck a pact with the Archons. In exchange for superior technology, Germany conquered the world for them and hybridized much of the human population. Their agenda seems to be the same as on our own Earth—that their race's genes live on.

"Also in the file was a mention of a Colonel Thrush, who apparently acted as the Directorate's frontline observer. She—I—assumed that this colonel was the ancestor of the field marshal."

Grimly, Kane said, "More than likely they're the same man or thing. What about the Totality Concept? Anything pertaining to gateway units or time-travel experiments?"

She shook her head. "No. I surmise that once Germany was given the secret of atomic weapons and they won the war, there was no need for it. As we know, the Totality Concept on our Earth was little more than subterfuge, a fifty-year plan to bring about a global holocaust.''

''Which this casement avoided when the Third Reich won World War II.''

He sucked on a tooth reflectively. ''There are a lot of similarities between the two Earths, especially the Purity Control Foundation and the obsession with eugenics. But what part does Thrush play in all of this? I mean, everything has been accomplished, right? He should have proclaimed himself Glorious Grand Emperor of the Universe by now, and not play solider.''

''He doesn't operate like that,'' Brigid said thoughtfully. ''There was another reference to him in that old wartime file—he was called keeper of the keys. It meant nothing to her.''

''But to you?''

Frowning, Brigid sat down beside him. ''Is it possible,'' she ventured, ''that on this casement Thrush has possession of and can interface with a version of the Trapezohedron?''

Reviewing their contact with the field marshal and his conduct, Kane answered, ''I think we should assume he does. He repeated to me the last thing that version of him said to me in Newyork—'Another time.' It was like he was trying to push my buttons.''

''And the mission he assigned you for tomorrow? You seemed to think that was unusual.''

''It is. To send two senior officers on a pacification mission is out of order. He's got something planned.''

Brigid eyed him worriedly. ''Like what?''

Kane shrugged. ''I can't say. I have no idea. I

don't have any suspicions of Thrush on this casement, but I don't trust Salvo, even if he is my genetic twin. The more things change, the more they stay the same.''

He turned his head toward her, trying not to dwell on how beautiful she looked or the fresh memory of their lovemaking, something they would not dare to do on their home casement for unexplainable reasons.

''What next, Baptiste?''

''First,'' she answered with a sheepish smile, ''we should get dressed. Then we need to make contact with Grant and find out if he's achieved fusion. And after that, Lakesh.''

Startled, Kane echoed, ''Lakesh? Why him?''

''Like our Lakesh, I have an intuition this one is far more than he appears to be. And it may be that Thrush suspects it, too.''

''Do you think he might have something to do with Domi?''

She grimaced at the mention of the girl. ''It's very possible. Thrush had a good point—she couldn't have gotten as far as she did with that virus unless she had inside help.''

She stood up quickly, but Kane took her by the hand. ''Wait.''

Brigid tensed but did not try to pull away. ''What?''

Tongue feeling clumsy and thick, he said, ''You know, there was a reason why we did what we did.''

She did not respond for a long moment, not wanting to meet his gaze. Finally, she did. In a soft, subdued tone, she replied, "I know that, Kane. I don't regret it, if that's what you're getting at."

Kane could only look at her, wondering why they had always concealed and bottled up their passion for each other.

Gently, she disengaged herself. "But not regretting it and wanting to talk it through are different things. We don't know how long before the minds of our dopplegangers reassert control and drive us out. Right at the moment, time and life are on the wing."

Kane smiled a little bitterly and reached for his pants. Brigid stroked his face, a quick apologetic caress. In a throaty whisper, she said, *"Anam-chara."*

It was an ancient Gaelic term that both of them had learned during the op to Ireland. It meant "soul friend."

Kane chuckled, but the sound had little genuine mirth in it.

WITH A BLOODTHIRSTY snarl, Grant drove his right fist into the face and watched it shatter into a dozen razor-edged fragments.

The shards of the mirror tinkled to his feet, but their semimusical chimes didn't make his headache go away, nor the haunting sight of the little albino girl, lying dead and bloodied.

He had been fully prepared to beat Salvo to death when he sadistically hurt her, and he had no idea why. It was if he had been temporarily possessed by someone else, moving on a primal protective impulse.

Grant was impressed by the girl's courage, but he

had tortured many a brave, tight-lipped outlander and Roamer. He had witnessed more than one commit suicide, so he couldn't understand why this one, this Domi, affected him in such a profound fashion.

He was ashamed of himself and more than that, mystified why Kane would step to his defense rather than instantly pouncing on his weakness.

Grant felt a smile tugging at the corners of his mouth when he recalled how Kane had tried to defuse the tense situation with a ridiculous bit of humor. Its meaning had eluded him at the time, but in retrospect he admired Kane's quick wit. But then he was always cracking wise and making sarcastic asides—

Grant shook his head furiously, which only increased the level of pain. Kane had never expressed anything remotely like a sense of humor before, in all the years he had known him. He was a true ice man, guarded and reserved. Even asking Domi if she wanted to be reasonable before the measured application of agony began was so out of character he wondered if he weren't the man possessed.

But then, considering the degree of grief he was battling over the girl's death, Grant didn't feel like the same man, either.

He had tried to sleep, but every time he closed his eyes visions wheeled and flitted and streaked through his mind. None of them made sense, not the ones where he wore black armor, nor those where he struggled to break a stranglehold placed on him by an enormous, repulsively fat man. In those Domi was there, slashing and stabbing with a long, serrated knife. And with the images came pain, severe and unrelenting.

Finally, he gave it up and got dressed, acting on the impulse to confront Kane. He lived on the floor above him, but he hadn't heard any sound from up there since he returned to his own flat an hour or so before.

When the rap sounded on his door, he whirled in surprise, stomach muscles clenching in an adrenaline-fueled spasm. He reached for his gunbelt, draped over the back of his one chair. At close to 2:00 a.m., only internal security agents made house calls. But they never knocked before entering.

"Who is it?" he barked.

Instead of an answer, the door swung open, pushed by Kane. He was followed by Captain Baptiste, and they both looked strange to him—no, not strange, just different in an unidentifiable, ineffable way.

"What are you doing here?" he demanded.

Kane glanced at the scattering of broken glass on the floor, smiled and asked dryly, "Having something of an identity crisis, Major?"

Grant didn't understand the query so he opted to ignore it. "I asked you two a question."

"How are you headaches?" Baptiste inquired.

"Worse, if you must know. How are yours?"

"Gone," Kane replied. "For the time being. We might be able to help you with yours."

Grant lowered his eyebrows and glared at him challengingly. "As far as I know, neither one of you is a medic."

"That's true," Baptiste stated matter-of-factly. "But we *are* your partners."

"Partners?"

"More than that," Kane said. "Friends."

In a low, menacing rumble, Grant asked, "Since when?"

"Me and you for about twelve years, since the time I pulled you out of that Roamer ambush."

Grant stared at him hard as if he had gone mad. Then a half memory flickered in his mind, of Kane treating his injured leg.

"Funny thing," he remarked darkly, "I don't seem to remember that."

"That's because it didn't happen to you," Kane replied, "it happened to another Grant. The one whose mind is locked up in your brain and is giving you headaches as he tries to get out."

"Oh." He stared at both of them blankly. "And I thought you were going to spout some bullshit about brain tumors. This explanation is much better."

"Telling him the truth won't work," Baptiste said to Kane. "He'll never believe us."

Grant lunged for his gunbelt. His fingers had just brushed the butt of his Sin Eater when Kane flung himself on him, trying to secure a hammerlock. "Hear us out—"

Kicking himself backward, Grant slammed Kane hard against the wall, pinning him there. Brigid leaped forward, trying to wrestle the gunbelt out of Grant's grip, digging her nails into the back of his hand. He shouldered into her, sending her stumbling backward.

Gritting his teeth, Kane jacked up on Grant's captured arm, increasing the pressure. The big black man snapped his head back, trying to butt Kane in the face.

Kane managed to dip aside and the back of Grant's skull smashed loudly against the wall, denting the plaster. He grunted in pain.

"Bet that didn't do anything for your headache," Kane hissed into his ear.

The hiss turned into an agonized *whoof* of forcefully expelled air as Grant drove an elbow deep into his solar plexus. Biting at air, Kane's grip on Grant's arm loosened and he shook free, whirling as he yanked his Sin Eater out of its holster.

Despite having almost all of the wind knocked out of him, Kane was a tenth of a second faster on the draw. Both men aimed their pistols at each other, fingers hovering over the triggers.

"Get that blaster off me," Kane ordered.

"Get yours off me first," Grant grated.

The tableau held, frozen, as Kane and Grant glared into the hollow, cyclopean eyes of the autopistols' bores.

"Do what he says, Kane," Brigid spoke up. "You know you won't chill him."

Kane shifted the barrel of his Sin Eater downward. "No, but I'll damn sure disable him. Maybe break the same leg here as there."

Confusion momentarily clouded Grant's eyes, then they squinted in pain. "What the fuck are you talking about?"

"Kane—" Brigid said urgently, warningly.

Kane inhaled slowly. "I'm going to disarm. I'll put my blaster on the floor. Then you can do whatever you want to do, but I know you won't chill me."

Grant tried to mold his features into a contemptuous smirk, but he failed. A slight tremor shook the barrel of the automatic. "Just how do you know that?"

"Because I know you."

Moving slowly, Kane bent and placed his side arm on the floor, then toed it over toward Grant, where it bumped against the tips of his boots.

"Baptiste is armed, too," Kane said quietly, reasonably. "But you might notice she's kept her blaster leathered. If we meant you harm, she could have chilled you five times over."

The trembling in the blaster's barrel increased. Grant flicked his eyes sideways in a feverish glance toward Brigid. His internal struggle was very evident on his face. "I think you two are trying to set me up for something. That's why I'm no good to you dead."

Kane gestured in frustration. "Come on—"

"Let's try some word association," Brigid said.

Both men looked at her in disbelief and their demand of "What?" was very nearly simultaneous.

Affecting not to have heard them, Brigid stated calmly, clearly, "Cerberus. Gateway. Trapezohedron. Domi."

Lines deepened around Grant's nose and mouth. "Shut up."

"Cobaltville. Magistrate," Brigid continued. "Guana Teague. Sindri."

Kane broke in with one whispered word. *"Olivia."*

Grant's eyes flicked to Kane. They widened, then narrowed to slits. The tremor in his hand worked its way up his arm, and for a second his entire body seemed to be jolted with high voltage current. The blaster dropped from his fingers, and his knees buckled. Sagging to the floor, he clasped both sides of his head, lips writhing back over his teeth in a rictus of silent agony.

Kane and Brigid caught him, holding him up.

"Who's Olivia?" Brigid asked.

Kane shook his head, putting a finger to his lips.

The seizure passed and Grant panted, "Nice strategy, Kane. You always know the right thing to say. Now I *do* regret not shooting you."

Rubbing his tender midsection, Kane said ruefully to Brigid, "On second thought, this might have been easier the way you and I did it."

Chapter 21

Salvo pulled off his coal scuttle helmet and dabbed at the perspiration on his broad forehead. "When the fuck are they going to get air conditioners that really work in these steel coffins?"

Seated across from him, Kane forced a sympathetic smile to his lips. "Ours is not to reason why."

Salvo frowned at him irritably. "What's that supposed to mean?"

Kane almost told him it was a line from a very old poem, then realized he would also have to tell him where he'd read it—in a book called *Heroic Ballads* he'd found in the Cerberus library. Few mass public book burnings had been staged over the past century and a half, but that was due in the main to having fewer books to burn.

The jump seats in which they and thirty of the Battle Class breed were strapped quivered as the treads of the huge personnel carrier crushed rocks and uprooted saplings.

The vehicle was known as an OGRE, but Kane couldn't help but think of it as a war wag. However, it made the one that Sky Dog and his people found seem like a baby buggy in comparison.

The OGRE combined the best elements of an APC, a ground assault vehicle and a battleship in its eighty-foot length. The ten-inch-thick vanadium armor plate protected the crew against chemical and light conventional weapons. The multispigot mortar launcher tubes possessed a range of four hundred yards, and the angle and rate of fire were adjustable. Four turrets contained six-barreled MG-1 A-9 miniguns that fired high velocity rounds at up to one hundred per second.

And then there was the Blitz or lightning cannons. The weapons accelerated electrons to fantastic speeds and spit them out as coherent beams. The tremendous energy discharges broke down the molecules of the very air and ignited sparks that resembled lightning bolts. Anything they touched went up in flames.

Six closed-circuit television screens, three to a side, were bolted on the bulkheads, displaying exterior images transmitted by the video cameras placed at strategic points on the hull. The people in the compartment could get a fairly close approximation of a 360-degree view of their surroundings.

Early that morning a big cargo plane, escorted by a pair of fighter jets, had flown out of the Dulce air base. It ferried Kane, Salvo and thirty of the so-called Battle Class breed to a military base in the Dakotas.

Kane thought the title Battle Class a misnomer if ever there was one. The troopers were slender of build and so blank of expression they might have been mistaken for mannequins dressed in soldier finery. The helmets made their paper-pale faces seem ridiculously small and elfin. The big eyes beneath the overhang of their headgear barely blinked, and their small baby mouths did not so much as twitch. Their long, artistic hands cradled their Sturmgewher auto-rifles with a lightness of touch that was almost effeminate.

Grenades hung from their wide leather belts, and the thick flak vests encasing their slight upper torsos made them appear weirdly barrel-chested.

After a two-hour flight, the plane landed at the base in the South Dakota badlands. There they underwent an annoyingly superficial briefing by First Flight Sergeant Whitcomb.

"We're not certain of the number of the opposition," Whitcomb told them. "Just that they're there and more keep arriving. For the past couple of days they've had a camp at the base of the monument. We don't have a clear idea of their armament either, but I'd judge this is the same bunch of scum who raided the Bismarck depot."

"And they're probably the survivors of the Canadian border campaign, too," Salvo grated. "We can expect some casualties."

Sergeant Whitcomb flicked his eyes toward the quiet ranks of the Battle Class. "More where they came from, right?"

Kane responded to the rhetorical query with a direct one. "If this group has been here for a few days, with more arriving, why haven't they defaced the monument if that's their intent?"

Salvo gave him supercilious stare. "Come on, Brother. Who can figure out what the subbreeds will do or why they do it? If they had any sense, they would have turned themselves in at the rehabilitation camps a hundred years ago."

At noon, they all filed aboard the OGRE. As soon

as Kane spied it, he experienced an unsettling sensation of déjà vu. He knew he had done all of this before, but the double tap-line of memories did not provide a clear recollection.

He tried to make himself comfortable, but it was almost impossible with the constant jouncing of the deck underfoot and the hard metal chairs. Although he was tired, having gotten only a couple of hours' sleep before embarking, he remained alert.

He wondered what Grant and Brigid were doing, if they had managed to implement the plan concocted hastily during the predawn hours. Kane sensed their time controlling the bodies and minds of their analogues was nearing its end. Already a restless stirring, a pressure was building within his head. He knew without knowing how he knew the pressure would soon become pain and the struggle between minds would begin anew. He grinned as he thought of how their dopplegangers would react if they knew what their bodies were doing.

Once Grant had oriented himself, even his doubts about seeking out Thrush on the parallel casement had been laid to rest. He hadn't reiterated his earlier arguments that revolved around attending to their own world, their own so-called reality, before getting involved in others.

Kane couldn't help but suspect that the only way Grant came to terms with this particular reality was not to examine it as a reality at all but to relegate it to the status of a dream from which he would soon awaken.

But Thrush wasn't a dream. Despite the history his

analogue knew regarding Germany's victory in World War II, Kane knew on a gut, primal level that it could not have come about without Thrush.

Kane had never devoted much thought to the concept of evil, pure or otherwise. He ascribed the motivations of his enemies to simply operating on a set of behaviors in opposition to his own. He was a pragmatist not a philosopher, and to him morals and ethics were sets of subjective, personal standards, not absolutes.

But if anyone—or thing—came close to meeting his amorphous definition of evil, it was Colonel Thrush. It wasn't the evil of a human being Kane could understand and deal with on his own terms. Whoever or whatever Thrush truly was, he was far more alien than even Balam.

Kane almost shuddered and decided to think about something else.

The OGRE creaked and yawed as it traveled through the badlands, following a rugged hellway up and over castellated hills, down gullies and around the bases of monstrous rock formations.

For the first couple of hours into the journey, Salvo was inclined to be chatty, mainly about mundane matters, occasionally bringing up past events. After a while, the reminiscences became more frequent and Kane suspected he was being tested. Fortunately, he fielded all of Salvo's inquiries with little difficulty.

"I saw Beth-Li going into your place yesterday evening," Salvo said with a smirk. "Was she as good the second time around?"

Kane answered with a grunting monosyllable, signaling he didn't care to discuss the woman.

Salvo affected not to notice Kane's apparent lack of interest in the topic. "You should have seen the cow I was matched up with last. I get the rank, but you get the prime meat. Something's wrong with that picture."

"There's got to be some balance," Kane replied noncommittally.

"Yeah," Salvo drawled. His mouth smiled, but his eyes glittered like chunks of black ice. "You get knighted, I get promoted. You get Beth-Li, I get the cows. That's some real balance at work there... Major."

A surge of anger boiled up in Kane, but it rose from two different sets of memories, two different sources of resentment. Yet, they all ended at the same place.

Trying to maintain a neutral tone, he said, "I was knighted for heroism. You weren't."

"I was in the same engagement."

"And you stayed safe and sound in the bunker while my squad was cut to pieces in that butterfly minefield. I took out the enemy emplacement, not you."

"Yeah," came the slightly mocking drawl again. "You made sure to mention that in your report, too. So much for brotherly loyalty."

Kane struggled with the irrational urge to draw his Sin Eater and shoot him dead in his seat. He snarled, before he could stop himself, "You tried to chill Baptiste, you tried to chill Grant, you tried to chill *me* and you think I give a shit about your idea of loyalty?''

Salvo's face twisted in stunned disbelief. ''What the fuck are you talking about?''

A cold fist of dread closed around Kane's heart. ''Forget it,'' he mumbled.

''No, I won't forget it,'' Salvo snapped. ''Those are pretty outrageous charges you just leveled against a superior officer. When was I supposed to have done this?''

''Forget it, I said. I apologize. I was out of line.''

Salvo plunged on as if he hadn't heard. ''Besides, why do you care what happens to those two, especially Grant? He's more of your rival than I am. As for Baptiste, I hear she's fucking Colonel Oberntiz. If anybody is going to have her killed, it's him.''

Kane folded his arms over his chest and leaned back, tipping the rim of his helmet down over his eyes.

''Then again, maybe she'll just be stripped of her rank and thrown to the Breeder Division. That's something to look forward to.''

Kane realized Salvo was doing his damnedest to provoke him, and Kane was doing his damnedest not to rise to the bait. All the thinly concealed hatred, jealousy and manipulation his own Salvo had directed toward him was mirrored here, in his analogue. Evidently, knowing from birth they were genetic twins hadn't made a difference in their relationship on this casement.

After a few more remarks about what a delectable morsel Captain Baptiste seemed to be, Salvo fell silent, although he strained mightily to keep the taunting leer stitched on his face.

As the day wore on, now and then he caught the eyes of Salvo, cold and deadly, watching him. It did not frighten him, but the poorly veiled hostility did begin to bore him, despite his familiarity with it.

The OGRE chugged on, angling across the flatlands, splashing through creeks, churning up and down bluffs.

As the sun began to sink, a tension grew in Kane. He looked up to the cockpit and through the ob port saw twilight painting the sky above the Black Hills in purple-red pastel tints. Towering in the distance he could discern five faces staring out from the edges of eroded butte rock. He tried to focus on the fifth face, the carved image of Hitler, but he swayed in his seat as the OGRE clanked its way down the side of a bluff.

"Not long now," Salvo commented.

The pilot of the vehicle downshifted, and the huge machine shuddered through the gears until it achieved a slower speed.

"Time," the copilot announced over the public address system.

Kane unlatched the seat restraint and made his way along the aisle and up the short ladder to the cockpit. Gazing out of the port made of triple glazed thickness of bulletproof glass, he saw flames dancing in the dusk from at least twenty bonfires.

In consternation, he said, "The Roamers don't seem too worried by our arrival. I'm sure they have outriders with radios. They've probably known we were coming for an hour or more."

The pilot, a wiry little man with a blond crew cut and rawboned face, didn't answer. He nodded tersely to the copilot. The man flipped up the cover on the fire-control board and his hands hovered over the keys, like a concert pianist preparing to go through the scales.

"I didn't give you an order," Kane snapped.

The pilot retorted, "Field Marshal Thrush instructed us to follow standard engagement procedures. That's what we're doing. Sir."

The man sounded as if he could barely summon up the energy to voice the honorific.

A dim blur of motion appeared in the path of the OGRE, fifty yards distant. Kane commanded, "Hit the spots."

The copilot flicked a toggle switch, and funnels of incandescence speared out from the array mounted above the ob port. Kane stiffened, gaped and muttered, "What the hell is going on?"

In a loose parade formation, dozens of men, women and children trudged toward the armored vehicle. They wore rags, buckskins and scraps of old uniforms from the Calgary campaign. In the blazing wash of the spotlights, they looked like the walking dead, many of them horribly scarred by poorly healed wounds. The children were even worse, sporting bellies swollen from malnutrition, their limbs stick-thin.

A limping man led the parade over the rock-strewn ground. From a long pole, obviously cut from a pine sapling, fluttered two banners. One was a tattered and scorched American flag, the stars and stripes perforated by a patchwork of bullet holes. Below that hung a white cloth. Actually, it was more gray than white, but it was probably the closet thing to the traditional flag of truce the Roamers could scrounge up among their meager belongings.

"They're surrendering," Kane said in surprise.

From behind him, Salvo's gloating voice declared, "That's their plan, anyway."

Kane gave him a hard, questioning, over-the-shoulder glance. "Their plan? Explain."

A grin of pure enjoyment split Salvo's sallow face. "Yeah, the Roamers and the outlanders made overtures that they wanted to come in, that they couldn't run or fight anymore. The field marshal's been playing along with them for months. He finally persuaded all the bands to agree to meet here and sign a formal declaration of surrender and loyalty oath. The stupid subbreeds think the OGRE is full of food and medicine and even a doctor or two."

A low chuckle bubbled at the back of his throat. "And I guess we *do* have the cure for what ails them."

Raising his voice, Salvo said, "They're in range now. Open up with everything we've got. The works."

The copilot's fingers tickled the keys. The mortar launchers gouted thunder and smoke, the minigun emplacements roared in a stuttering rhythm, tracer rounds cutting threads of phosphorescence through the twilight.

Kane caught a glimpse of the man bearing the flags spinning, clutching at himself as the bullets clawed open his chest, sending fragments of clavicle and rib bones spinning in all directions, propelled by crimson sprays. Bodies flew up, out and apart amid mushrooms of yellow flame.

The copilot stroked more keys. Arcing tendrils of electricity reached out with crooked fingers, touching and tapping. Running human figures became leaping, careening scarecrows made of fire.

The OGRE rumbled on, the thickness of the armored hull muffling the detonations of the mortar rounds and the drumming of the miniguns. The shrieks and screams couldn't be heard at all. Kane drew away, shaken and sickened, not caring if Salvo noticed his reaction.

Bullets began rattling on the OGRE's steel sides like hail. Kane barely made out muzzle-flashes from a hilltop and a brush-clogged draw. Unless the Roamers had HE rockets or heavy AP rounds, they might as well have been throwing rocks. After all, even the prototypes of the OGREs had repelled the invasion of Normandy two and a half centuries earlier.

Salvo alternated looking at the black-and-white images on the monitor screens with peering through the ob port. He grinned broadly, his eyes shining like chunks of wet obsidian.

Kane couldn't deny it was a beautiful betrayal, well-laid and lethally executed. He caught that ruthless thought snaking through his head and tried to chase it out. He didn't wonder at where it came from.

The OGRE bounced and groaned onward, pushing

through the billows of smoke and dust. The copilot switched on the targeting scope. It reduced the running, falling, flaming chaos to a set of sterile, computer-generated, radar-fed images, but it was certainly more accurate than shooting blind through the shifting curtains of grit and vapor.

"Time to give our new recruits their first field test," Salvo announced.

"Test them against what?" Kane did a poor job of repressing the icy disgust in his voice. "The Roamers are in full rout. We can just sit tight in here and chase them back to Canada."

Salvo's eyes widened in ingenuous surprise. "Why, Major, you know those aren't the field marshal's orders. We've got to run the hounds, so to speak."

The mildness vanished from his tone, a steel edge replacing it. He hooked a thumb over his shoulder. "Get them ready."

Pushing past him, Kane marched down the aisle between the seated soldiers. Their blank, masklike expressions had not altered, and their placid eyes did not follow his movements.

Taking up position astern, Kane barked, "Troops at attention."

Their erect carriages were ramrod straight in the first place, so the only change that took place was a shifting of their weapons, aligning them with a mathematical precision.

The OGRE's brakes squealed, the hull shivered and trembled as the vehicle shuddered down to a clanking halt. From the undercarriage came the hissing of pressure valves being vented.

"Remove seat restraints," Kane commanded.

As one, in absolutely perfect and unnerving synchronization, thirty hands pressed thirty catch-release buttons. The personnel compartment filled with one very loud *snap-click.*

"On deck!"

The black-clad soldiers all stood in unison, their weapons held at the same twenty-five-degree angle across their padded chests. Kane's memory drifted back a few months, to the droids he had encountered during the mission to rescue Lakesh. Briefly, he contemplated the possibility that the Battle Class breed might be things of metal and circuitry sheathed in a synthetic flesh. Or worse, hybrids of man, machine and something else, like Colonel Thrush.

The soldiers stood on a narrow metal channel running the length of the compartment. The flooring of the aisle began to descend with a hum and a series of clicks. As it lowered, the overlapping sections became shallow risers, forming a staircase.

Kane glanced at the opposite end of the compartment and met Salvo's eye. "Awaiting your word. Sir."

Salvo nodded. "The word is given. Banner man, point position."

A soldier stepped down on the ramp, unfurling the flag of the Reich in a single snapping motion. He extended the narrow telescoping pole to its full length.

"Disembark," Salvo continued. "Standard deployment of personnel and firepower. Observe rules of engagement until otherwise ordered. Comm-link frequencies open.''

The Battle Class breed marched forward and down, moving with an almost silent grace. After the last one had exited, Kane and Salvo joined them, one hand on the butts of their Sin Eaters, the other on their subguns.

Kane sniffed the hot, electric smell sizzling in the smoky air, and his stomach lurched at the thick stench of roasting human meat.

The Battle Class breed spread out in a line along the side of the OGRE. Men appeared, climbing over the rocks a hundred yards distant, leaping from them, scrambling on in a terrified retreat. The miniguns opened up again, the bullets crashing against the rocks, the stream of autofire tearing them to blood-streaked ribbons.

''Cease firing,'' Salvo shouted into his helmet comm-link. ''It's over.''

A man staggered up from a declivity near one of the war wag's treads, thin trails of smoke streaming from his hair. He started to run, stumbled, fell, dragged himself to his feet, took a step, then fell again. This time, he did not get up.

He raised a raw, blackened travesty of a face. His blistered, leaking lips writhed and he croaked, ''I surrender. Help me.''

Salvo fired from the hip, a short burst from the subgun slung over his shoulder. The man's burned features dissolved in a wet, red spray. The bullets knocked him backward into a tread-dug ditch.

Salvo chuckled. "So the rebellion ends with a whine for mercy, not a bang." He threw a grin at Kane. "A little anticlimactic, isn't it, Brother? Move in."

"Those aren't Field Marshal Thrush's orders," Kane replied. "He told us to set up a perimeter around the Rushmore zone, to keep the Roamers from escaping—"

Salvo cut him off with a sharp, savage gesture. "Do it. I'm in command here. You take point."

Kane moved forward, using hand signals to tell the troopers to fall in behind him. He glanced up once, as the gigantic stone faces loomed above him, and a trick of the light made them appear as if they were silently and grimly judging him—all except for the Hitler effigy. Beneath the square stone mustache, his huge lips seemed be curved in a smile of satanic anticipation.

Kane went quickly over the rocky ground, and it wasn't until he had crossed ten yards that he noticed the soldiers had hung back. He turned, opening his mouth to shout an order. He didn't. The sensation that he had been here before, executing the exact same maneuver overwhelmed him. The pressure in his skull built, not yet a pain but only a whisker's breadth from it.

Wheeling, he saw a small round object arcing overhead, dropping between him and the troopers. Without hesitation, Kane dived forward. He hit the ground, going into a shoulder roll. He was still rolling when the grenade detonated with a hot orange flash, a fireball ballooning outward. Clods of dirt and shrapnel rattled against the OGRE's hull.

The shock of the concussion slammed into Kane, bowled him over. As he somersaulted, he felt the brief wave of searing heat against his back.

When his head-over-heels tumble ended, one thought dominated his mind—it was a military grenade, exactly like the ones attached to the combat belts of the Battle Class troopers.

Elbowing himself onto his back, his stunned eardrums registering little but a surflike throb, Kane peered through the ragged scraps of smoke and settling dust. He knew in his marrow Salvo had ordered the grenade to be thrown at him. He drew his Sin Eater, thumbing the selector switch to fire 3-round bursts.

A soldier slid through the drifting, gray pall. Without hesitation, he fired at him, neatly grouping the shots right over the heart. The trooper looked down at the watery red mess the AP rounds had produced on his flak vest, then raised his big eyes and stared dispassionately at Kane. Then his body went into a series of strange, almost mannered convulsions.

With each motion, the Battle Class solider changed, as if he were shedding a larval cocoon at an inhuman speed. His fingers lengthened, spurs of bone thrusting from the tips of his fingers amid little squirts of blood. The curving claws looked like twigs that had been used to stir thin red paint.

The trooper's helmeted head sank between his shoulders, while thick ropes of muscle and humps of sinew writhed on his upper back and swelled his triceps. His lower jaw extended, popping out like a cabinet drawer, and dark membranes suddenly veiled his eyes.

His mouth hung wide, revealing double rows of serrated teeth, pushing up through the gums like ivory-colored nails.

The entire transformation occurred between one heartbeat and the next. Kane's belly shrank with terror as he struggled to comprehend what was happening. Then he understood how the Purity Control Foundation had scored a stunning victory with the Battle Class breed.

The trooper launched himself forward, kicking off the ground in a broad jump. Flame wreathed the muzzle of his Sturmgewher. Fountains of dirt sprang up all around Kane as he frantically returned the fire and tried to dodge at the same time.

One of his rounds struck a spark from the frame of the autorifle, ripping it from the soldier's hands and sending it spinning end over end.

Kane managed to achieve a half crouch and ducked as the trooper sailed over his head. He stood and started to pivot, leading with his pistol. A living weight landed on his back, and arms whipped up and around his throat, cinching tight.

Kane put all of his strength into a wild, adrenaline-fueled surge to break the chokehold.

It did not break.

Chapter 22

Lakesh wheeled his chair away from the trestle table loaded with a complicated network of glass tubes, beakers, retorts and Bunsen burners. The rubber tires squeaked on the polished floor, and he regarded Grant and Brigid with a polite curiosity.

"Two visits in two days," he rasped. "Should I feel honored or afraid?"

Brigid fielded the question smoothly. "We're only following up on yesterday's unfortunate incident."

"Really? Since when is a cryptographer dispatched to follow up on unfortunate incidents?"

"If a failed intrusion was all it was, then our investigation would be over," Grant said gruffly.

Blinking up at him in annoyingly familiar fashion, Lakesh remarked, "The field marshal said nothing about you two coming out here today to annoy me and waste my time."

"Does he tell you everything that's going on?" Brigid asked testily.

Lakesh laughed and rolled himself to a control console that spanned the length of the far wall. He glanced at the glass-encased readouts and gauges before saying, "As a point of fact, he does. He devotes an anally retentive attention to this facility. Almost obsessive. This is his place, you know, his sanctum sanctorum. I just work here.''

''Regardless,'' Brigid said with a breezy officiousness, ''we are here, and you will answer our questions.''

Lakesh cackled wearily. ''My dear young woman, dearest Brigid, I don't have to answer questions put to me by anyone other than Field Marshal Thrush. Don't you understand that with one word from me, I can have you and your overbearing companion ejected? At another word from me, I can have you standing before a disciplinary tribunal.''

Lakesh stirred in his chair. ''Which brings me around to another point—why don't you know that?''

Both Grant and Brigid sifted through their memories. Lakesh was in there, but a ghostlike, indistinct figure, a man of mystery linked in some indefinable fashion with another mystery man, Field Marshal Thrush.

''You're not so powerful that you're exempt from being questioned in matters of national security,'' Grant growled.

The patronizing smile on Lakesh's face became one of pity. ''Young man, I *am* national security. This facility represents the future of the Reich. Not virtually, not figuratively, but literally. It is the citadel of that destiny.''

Bitter sarcasm undercut the old man's tone. ''When you dare to question me, you are questioning the foundation of the Reich itself and why we fought so long, why so many warriors fell in battle so we could reach this point in our mutual evolution.''

The speech was obviously dogma, delivered by rote, and Lakesh voiced it with a slightly mocking edge. "We have the stepping-stone in place to reach further than even Hitler's ambitions, and we are all unified to achieve that goal."

Brigid pretended to flick a speck of dust from her uniform sleeve. Casually, sounding almost bored, she inquired, "This stepping-stone—is it by chance black, in the shape of a trapezohedron with Sanskrit characters inscribed along one side?"

Grant kept his surprise at Brigid's offhand inquiry from showing on his face. At the same time, he scrutinized Lakesh, expecting him to either react in utter confusion or as if he'd been gut shot.

Neither occurred, and Grant was a little disappointed. The old man sat perfectly motionless in his chair. Only his eyes moved, the fleshy lids fluttering like the wings of a butterfly desperate to take panicked flight. Brigid and Grant stood and watched and waited.

Even though he couldn't see it, Grant was pretty certain the laboratory was equipped with a spy-eye sec cam and more than likely a sound pickup.

When Lakesh finally spoke, it was in a normal tone of voice, stronger, not as reedy or raspy. "This area is a blind zone. I saw to that. The video system is focused on that section over there."

His head gave a backward jerk. Grant and Brigid looked in that direction. On the far side of the room, they saw a trestle table holding equipment identical to that on the table they stood near. The control console on the wall was an exact duplicate as well. The subterfuge was almost artistic in its simplicity. Even the most suspicious minds wouldn't notice the twin effect.

"You're a master of diversion even here," Grant remarked. "We should have guessed."

Lakesh acknowledged the observation with a gracious nod. "Through long experience and necessity. Would I be correct in assuming that although you appear to be Major Grant and Captain Baptiste, I am actually addressing silent invaders from a parallel casement?"

The question, posed so mildly and phlegmatically, stunned Brigid and Grant into a long period of speechlessness.

Lakesh chuckled. "You are either what I assume you to be, or I am very, very wrong and you'll report my dementia to the health authority. If the latter is the case, please don't waste your energy or my limited time humoring me. Just go, make your report and I'll wait here to be wheeled off to the assessment room.

"On the other hand, if I'm right, then please confirm it and stop gaping at me. As I said, no one can see or hear us in this spot."

Tentatively, Brigid said, "For the sake of argument, let's agree your assumption is dead-on. Which of course leads me to a very pertinent question."

"How could I possibly know enough about such a fantastic concept as parallel worlds so I could even hazard such a wild guess?"

"That's about it."

Sighing, Lakesh tugged absently at his long nose,

a gesture that was all too familiar. "As is apparent, I am very old, but I am far older than you might guess."

"Let me try," Grant put in. "Around 250 years?"

Lakesh smiled at him appreciatively. "The Major Grant of this world would not have known that, since it's one of the deepest secrets of the Reich. Only Thrush knows. I take it the Lakesh you know is of the same age and with a similar background?"

"The Lakesh we know is a physicist," Brigid stated, "not a geneticist, though he dabbled in that field. But the age is the same."

"He's in a little better shape than you are, though," Grant said.

Lakesh shrugged his knobby shoulders. "For a man with no stomach to speak of, an artificial heart, replacement eyes, one lung, no kidneys, legs that haven't moved in over thirty years and who subsists primarily on intravenously introduced liquid protein, I'm in the best shape of my life."

"Our Lakesh had the benefit of cryogenics and advances in prosthetic surgery," Brigid said kindly.

"Tell me about him, about your casement of origin."

"Tell us," Grant rumbled, "how you even know about such things and why you called us 'silent invaders.'"

"I asked you first," the old man snapped with some asperity. "Neither of you would have come here if you didn't need me for something. Therefore it's to your benefit to get on my good side."

Grant's brow knitted in a ferocious scowl. "And

we can just walk out of here, tell Thrush you've fused out and have you placed in room with nice soft walls.''

Lakesh cackled, coughed, put the oxygen mask over his face and breathed deeply for a long moment. Removing it he said, ''Your naiveté astonishes me, Major, or whatever you are. If it wasn't for Thrush, I'd know nothing abut the multiverse or the lost Earths or the danger of silent invaders. That's what he calls visitors from parallel casements.''

''Have you had many of them?'' Brigid asked, interest glinted in her green eyes.

''As far as I know, you two are the first. However, all I'd have to do is report to the field marshal that you two—and probably Major Kane—are not devoted servants of the Reich but silent invaders from the hyperdimensions. If he didn't torture you for information, he'd have you executed.''

''What good would that do?'' Grant demanded. ''The bodies would be killed, but not us, the invaders.''

Lakesh crooked an eyebrow. ''Are you so certain of that you would want to risk it? At the very least, your mind energy would be driven out of your host body. You would either return to your home casement and never be able to return here, or you'd float around as a disembodied electromagnetic pattern.''

Grant found the possibility too horrifying to dwell on, and he said nothing.

Brigid retorted impatiently, ''Let's stop swapping threats, shall we? What do you want to know?''

Lakesh stopped short of smirking triumphantly, but

he posed a number of simple questions that were simply answered. All he required was a superficial knowledge of their world. He asked nothing about the Archon Directorate or the Trapezohedron, and Brigid supplied no information. She told him of their encounters with Thrush in the past time line of their casement.

Lakesh's eyes went watery and vacant when she mentioned Domi and how she had witnessed Thrush executing Adolf Hitler.

"What happened to the child?" he asked in a faint voice.

"She's alive and well at the installation I told you about," Brigid replied. "She was wounded a while back trying to save you—save your doppleganger, that is."

Grant thrust out his jaw truculently. "You were behind Domi's attempted insertion here, weren't you? You supplied her with the equipment to breach the sec system and the virus."

A tear slowly spilled from Lakesh's left eye and worked its way down his deeply seamed cheek. "I was. Not personally, of course, I went through several levels of intermediaries. But the plan was mine. And if you're aware of that, the field marshal is aware of it, too."

"You sent that girl to her death," Grant grated.

"She volunteered. As a field operative for the Preservationists, it was part of her oath."

The reply dampened a bit of the angry heat in Grant's eyes. "There's a Preservationist group here?"

"Yes, and I am one of the cell leaders. I take it from your reaction you have something similar on your home casement?"

Brigid shook her head. "Similar in concept. There it's a myth crafted by your other self. It's only a diversion."

"Here it is very real. Its formation stretches back to the day of the Reich victory. It is an underground resistance movement, drawing from the ranks of disenfranchised Americans. There are many of us, in all walks of our society, but I obviously don't know the true number."

"Doesn't look like the Preservationists have accomplished a hell of a lot in two and half centuries," Grant said grimly. "It might as well be the myth it is back home."

Lakesh nodded sadly. "I wish I could argue with you, but I cannot. The winter of the human race is at hand."

Softly, in a rustling whisper, he quoted, "'For we wrestled not against flesh and blood but against principalities, against powers, against the rulers of the darkness of the world.'"

"*Ephesians* 6:12," Brigid said quietly. "There's not much future in being a Biblical scholar on my world, either."

Suddenly, she winced and her hand flew reflexively to her head.

Lakesh observed sagely, "The fusion link is weakening. Soon you'll be driven out or forced to concentrate completely on maintaining control."

Brigid lowered her hand. "How do you know that?"

"I was told."

"By whom? Thrush?"

Lakesh wagged his head from side to side. "No, he told me very little about silent invaders from the lost Earths. If he knew I was talking to you, he would probably execute me with his own hand."

"It wouldn't be the first time," Grant remarked enigmatically.

Lakesh looked to be on the verge of asking him to explain, but Brigid pressed, "Then who told you? It's more than a little significant that you use the term lost Earths to describe parallel casements."

Lakesh blinked up at her in mild curiosity. "Indeed? Why is that?"

Grant made a sharp dismissive hand gesture. "Enough. It's our turn to ask questions. Domi's mission objective was to screw up the so-called Battle Class breed. Why that breed? From what I've seen, you've got hybrids pretty much integrated in this society."

"You seem passingly familiar with hybridization."

"We've had our own problems with it," Brigid said dryly.

"I figured as much." Lakesh's gnarled hands gripped the wheels of his chair. He rotated it and headed toward the door. "Just like I figured you've had problems with the Archon Directorate. Come with me."

BRIGID PUSHED Lakesh's chair into the wire-enclosed lift cage at the end of the catwalk spanning the mezzanine. The elevator was cramped, and Grant had to suck in his stomach to accommodate the handles jutting from the chair's back. Sourly, he noted that this Grant's body was a bit trimmer than the one he had grown accustomed to.

With an electric whine, the cage descended. As it did, Lakesh said, "I know very little about the so-called Archons and their dealings with the Nazis. However, if there ever was a Directorate, it was long ago."

Brigid and Grant exchanged surreptitious glances. The lift clanked to a halt, and Brigid rolled Lakesh out into the vast, cavernous space. He nodded toward a large-skulled, big-eyed figure examining a power cable snaking from the base of the rotating cube generators. The floor transmitted the never-ending drone.

"The hybrids of human and Archon genetic material are all that is left of a Directorate."

"Tell us what you know," Brigid urged.

"I intend to do more than that."

He directed them through the huge chamber, past large bulky machines. It was all medical equipment—fluoroscopes, oscilloscopes, centrifuges, electron microscopes, distillation tanks and a chromatograph.

As they approached the interlocking glass cubicles in which the fetuses floated, he began speaking of his past and of secrets he had learned. Not surprisingly, his background was very similar to that of the Lakesh they knew—born in Kashmir, India, in 1952 and educated in America. However, his scientific aptitude and staggeringly high IQ was not channeled to physics, but to biology.

"Since the major tenet of the Third Reich was to change the image in which evolution shaped man, that was the focus of my work. A true master race. I learned several years into my career that the expertise and material to make the dream of an invincible master race was available…and it derived from the same source that allowed Germany to develop superior technology to win its global conquest."

They reached a door bearing a keypad instead of a knob or handle. Lakesh pushed a combination of buttons, and the door swung open silently. As they entered a cool, white corridor, Lakesh said, "Of course there were blunders along the way, but it is from those that science learns."

They turned right at the corridor's first intersection. It stretched for what seemed like miles, lighted by suffuse neon tubes.

At regularly paced intervals, recessed into the walls, instrument panels blinked and flashed. Each one bore a small monitor screen. Lakesh continued speaking as they went down the passageway. "The first thing a geneticist learns when he sets out to redesign the human animal is just how appallingly frail we are, the ease with which we can be damaged and our vulnerability to disease.

"If one was laying out a blueprint for a superior breed of man, one would first design an epidermis that would not tear so easily and bones that would not break so readily. Next, one would want to give him the capacity to recover completely from injuries by regenerating tissues and regrowing limbs and organs.''

"So far," Grant muttered bleakly, "this has a familiar ring."

Lakesh did not respond. "In order to make those modifications, one must do so for the purposes of war. After all, nature itself has engineered specialized warriors. But nature rarely blunders. Science, unfortunately, has that tendency."

He paused by the second instrument panel. "If you care to, you may see one of the blunders."

Grant and Brigid looked at the image flickering on the small screen. At first glance, what appeared to be a nude, normal human male paced restlessly within a stainless-steel room. The expression on his face was utterly mindless. On a second glance, they noticed the disproportionate length of his arms, how the forearms seemed extended. They terminated in stubby fingered hands, the palms callused an inch thick. Sprouting from the fingertips were cartilaginous masses, like dull claws with spongy surfaces.

"What's wrong with him?" Grant asked.

"Nothing, really. Observe." Lakesh depressed an intercom button on the console and said, "How are we doing today, good fellow?"

The man ignored the question. He continued pacing, not so much as blinking at the sound of this voice.

"Is he deaf?" Brigid wanted to know.

"No, just programmed to be oblivious to any aural

stimuli other than this.'' Lakesh reached over and tapped a button. A soft electronic beep sounded.

The man in the cell reacted to the inoffensive sound by bounding backward, as if he were performing a reverse broad jump. Slamming into the wall, he bounced forward and fell to his hands and knees. Throwing back his head, neck tendons arching, he howled long, loud and hard. As Brigid and Grant stared in horror, the man's body shook and shuddered with a series of convulsions. With each spasm, sinews rippled and bulged under his flesh, the muscle mass seeming to thicken. The skin over his shoulder blades stretched up and outward, splitting amid crimson sprays to allow spikes of sharp bone to protrude.

The man wailed in soul-deep agony all through the transformation: his spur-tipped fingers wildly scraping the floor; his dripping tongue protruding from between his wide-hanging jaws; a thick, yellow-gray discharge oozing from both eyes.

Falling onto his right side, he kicked and thrashed. His bowels evacuated, and he smeared the excrement all over himself and the floor.

''This particular subject was programmed to morph at the sound of a certain tone.'' Lakesh's voice was eerily calm, completely unmoved. ''An interesting variation on the glandular trigger.''

Voice cold with disgust, Grant said, ''Not to mention the extreme pain it puts the poor bastard in.''

''We did not always get results we wanted. In the instance of this level of the breed, work on the nervous system and skeletal system had to be refined.

The glandular response caused too much pain for the subjects to be of any use in combat situations.''

Brigid looked away from the image of the convulsing man on the screen. ''Blunders, you said. That man was one of your early experiments to develop the Battle Class breed.''

''Not early. He represents a midrange stage. Some of the very early hybrids had upper vertebrae that would break loose from the body entirely during the morphing process. Others could not control the release of testosterone, adrenaline and other hormones. They had the habit of bashing out their brains on the walls or ripping out their own eyes. We even had one who torn off his own genitals and devoured them.''

Growling a curse, Grant snatched the handles of the wheelchair and roughly spun Lakesh to face him. ''Enough of the bullshit, old man. What's this got to do with anything? He's like no hybrid we've ever seen, and we've seen a lot of them.''

Lakesh glared at him, clapped the respiration mask over his face, inhaled several times, then spit angrily, ''He represents the progenitor of an entirely new species, a different method of splicing human and other genetic material. It's been the entire point of my work for over a century. It's finally been achieved.''

Lakesh's hands tightened on the armrests of his chair. His furious blue gaze swept over Grant and Brigid. ''Don't you understand? With all the defects finally removed from the Battle Class, the master race has at last been born, unlike that conceived of by either Nietzsche or the Nazis. Humanity is now extinct. Literally!''

"Yes," agreed a silky voice from behind them. They turned to see Field Marshal Thrush sauntering casually down the corridor on soundless feet. The overhead lights made him look more like a cadaver than ever.

"Humanity is now extinct," he said quietly. "They just don't know it yet."

He touched a gloved finger to the brim of his cap. "Miss Baptiste, I trust you and Mr. Kane enjoyed yourself on New Year's Eve. If not, that is unfortunate. I can assure you that you have little to celebrate now."

Chapter 23

Kane gagged as the steel-thewed arms around his neck compressed his windpipe. He heard a husky snarl, even though his hearing was still impaired.

A stabbing pain suddenly lanced through the back of his neck. He would have screamed, but he didn't have the air for it. Struggling madly, he whirled, utilizing every trick he had been taught or even heard about to dislodge the demon on his back.

The soldier's pointed teeth sank into the thick muscles and tendons running up his shoulders, tearing at the flesh, gnawing down to the bone.

Kane twisted, trying to plant the bore of the Sin Eater against the trooper's lower, unarmored body. A booted foot lashed up, the steel-reinforced toe catching his wrist. The pistol fell from his suddenly nerveless fingers.

Clawing backward with both hands, he strove to fit his fingers between the jaws of the Battle Class soldier, to pry them apart by sheer strength. The trooper only tightened the inexorable grip of his arms and clamped down harder with his teeth.

Hooking his fingers, he jammed them into the soldier's eyes, but they only slipped across the surface of the tough protective membrane. Kane felt his knees buckling, his sight growing dim, his lungs on fire.

He allowed his knees to bend, as if he were losing consciousness, and the trooper shifted position to keep his body upright. Kane straightened his legs, springing up, hurling himself and the thing attached to him forward.

With a whiplash motion of his body, Kane turned in midair, and when they hit the ground, the trooper was underneath him. The impact jarred the chokehold and the teeth loosened their grip. Not much, but enough for Kane to fight loose in a flailing frenzy of kicks and elbow punches.

The soldier was up quicker than he was. He rushed at Kane, slashing with his claws. Gasping loudly, unsteady on his feet, Kane did not completely avoid the spurs of bone. Two of them raked twin bloody furrows across his face.

Instinctively, he lashed out with the edge of his right hand, striking his adversary across the back of the neck. The vertebrae should have snapped, but cushioned by the dense lumps of tendon and muscle, his hand only rebounded.

Still, the force of the blow sent the trooper stumbling a few paces forward, giving Kane enough time to unsheathe his combat stiletto. The soldier spun gracefully and bounded at him with lupine speed.

Kane sidestepped, thrusting in and out with the knife. He felt the blade sink with a crunch halfway to the hilt in the soldier's upper thigh. It was like stabbing pure gristle. The blade showed no blood whatsoever, only a faint sticky smear as of sap.

The trooper pivoted on the balls of his feet and surged forward again. They writhed fiercely for a long, eternal moment, Kane stabbing and hacking, the claws slashing and raking. Kane struck repeatedly in a madness borne of terror because nothing he did had any effect.

He briefly flashed back to Baronial Guards he and Grant had fought in Cobaltville's Administrative Monolith. In comparison to the Battle Class breed, the genetically enhanced men were slow, clumsy and about as dangerous as a bowl of ice cream.

Kane hurled himself back and away, his limbs quivering from the violent whirlwind of combat. His tunic was torn where the bone spurs had grazed him, blood trickling from the lacerations.

In the smoke-laden twilight, it was as if he fought with an unkillable monster conjured from one of his nightmares. He knew the trooper would not stop until Kane's maimed body hung limp from his taloned hands. The ex-Mag had shot him, punched him, stabbed him and the creature wasn't even breathing hard.

The trooper bared blood-filmed teeth in either a grin or a snarl and charged to the attack again. Tossing up his stiletto, Kane's thumb and forefinger closed around the tip. He cocked back his arm and hurled the knife at the solider's face, putting all of his upper body strength into the throw.

The point of the blade struck true, precisely on the soldier's fathomless left eye. The knife bounced away, scoring a faint scratch on the membrane. The trooper did not react at all, nor did his swift pace falter.

Abruptly, the black-clad figure stumbled and almost fell, checking in his headlong rush. He recovered, began to run again, then staggered. He fell to his hands and knees, jaws opening and closing spasmodically, as if he were dry heaving.

Kane wasted only a fraction of a second watching and wondering. He dived for his Sin Eater, snatched it up, whirled and triggered a 3-round burst directly into the trooper's face at a range slightly under seven feet.

A wave of almost religious joy splashed over him when the AP rounds shattered the serrated teeth into a handful of flying splinters, smashed an eye into a gelid smear resembling blackberry jam and pounded the lower jaw into a ragged mass of tissue and bone.

The triple sledgehammer impacts knocked the trooper's body half erect before dropping him in a limb-twisted heap on his back. Kane went to one knee, panting heavily, wincing at the flares of pain igniting from various parts of his body. Gingerly, he explored the mangled flesh at the back of his neck, and his fingers came away coated with wet scarlet.

"Thirty-two seconds," Salvo's voice announced. "Not too bad considering the three rounds you put through his pump. But then, modifying the cardiovascular system was the last hurdle."

Dully, Kane watched Salvo, flanked by a quartet of the Battle Class soldiers approach him. Although their eyes were clear and mild, the muzzles of their Sturmgewhers were trained on him. Kane fought back the impulse to aim his own weapon, recalling that such a threat had precipitated the trooper's transformation.

"The master race," he intoned colorlessly.

Salvo grinned. "Exactly. And we're the masters of the master race."

Moving slowly and carefully, Kane pushed himself to his feet, the Sin Eater dangling at the end of his arm. "Who is 'we'?"

Salvo tapped his chest. "Me, of course. A consortium, a cadre in different parts of the world. Only the best of the best were recruited." His grin broadened. "In case you were wondering, you didn't make the final cut."

"And of course Thrush is the master of it all," Kane said.

"Somebody has to be. The Reich hasn't had a true leader since Hitler died." Salvo squinted toward him. "Since you survived the test with the trooper, maybe you can tell me why the field marshal all of a sudden wants you dead."

"He didn't tell you?"

"He didn't say and I didn't ask. You know how it works. Not that I'm upset, mind you—I'm just curious, seeing as you've been a favorite of his ever since you were knighted."

"News to me."

All the forced good humor vanished from Salvo's face and voice. "Not to me, Brother."

Kane gestured around him with his left hand. "He didn't arrange all of this just so I could be eaten alive by those pet monsters of his?"

"Of course not. Like I said, this operation has been in the planning stages for months. But if you got yourself killed during it, hey, just a casualty of war. We'll have big a hero's funeral for you, a pyre and everything."

"Why not just have me arrested and executed?"

"You're a *knight*, remember?" The bitter emphasis on the word passed Salvo's lips as if it were an insult. "Knights can't be charged with treason. It's bad for morale."

"So you think I'm a traitor?"

"No, I think you're a full-of-himself, arrogant prick who got lucky once and played it to the hilt. Luck, like anything else, has a tendency to run out."

Salvo pulled in a long breath through his nostrils. "Are you going to tell me or not?"

A slow smile played over Kane's face, and he showed an edge of teeth. "Why not, since you're going to kill me anyway? I'm not really the Kane the you know. I'm from a parallel universe. You're there, too. Or you used to be."

Salvo stared at him with a mocking condescension. "Really? Where am I now?"

"Dead on a rooftop. I chilled your slagging ass myself."

For an instant, Salvo looked confused by the vernacular, then angry incredulity glinted in his eyes. "Are you trying to make me believe you're crazy and so let you off?"

"I was just giving you the reason why Thrush wants me dead, since you asked so nice and all. He knows the Kane I am now isn't the Kane who is his favorite.''

"He knows you're from another planet." Salvo's voice was flat.

"Not another planet, the same one. A parallel Earth. And so is Thrush. A lot of them probably, since he gets around. Wherever he goes, he fucks it up. Like this place. In my universe, Germany lost World War II. Thrush was so disappointed in Hitler, he blew your precious Füehrer's brains out.''

Salvo gaped in genuine, goggle-eyed shock. The concept was more than insane, it was blasphemous. His lips worked but no sound came out. Finally, he managed to spit, ''You really *are* crazy—and a fucking traitor to unity. No wonder the field marshal wants you dead.''

"Thrush want me dead because I know what he really is—or what he's not. He's not human. I'm not even sure if he's really alive. We crossed paths once before, but he seemed to know we'd meet again at another time.''

Salvo wagged his head doggedly. ''You're crazy, you really are. I'm glad we're only half brothers. I'd hate to think this is a family trait.''

Gusting out a sigh, he took a step backward and said loudly, ''Standard rules of termination. Implement.''

Kane tensed himself, wondering if he could drill Salvo before he himself was blasted to pieces by the barrage of high-velocity rounds.

A fusillade of cracks ripped through the darkness, one coming so fast on the heels of the other they sounded like one long report. Two of the Battle Class troopers twirled on their toes, performing grotesque pirouettes as bullet struck sparks from their helmets.

The other two staggered sideways, hit in the body and colliding with each other. Salvo slapped at his right hip, blurting wordlessly in surprise and pain. Divots of dirt and rock exploded from the ground, and as several spurted up around Kane's feet, he raced with furious speed toward the nearest of the ditches plowed by the OGRE's treads.

He threw himself into it as bullets chewed up the heaped dirt on either side of the depression, one grazing the top of his helmet. Salvo's voice bellowed, but he couldn't hear make out the words over the din of full-auto fire.

The Battle Class breed triggered their Sturmgewhers, and stuttering roars overlaid the continuous volley fired from the shadows. Kane didn't dare raise his head to see what was going on. Bullets thumped the air above him, banged loudly against the hull of the OGRE and screamed off.

He was fairly certain of what was happening. Drawing on his doppleganger's memories of the Calgary campaign, he figured that a heavily armed contingent of Roamers had hung back, waiting to see if the Reich's representatives intended to honor the truce. Now they were paying back the betrayal with interest.

It was a big group, judging by the popping quality of the massed single shots interwoven with the bull-fiddle roar of full-auto bursts. Roamers were generally frugal with their ammo, but now they intended to make a last bloody stand.

The field of fire shifted, concentrating on the Battle Class troopers who shot back. Using his elbows and the sides of his feet, Kane began crawling forward, toward the rear of the OGRE. Mortar rounds burst from the launch tubes of the vehicle, and the detonations smeared the night with distant orange flashes. Veiled by smoke and dust, the explosions were dim, like distant heat lightning within heavy cloud cover.

Over the cacophony, Salvo's maddened voice screeched, "Advance! Terminate! Advance!"

Salvo had lost whatever cool he might have had, ordering his soldiers to charge into the teeth full-auto fire. The wisest tactic would have been to order a retreat, back to the OGRE. Once inside, all of its on-board weapons systems could be brought to bear while everyone sat in safety.

A body thudded into the ditch in front of Kane. The trooper thrashed around and kicked up clods of loose dirt, trying to force his bullet-riddled body to obey Salvo's command. His pointed teeth champed impotently at the air; his clawed fingers tore up the soil.

Kane watched his mad struggles, the sweat of fear breaking out all over his face, flowing into the scratches on his face and making them sting. The ripped, gnawed flesh at the back of his neck hurt with a bone-deep ache.

The more human features of the trooper were subsumed by their bestial aspect, increasing the overall horror of his death throes. The soldier fought to stay alive only so he could kill. He turned his obsidian eyes toward Kane, staring at him without seeing him.

With a quiver of loathing, Kane realized the trooper symbolized how ancient man viewed Balam and his folk, as demonic, utterly inhuman monstrosities. The Battle Class breed was millennia-old superstition made a terrifying reality.

The soldier's struggles ceased abruptly, his limbs locking stiffly in unnatural angles, mouth agape, face turned toward the sky. Although it made his heart pound, Kane forced himself to crawl over the corpse, thinking the trooper was almost as ghastly dead as alive. He noted the multitude of bullet holes in his body, too many to count. However, there was very little blood, only a watery gruel mixed with the sticky ichor.

As Kane lifted himself over the corpse, he risked a swift glance over the heaped dirt rimming the furrow. He saw a confusing turmoil of running shapes and smears of orange flame from weapons. From out of the shifting planes of dust and smoke plunged a howling mob of crazed Roamers, shrieking bloodthirsty cries. They fired their blasters as they came.

The trooper swarmed to meet them like slinking black shadows with unblinking soulless eyes and misshapen, vulpine jaws open. They moved with a blurring speed, in great leaps and bounds.

The two forces crashed headlong into each other. Wherever a clawed hand found a hold on a human, it began to tear him apart. The Roamers shot, battered and clubbed them in maniacal fury, but where one trooper fell, three of their own number went down.

Kane didn't spy Salvo anywhere in the screaming mass, so he increased the speed of his crawl to the OGRE, resisting the insistent urge to leap up and participate in the battle. The problem was, his desire to join one side or the other seesawed. Kane, the knighted warrior of the Reich, had his devotion to duty to adhere to. Kane, the exile, the invader, had the fierce urge to help the humans wipe the genetically engineered abominations off the face of the Earth.

More than likely if he surrendered to either impulse he would instantly be killed by whatever side he chose to join.

Reaching the rearward tread assembly, Kane wriggled out of the ditch it had dug in the ground and crept to its far side. He paused to catch his breath. No more bullets struck the OGRE's heavy metal hide, and no more mortar rounds belched from the machine's launch tubes. The two battling factions were locked too closely together for even the most precise targeting to do more than blow up both man and nonman.

Rising to his feet, Kane ran in a crouch beneath the underbelly of the OGRE, the cloying smell of grease and fuel filling his nostrils. He reached the ramp and clambered over its side, sprinting up into the personnel compartment. He used the jump seats as stepping-stones to reach the cockpit.

The door was down, and he hammered on it with the butt of his Sin Eater, shouting, ''Open up, damn you! It's Major Kane! Open up!''

He gambled the pilot and copilot hadn't been informed of the kill orders on him. Even if they witnessed the fight with the trooper and his confrontation with Salvo, they wouldn't ask any questions. As highly trained soldiers, they should, by all rights, immediately obey the commands of a superior officer and a knight.

The inch-thick metal portal slid up into slots, and Kane bulled his way into the cockpit. The two men gave him tense, bright-eyed stares as he stood behind their chairs. Salvo's tinny, stressed voice shouted from the comm-link channel.

A glance at one of the monitor screens showed him black-clad figures pursuing the Roamers into the smoke-shrouded shadows, pulling down man after man. He saw nothing of Salvo in the milling, running confusion. He palmed the door button on the bulkhead and the portal slid down, closing off the cockpit.

"Raise the ramp," Kane ordered.

Both men looked at him in disbelief. Covered with dirt, smeared with blood, his tunic ripped and torn, they instantly suspected he'd lost his grip, giving in to panic.

"Sir," ventured Dent, the pilot, "our forces are driving them off, so there's no need—"

"Do it," Kane broke in harshly.

The copilot swallowed hard. "With all due respect, Major, I cannot see why—"

Kane used the Sin Eater as a bludgeon, rapping the barrel sharply on the copilot's head. Metal collided against bone with an ugly crunching thud. The man sagged in his chair, blood rivering from his laid-open scalp.

Half rising from his chair, Dent shouted, "Sir!"

Kane covered him, his teeth bared in a snarl. "Sit down, stupe, or I'll turn your head into a canoe."

The pilot slowly relaxed into his seat, fear warring with anger on his face. Keeping Dent's head framed in the sights of his weapon, Kane reached over and tapped the appropriate buttons on the console. With a hum and a hiss, the ramp raised to join with the floor of the personnel compartment. It sealed with a dull clank.

In a faint voice, Dent said, "The Lieutenant Colonel is still out there."

Kane jammed the bore of his Sin Eater against the side of Dent's head. "I'm in command now. You'll follow my orders, or your brains will be in your lap."

The skin around the man's eyes and lips turned the color of old ashes. "Yes, sir."

Kane reached behind him to the fire-control board, relieved he recognized the buttons and what weapons they controlled. Glancing through the ob port he saw a group of black-clad Battle Class troopers savaging the Roamer dead, flaying the skin off their faces. His belly slipped sideways when he saw them shoving the ripped and bloody flesh into their mouths, using their long prehensile tongues to lick their claws clean of blood.

With a touch of two keys, he adjusted the position of the minigun turret. "What are you doing?" Dent demanded.

Kane gave him an ingenuous smile, then with his forefinger bent at a fey angle, tapped the key once.

Rotating spear points of flame flickered from the

multiple barrels of the machine gun. The 7.62 mm rounds punched a cross-stitch pattern in the dirt, the lines of impact scampering and intersecting with a pair of the troopers. They were flung around in mists of blood. The jackhammer roar was muted by the hull of the OGRE, but the results of its full-auto burst were not. At that range, nothing could survive the withering lead hail.

Kane tapped the key again and silenced the minigun. "Get us moving. Drive us closer to the monument."

Dent hesitated only an instant before shifting levers and pressing the gas pedal. The armored vehicle groaned and bounced along in first gear until the engine hit a high, straining note, then Dent upshifted.

Peering through the port, Kane saw three of the Battle Class breed run into the path of the OGRE, waving their rifles over their heads, trying to flag the vehicle to a stop. The pilot eased the pressure of his foot from the gas pedal.

"Run them down," Kane snapped.

"They're our own men!"

"They aren't men at all. Run them down, I said."

Dent paled but did as he was ordered. He slammed his foot against the accelerator, flooring it. The OGRE surged forward.

The troopers turned to run. One of them managed to leap out of the vehicle's path, but the prow of the OGRE slammed into the other two, knocking them down, crushing them beneath the ponderous, clattering treads.

The OGRE chugged its way up a slope, through a

stand of sagebrush and down into an arroyo. As the deeply fissured and creviced base of Mount Rushmore filled the ob port, the pilot asked, "Where are we going?"

"Not much farther," Kane replied. "Just until we're in range. I'll let you know."

Dent cast him a worried glance, but said nothing. After another minute of steady forward rumbling, Kane said, "Stop us here."

The pilot stamped on the brakes hard, and the OGRE lurched to a squealing halt. Kane kept the blaster trained on the man, smiling a knowing smile. He had expected Dent to try to throw him off balance and so had braced himself against the copilot's seat.

"Now what?" Dent was starting to show some attitude.

Kane's left hand deftly played over the keys of the fire-control board, realigning the mortar launchers, configuring the targeting scanner. The graven image of Adolf Hitler swelled within the scope, and Kane centered the crosshairs on his granite mustache. Then he brought his finger down hard on the key in a savage, stabbing motion.

The mortar tubes erupted with flame, smoke and noise. He launched them all, more or less simultaneously. Dent shrieked, his eyes bulging in hysteria.

The huge visage of Hitler disappeared beneath tongues of yellow flame and billowing puffballs of smoke. Chunks of rock erupted, rattling down on the OGRE's hull, beating like outraged fists. The pilot screamed with each detonation, clawing at his face, his gaze glued to the targeting scope. After the last warhead exploded, Kane waited silently for the smoke to clear.

Hitler's likeness was completely unrecognizable as either the leader of the Reich or as a man. Huge smoking craters dotted the massive face, completely obliterating his features. A pattern of cracks was riven deeply through the sculpture, and Kane figured the next half-decent storm would cause what was left of it to collapse.

"Do you think that's enough?" Kane asked. "Or should we give him a light once over with the Blitz cannon?"

Dent buried his face in his shaking hands. He made retching noises. "You bastard...you bastard..."

Kane rapped him smartly on the back of the head with the barrel of the Sin Eater. "Shut up. Get it together and get us moving back to the base."

Groaning between clenched teeth, Dent threw the machine into gear and steered away from the monument in a ninety-degree turn. Kane yanked the power cables from the radio set and put them in a pocket.

"Keep following my orders," he said, "and you'll live through this. Disobey a single one, and I'll leave you here for what's left of the Roamers to find."

He pointed to the unconscious, bloodied copilot. "The same thing goes for him when—or if—he comes around."

He pushed the button to raise the door and stepped down into the personnel compartment. Salvo chose that instant to hammer the butt of a Sturmgewehr into his groin.

Chapter 24

Grant and Brigid went for their side arms at the same time. Before either one had their weapons more than halfway out of the holsters, Thrush was aiming his own pistol directly at them. Grant froze, staring dumbfounded. He had only the briefest of impressions of a blur of movement before the Sin Eater sprouted magically from the end of Thrush's arm.

"Oh, yes," Thrush said quietly. "I *am* that fast. Surely your compatriots must have informed you of that."

Shoving his pistol back into the holster, Grant said, "I saw it for myself."

Thrush cocked his head questioningly. "Indeed? When or where was that?"

"Nearly two hundred years ago, in the basement of the Russian embassy in Washington. I watched you murder a man with a nerve poison."

Thrush moved his head fractionally. "Oh, yes, Felix. So that was you I sensed. I'm able to detect anomalous electromagnetic signatures, but I'm not always able to identify them."

"So you're not perfect," Brigid commented.

"I don't recall ever making that claim. But then, I've made so many claims in so many places it's possible I might have implied something along those lines.''

Thrush's dark-lensed gaze shifted to Lakesh. ''And I've extracted so many troublesome factors. It becomes wearying.''

He wagged the barrel of his weapon. ''Let us move along and continue with the tour. I'll take over from this point onward.''

Lakesh displayed no fear whatsoever, not even a mild anxiety. With a touch of disdain, a whiff of defiance he inquired, ''So you're a silent invader, too, aren't you?''

''Don't employ my own euphemism against me, Administrator,'' Thrush retorted. ''I've been here longer than you. This is more my world than yours, since I helped to shape it.''

''When you warp and corrupt worlds,'' Grant said, ''they become yours, is that your reasoning?''

Thrush smiled. ''Rather more melodramatic than I might have phrased it, but you're essentially on track.''

With Thrush behind them, they moved down the corridor. Brigid said conversationally, ''I did a bit of research on the phenomenon you're associated with, Field Marshal.''

''And what phenomenon is that, Miss Baptiste?''

''The Men In Black. MIBs, to use the old vernacular. It's assumed that MIB reports dated back only to the twentieth century and were linked to UFO sightings. I learned that history is replete with legends about Men In Black whose origin is uncertain.

Many times they were involved in pivotal points of human development.''

"Is that so?" Thrush inquired in a thoroughly bored tone.

"It's so," Brigid answered. "Men In Black figured peripherally in many of the greatest inventions, from the printing press to the steam engine. And of course, they figured a bit more prominently in political events, like assassinations, wars and religious upheavals. According to testimony, a Man In Black was the instigator of the Salem witch trials."

"A very long time ago," Thrush commented.

"In more recent history, Lakesh—our Lakesh—saw you at the Overproject Whisper facility. Not coincidentally, it was located under the Archuleta Mesa. He claimed you were always around when Operation Chronos experiments were scheduled."

"What are you trying to make me out to be, Miss Baptiste?" Thrush asked blandly. "Chaos incarnate? Shiva the Destroyer? The devil?"

After a second's contemplation, Brigid retorted, "Why not? If it looks like a duck and walks like a duck, then it probably is a duck."

Field Marshal Thrush only laughed.

They continued traveling down the corridor, which seemed to stretch on endlessly. "Where are you taking us?" Grant demanded.

"To a place where your curiosity is satisfied, sir. I am nothing if not accommodating."

After a few more yards, Thrush ordered a halt, instructing them to face the left-hand wall. It was a blank white expanse, broken only by a recessed toggle switch nestled within a small round collar. He pointed to it. "Miss Baptiste, be so kind as to throw the switch."

She hesitated, then did as she was told. A section of the wall split in two and parted, like rectangular, floor-to-ceiling curtains. It revealed a transparent barrier, and on the other side of it stood a figure.

Beneath the pitiless glare of neon tubes overhead, it might have been a statue crafted from smooth, whitish stone. But they saw the steady rise and fall of its chest and the flicking of its long tongue. They stared in horrified fascination, then revulsion.

The creature regarded them with no expression on its face, though it was difficult to tell. It stood perhaps five feet eight inches tall and was of human configuration. The hairless head looked strangely swollen in the rear. Strips of muscle tissue ran up from the jaw hinge and joined at the back of the skull to make a sagittal crest.

The lower portion of its head was snouted and fanged, and a long black tongue writhed restlessly between the open jaws. The eyes were like little pools of onyx, with no visible pupils, irises or whites.

The arms were very long, the hands slender, the fingers terminating in curved claws. The digits on the bare feet were similarly tipped.

Its entire body looked to be all muscle, from the washboard-ridged belly, to the well-developed biceps and triceps, to the thick ropes of tendon and sinew enwrapping its shoulders and upper back, forming an unnatural hump. It possessed no genitals, only smooth pale flesh at the juncture of its thighs.

Both Grant and Brigid had seen any number of hybridized creatures, but not one like this. It looked like predatory death stripped down to its bare essentials. It occurred to her that it faintly resembled a cross between Balam and the body they had seen of Enlil, the last Annunnkai.

"The master race to inherit the Earth," Thrush intoned pridefully. "Free of carnal appetites, with no hunger for affection or ambition. The ultimate warrior, history's darling and humankind's despair. He and his brothers are pure predator, created and existing only to kill."

"Kill whom?" Brigid wanted to know.

"Whomever they're told," Thrush replied. "In this instance, human beings."

"Certain human beings," Grant ventured, "or human beings in general?"

"Not in general, specifically," Lakesh said quietly. "*All* human beings."

"Why bother breeding a warrior race?" Grant demanded. "The Reich rules the world and owns all the blasters. Even where we're from, if the blaster is big enough, it makes the soldiers who use them pretty unimportant."

"Very true," Thrush said agreeably. "Tanks and automatic rifles make any advantages that can be gained from breeding superior physical properties into soldiers marginal."

Brigid looked at the creature again. It stood stock-still, as if it were asleep. "Then why go to all the trouble?"

Thrush glanced at Lakesh. "Why don't you tell

them? The same question plagued you for many years until you eventually reasoned out the answer.''

Lakesh cleared his throat. ''The term Battle Class is something of a misnomer, deliberately so. They would be more accurately named the Genocide Class. They were bred to view humankind as their natural prey, as a wolf views a rabbit or a killer whale a seal.''

Grant's lips twisted. ''If the aim is to make humanity extinct, turning loose a bunch of dickless, bioengineered muties doesn't seem the way to go about it.''

''Really?'' Thrush asked. ''Presented with the same problem, how would you solve it? A long, destructive and chaotic war in which natural resources are as in as much danger of extermination as the enemy?

''Nuclear weapons that render much of the Earth completely uninhabitable for many years? The release of biological and chemical weapons that befoul the atmosphere and toxify ecosystems for generations? No, my plan is much better, much neater and fits in with nature instead of opposing it. Survival of the fittest.''

Brigid scrutinized the creature again. ''You really think things like that can remove all of humanity, conduct a globicide? No matter how depopulated the world is right now, the introduction of a new predatory species still seems inefficient. They might be tough, but they're still mortal. You'll have losses, and it doesn't appear they can reproduce in the conventional fashion.''

Lakesh spoke up. "The Battle Class breed has sensory organs reduced and shielded. Their minds are controlled by means of communications filaments grown by the electromagnetic energy of the brain itself. Their skin is very tough, and the pores can be closed autonomically to prevent the introduction of bacteria or toxins. Almost all of their orifices can be sealed at will. Their eyes are equipped with a protective outer lens with adjustable transparency that keeps the eyeball moist. The skeleton is streamlined, and all of the internal organs simplified. In the stage of the metamorphosis you observe in this subject, the lower abdomen and pelvic girdle have been modified so that the genitals are withdrawn into the body for protection. So, yes, they can reproduce conventionally."

Field Marshal Thrush chuckled. "Once we get around to breeding females, of course."

"For vicious predators," Grant said, "this one seems fairly well-behaved."

"That's because his organic trigger is switched off," Lakesh replied.

"What happens when it's on?"

"Their systems are flooded with vast amounts of adrenaline, testosterone and other hormones. They undergo a feral 'flight or fight' reflex, which is shifted toward aggression and hostility."

Brigid studied the creature's fang-filled jaws. "You've obviously designed it to be a carnivore."

Thrush nodded. "Aren't all predators? And don't all predators eat what they kill?"

Grant and Brigid swung their heads toward him

sharply, faces registering repugnance. "They're cannibals?" Grant demanded.

"Cannibals devour their own kind. Humanity is not their own kind, though of course they have human genes. That is where the vicious killer-instincts come from."

"How do you plan to introduce your predators into human environments?" Brigid asked. "Just turn them loose in a wild, disorganized horde on communities?"

"Wild, perhaps. Disorganized, not at all. Have you ever heard of the Wild Hunt?"

Brigid started, eyes going wide. "A pagan ritual, probably dating back to prehistoric times. Cerunnos, the Horned God, represented the hunt, the killing of prey and the winter months. The Wild Hunt was performed every year in his honor and ranged far and wide. People who were criminals or unproductive were the designated prey. They were hunted down, killed and allegedly eaten in a ceremony.

"Cernunnos himself often led the hunt. Some texts describe him as half animal, but most of the time he manifested himself as a Man In Black."

She eyed him speculatively. "You're not claiming you're Cernunnos, a pagan deity, are you?"

"As I said, I've made so many claims in so many places they tend to slip my mind. Have you seen enough here?"

Not waiting for a response, Thrush flicked the toggle switch to the down position, and the wall portal closed again. Brigid wasn't done with the topic. "I suppose it's conceivable you're the basis of Cernunnos, since you can travel through the hyperdimensions as easily we walk through a room. It's equally possible you formed the foundation of many myths and legends as control mechanisms for the human race. The Battle Class breed is the latest in a long line of control mechanisms, isn't it?''

"Anything is possible, Miss Baptiste." Thrush motioned to them with the blaster. "If not in one universe, then certainly in another.''

Grant stood his ground, eyes seething with hatred. "Maybe so," he grated, "but you seem to have the same agenda in every one of them."

"The way I approach that agenda varies as to circumstance.''

"Who gives you your marching orders?" Grant demanded. "The Archon Directorate?"

"As I indicated, everything is variable depending on the circumstance.''

"Let's talk about these circumstances," Brigid challenged. "The Archons definitely figured into World War II on this casement as on our own. How did that involvement with the Nazis come about?''

"Start moving, please," Thrush said politely. "And I'll explain a bit of it to you.''

Reluctantly, they obeyed his order, Grant pushing Lakesh's wheelchair ahead of him. Thrush walked behind them and spoke in a calm, uninflected voice.

"As on your casement—on all of them that I have visited—the Nazi Party in and of itself was nothing more than a red herring, a public-relations front to hide the workings of an ancient secret society with links to Asia, whose symbol was the reversed swastika. Even the most fanatically patriotic German would not have been able to stomach what the Thule and Vril societies were up to, or what deeds Hitler performed in their service.

"Hitler, as well as the men who became his inner circle of advisers, were initiated into this secret lodge. Rituals were common, and some of them revolved around a fragment of a mystical black stone. They used it to affect and alter outcomes of events."

"Alternate event horizons," Brigid murmured.

"Just so. As you have no doubt learned about the stone, the Trapezohedron is a discrete quanta packet that interacts and interfaces with the basic units of reality."

Grant threw a scowl over his shoulder. "What the hell are basic units of reality?"

"Essentially," Thrush replied, "any action that triggers a reaction. In essence, their rituals with the facet of the Trapezohedron opened a door and something came in."

"The Archons," Grant said matter-of-factly.

"No," Thrush replied, "not on this casement or your own. An emissary arrived first, one that easily moved among the decision makers, observing and assimilating knowledge, extrapolating and recommending whether an alliance would prove profitable."

"Who was the emissary?" Brigid asked suspiciously.

"The emissary was capable of independent thought and movement, could make value judgments, but was bound within strictly circumscribed parameters of duty."

"You sound like you're describing a computer program," Brigid said, "not an individual."

"A program, yes. But not necessarily a computer's."

They turned a corner and Grant said, "She asked who was the emissary, not what."

"There is little difference in this case," came Thrush's unruffled response. "Yes, I was the emissary, a traveling diplomat without a portfolio, a mobile embassy if you will. What you refer to as the Archon Directorate wanted to make sure I could arrange the best deal in exchange for their involvement in a global conflict. But Archon priorities had to take precedence."

"What the Third Reich got out of the deal is obvious," Brigid commented. "What were the Archon priorities?"

"A world without chaos, humanity depopulated, unified and made productive. As you know, this is their planet, too, and they were willing to make sacrifices in order for it to be secure."

They reached a T junction, and Thrush pointed them to the left. "However," he went on, "after the Reich victory and unification, I came to realize that the true gift the Archons offered this world lay not in the superior technology they gave to Germany, but it lay within themselves."

Grant shook his head. "I don't get you."

"I do," Lakesh murmured.

"Draw on your own experiences from your home casement," Thrush suggested. "Think of the hybridization programs instituted by the baronies, the fixation with Purity Control, on improving the breed by the judicious mixing of Archon genes with human.''

''Yes,'' Brigid said impatiently, ''we learned from Balam that it was done in order for their race to survive in some fashion.''

''As here. But consider—why always the genetic material provided from the Archons? What makes it so unique?'' Without waiting for an answer, he declared, ''Their DNA is infinitely adaptable, malleable, its segments able to achieve a near seamless sequencing pattern with whatever biological material is spliced to it. In some ways, it acts like a virus, overwriting other genetic codes, picking and choosing the best human qualities to enhance. Their DNA can be tinkered with to create endless variations, it can be adjusted and fine-tuned. It is the human genes that cause blunders, not the Archon.''

Brigid recollected what Kane had learned about Balam's race during his telepathic communication with him. After an ancient global catastrophe, in order to survive, his race transformed itself to adapt to the new environment. Muscle tissue became less dense, motor reflexes sharpened, optic capacities broadened. A new range of abilities was developed that allowed them to live on a planet whose magnetic fields had changed, whose weather was drastically unpredictable.

They reached a door at the end of the corridor. Thrush punched in a three-digit number on a keypad in the frame, and it swung silently inward. Brigid and Grant hesitated on the threshold, staring.

"I only visited here once, many years ago," Lakesh murmured. "I never cared to come again."

They looked into a large chamber with a domed ceiling from which dim blue light shone down. The walls were of a dull green, the floor white. There were only three objects in the room. A stone pillar rose some four feet in height from the center of the floor. Atop of it rested a box of hammered silver, its hinged lid thrown back.

Beyond that was a pale gray man-shape seated on a raised dais. They stared aghast, first in surprise, then in recognition. The naked figure was very short, barely four feet tall and excessively slender. His high, domed cranium narrowed to an elongated chin. His skin bore a faint grayish-pink cast, stretched drum-tight over a structure of facial bones that seemed all cheek and brow, with little in between a vestigial nose and a small compressed slit of a mouth. Six long, spidery fingers, all nearly the same length rested on his crossed knees. The two huge up-slanting eyes were closed as if in sleep.

"Balam," Grant said hoarsely.

The blue-veined lids parted and the big obsidian stared at him, then at all of them, finally focusing on Field Marshal Thrush.

Voice purring with amusement, Thrush nudged Brigid in the small of the back with the bore of his pistol. "Go on in and meet the true father of the master race."

Chapter 25

Kane flopped onto his side, swallowing the bile rising up his throat in an acidic column. Pain radiated in throbbing waves from his groin as he lay doubled up on the floor.

Salvo kicked him on the thigh. "Are you just going to lie there, you traitorous bastard? Get up."

Blinking back the tear-haze swimming in his eyes, Kane saw his Sin Eater lying on the deck ten feet away, where Salvo had kicked it.

"Get up!" Salvo roared, kicking him again.

Kane looked up at him. Blood soaked Salvo's right trouser leg. A crimson streak painted his left hand and knuckles from another wound torn in his bicep.

"Fucking Roamers nearly beat us," he hissed between clenched teeth, his voice so thick with outrage it was nearly incomprehensible. "*Us*, the elite of the Reich. Sixteen of the Battle Class dead! Over half the squad!"

He stamped hard on Kane's thigh. "You did it! How can I face the field marshal now?"

Kane waited until he was certain he wasn't going to throw up before saying, "You don't have to face him."

"What the fuck do you mean?" Salvo's eyes blazed with a wild, crazed light.

"Do what a solider and a knight would do. Put a blaster to your head and pull the trigger."

Salvo hawked up from deep in his throat and spit on him. "That's what you'd do, right?" he asked scornfully.

"Yes, if I failed as miserably as you. And against Roamers and outlanders no less. It's the only honorable thing to do."

Kane paused and forced a taunting smile onto his face, though it caused the claw-inflicted gouges to sting. "But I keep forgetting, you're not honorable. That's why I'm the knight and get all the perks, and you get the rank but have to live in my shadow."

He watched and waited for Salvo's reaction. It was not long in coming. His facial muscles twitched in a nervous tic, his entire body trembled as if he were in a seizure and his hands clenched so tightly around the Sturmgewher the metal creaked.

Then, with a full-throated bellow of insane rage erupting from his throat, from the roots of his soul, Salvo lifted the rifle over his head, preparing to batter him to death.

Kane had gambled if he struck enough nerves, Salvo's ego-fueled fury would blind him to the easiest and most reasonable option—simply shoot him dead while he lay on the deck.

But Salvo was too consumed with the mindless, savage desire to beat him until he died or begged for it.

As Salvo whipped up the rifle, Kane's upper body catapulted from the floor, driving the crown of his head between Salvo's legs. He felt the testicle sac grind against the pelvic bone and he almost muttered, "Quid pro quo."

The butt of the rifle crashed against his back, between the shoulder blades, but it felt less like a blow than if Salvo had merely dropped the weapon on him.

A choked, keening wail burst from Salvo's lips as he jackknifed at the waist. Kane lunged up again, using the back of his head as a battering ram. Salvo fell down against a jump seat, lower lip split and spurting blood. He tried to kick him, but Kane made a dive for Salvo's neck and got both hands around it.

For a second, their bloody, sweat-sheened faces were only inches apart. Through gritted teeth, Kane hissed, "This is what I should have done to you that night in Mesa Verde Canyon."

He squeezed and pressed down with his thumbs with all this strength. Salvo clawed at him madly, his nails tearing at his face, trying to gouge out his eyes. He struggled and thrashed, his tongue protruding.

A shudder ran the length of the compartment, then the deck dropped out from underneath them. Kane had only the briefest impression of Dent gazing over the back of his chair, one hand resting on the ramp controls.

The OGRE was traveling at a fairly good clip, and the pilot didn't slow it. He obviously felt Salvo was an acceptable loss if it meant getting rid of the murderous, treasonous Major Kane.

Both men began sliding down the metal chute, but as the steps rose beneath their bodies, Kane was able to jam a foot against one and hold him and Salvo in place.

The end of the ramp banged loudly against a rock, sending up a flurry of sparks. The violent jounce nearly threw Kane over the raised lip of the side. He released his stranglehold on Salvo and slapped both hands on the edges. The roar of the engines beat at his ears like thunder, and the fuel fumes stung his eyes and seared his throat.

Salvo, his face a twisted, blood-spattered mask, attempted to drag enough air into his lungs to take action, but he succumbed to a coughing fit.

The ramp struck another rock, almost bouncing Kane straight into the personnel compartment. Salvo slid down, bumping against the risers, flailing to secure a grip on anything. His hands closed over the toe of Kane's left boot. Kane, hands braced against the raised sides of the ramp, strained to keep from being dragged down. Salvo's feet were only inches from the ground.

Gravel sprayed up, rattling against the metal, pluming dust contrails blinded them both.

"Help me!" Salvo screamed.

Kane tried to pull his foot free. The ramp began a back-and-forth fishtail swing, evoking a bleat of terror from Salvo.

"Help me!" he shrilled again. "For God's sake, you're my brother!"

"I thought I was a full-of-himself, arrogant prick!" Kane shouted back, but he doubted that Salvo heard him over the roar of the engine and the incessant, near-deafening clatter of the treads and return rollers.

Salvo lunged desperately, shifting his grip from Kane's foot to his ankle. He pulled, intending to climb Kane's leg like a rope. Arms trembling with the effort of keeping himself braced in position, Kane yelled, "Get your feet up on the steps! Do something to save yourself!"

Salvo's boots kicked futilely for purchase, but the ramp crashed violently into an irregularity in the ground. His near panic gave way to a burst of anger. "Fuck you!" he shrieked, fingers digging into Kane's leg.

Kane raised his left leg, bent it at the knee and straightened it, driving the treaded sole of his boot full into the middle of Salvo's face. The man's nose collapsed under the blow, blood sheeting out from both nostrils. He croaked "Fuck you" again.

Kane kicked Salvo in the head a second time, then a third. He drew up his leg for a fourth, but it wasn't necessary. Salvo's fingers lost their strength and as the ramp bounced, he pitched headlong over its side and out of sight.

Kane wasn't sure if he'd been caught by one of the treads or had his bones broken against the rocky earth. At the moment, he didn't give a damn one way or the other.

Carefully, with agonizing slowness, he inched his way back up the ramp, pausing every few moments to brace himself. Turning his head on his throbbing neck, he looked toward the OGRE's cockpit. The door was still open, and Dent alternated his attention between piloting the vehicle and glancing back every few seconds.

When he caught sight of Kane, his mouth fell open and he half rose from his chair, swatting awkwardly for the door's push button control.

Twisting over onto all fours, Kane set himself and ran up the risers of the rocking ramp, nearly falling over the side. Dent's hand slapped at the button, and the portal began sliding down. Kane dived under it, the edge clipping the heel of one boot.

He fetched up in a half-prone position beneath the control console and fended off the clumsy, one-legged kicks a squealing Dent launched at him. Fighting his way to his feet, Kane lashed out with the edge of his right hand, catching the man full across the neck. There was a mushy crunch, as of a stick of wet wood breaking, and Dent dropped dead into his seat. His foot fell from the accelerator, and the OGRE instantly slowed.

Kane dragged the pilot's body from the chair and sat down. He applied a steady pressure to the brakes and worked the gearshift lever, clumsily at first, then with more skill. The vehicle came to a full stop and sat idling.

He activated the ramp and raised it, although the metal frame did not perfectly join with the tooled slots.

After pulling Dent's body into the personnel compartment, he quickly examined the copilot. The man was dead, apparently from a fractured skull. He let him stay where he was. Removing the power cables from his pocket, he plugged them into the radio, and after a few moments managed to raise the air base. He identified himself.

"I need air evac immediately. We've got many casualties." He did not have to try to very hard to sound weary and racked with pain.

"From Roamers?" came the astonished reply.

"Roamers and the Battle Class troopers. They turned on us, went completely blood simple. I'll give the field marshal a full report. Have a medic and air transport back to Dulce ready for me."

He read off the coordinates from the instrument panel and cut the contact. He sat back in the chair to wait. What concerned him the most was not his various wounds, but the fact the pressure in his skull had built to a steady, insistent throb.

Chapter 26

Balam spoke, in a harsh, strained stammering whisper that did not change in key or timbre. "What is it you wish from me now?"

Grant's and Brigid's eyes strayed to Balam's skinny, elongated limbs. Both of them saw the marks of hypodermics, IV shunts and the scoop-shapes where innumerable skin samples were taken.

"This is a social call," Thrush said with a mocking, deferential smile. "The project is complete. The breeding cycle is successful. You have fathered a new species that will make this world secure."

The huge black eyes shifted to Brigid, Grant and Lakesh. They felt sad, as if they were looking upon a tragic figure, not a participant in a conspiracy.

"The new species will hunt the old into extinction," Balam said.

"That is the plan," Thrush replied. "You knew it from the start."

He gestured to Grant and Brigid. "They are my guests from far away. They arrived by the path laid down by your forebears."

He shifted position to stand beside the silver box on the pillar. They followed his hand wave, and their stomach muscles clenched and their heartbeats sped up. They stared at the shape within the box. It was a black Trapezohedron with many flat, surfaces, like the facets of a crystal. It did not touch the bottom of the box, but hung suspended by eight delicate silver wires extending from the container's inner walls. A radiance seemed to shimmer from it, an unearthly phosphorescence that was very nearly invisible.

Thrush met Brigid's questioning gaze. "The complete stone, the entirety of the Shining Trapezohedron. The fragments were scattered on this world, too. Here they were all recovered some two centuries ago, a feat that eluded the Third Reich on your casement."

Brigid started to speak, cleared her throat and asked, "And is that why the Nazis failed there?"

"One reason," Thrush admitted. "Only one among many."

Balam's strange, strained voice spoke lowly. "There are always reasons, always different paths. This is only one among many as well."

Lakesh wheeled himself closer to Balam, scrutinizing him keenly as if he were a specimen under a microscope. "You've been the source of all the genetic material for the Reich's breeding program for nearly 250 years, haven't you?"

"I should think that is patently obvious, Administrator," Thrush stated. "He is the last of his kind and therefore the bridge between the human race and the master race."

Balam's head slowly swiveled on his short, slender neck. He addressed Thrush dispassionately. "You corrupted a program that was meant to create a new race, the mixing of the best of two to create one so both would become greater than the sum of their parts. You have pent me up in here to do your bidding. Now it is over. Set me free."

"You should be grateful I kept you here, Balam."

"Like a host body should be grateful to its parasite?" Brigid snapped in sudden anger, eyes hot with green flames. "I've finally figured you out, Thrush—you're not an agent of destiny or the Archons. You're a tick, sustaining itself on the life fluid of any living creature who allows you to get close enough to it. You grew so bloated with ambition you decided you could control the hosts."

Grant looked at Balam again, and instead of an xenophobic cringing, he felt a shame, as if the guilt of the human race were laid on his shoulders.

"Why have you kept Balam alive all these years?" Brigid continued. "Surely you have enough DNA samples in storage. You claimed the most unique aspect of his genetic structure was its ability to adapt, to replicate. I think you need his mind to interface with the Trapezohedron, to keep all the pathways open to the parallel casements."

For the first time, Thrush's blank countenance registered varied emotions, none of which could be identified. In a low tone, he said, "I've seen oceans rise and engulf entire civilizations. I've watched empires go down into ruin, humanity climb from abysmal savagery, and always locked in bloody war after war. Do you think you're truly in any position to pass judgment on me?"

"Yes," Grant said vehemently. "We are. Humans might war with humans, we might hunt each other down, but that savagery bonds us together. It's something we recognize in ourselves, no matter how sickening it is. But you're from outside humanity. What are you? A cyborg, a hybrid?''

Thrush's lips twitched in a macabre caricature of a smile. ''I believe Miss Baptiste said it earlier…chaos incarnate, Shiva the Destroyer, the devil.''

Brigid snorted. ''I don't believe you're any of those things, though you've worked very hard to delude others into fearing that you might be. Maybe you've even deluded yourself.

''I think without the Trapezohedron and Balam as your basic reality unit anchor, you'd waste away until there's nothing left of you but a Cheshire-cat smile.''

An emotion very close to uncertainty flickered over Thrush's high-planed face. ''Desperate speculation, Miss Baptiste.''

''I think you're the one who is desperate, Thrush. I don't think you know yourself what you are. In Newyork you said there was no point in killing your body because Colonel Thrush was not an individual but a program. A few minutes ago, you said the program didn't originate with a computer. That leaves only one alternative—the Shining Trapezohedron.

''In conjunction with Balam's mind energy, it provides you with a delicate balance, an equilibrium of realities. Balam and the Trapezohedron created you and without them you're nothing.''

Thrush shook his head in pity. ''An interesting conjecture, Miss Baptiste. However, there is no way it can be proved empirically.''

"I think you're wrong, Field Marshal," Lakesh rasped.

Balam met Lakesh's gaze. The creature nodded almost imperceptibly, as if giving his assent. Flinging back the folds of his blanket, Lakesh raised a Walther PPK, gripping it tightly within his gnarled, arthritic fingers.

Thrush blurted a cry and swung his pistol in Lakesh's direction. He squeezed the trigger, but a shaved sliver of a second too late. The Walther made a hand-clapping bang as the bullet from Thrush's Sin Eater crashed through the back of Lakesh's head.

His body lunged violently forward as the front of his skull opened in a weltering fountain of blood and brain matter. Only the various tubes and shunts attached to his body kept him in the chair.

A speckled pattern of crimson sprayed across Balam's chest, mixing with that pumping from the blue-rimmed hole in his heart. Only Grant was a little surprised to note that the color of Balam's blood was the same as Lakesh's.

Balam trembled convulsively, his eyes boring in on Thrush. In a whisper so scratchy and faint it was barely audible, he said, "I give you a final reality among many."

Then he toppled backward, aligning his arms, drawing in and closing his legs. His eyelids drooped over his eyes.

At the same instant, the dim halo of radiance shimmering from the Trapezohedron faded completely, and the box held only a curiously shaped chunk of black rock.

Field Marshal Thrush froze in place as a shiver shook his body. The shiver didn't pass. Instead it spread, becoming more of a vibration and a loud, high-tension wire buzz cut through the chamber, from a source they couldn't locate.

Grant whipped out his Sin Eater and without hesitation fired it at point-blank range into Thrush, the thundering reports resonating and reverberating beneath the domed ceiling.

As Thrush staggered and doubled over, Brigid drew her own Walther TPM and triggered three rounds. Hands going to his middle, Thrush twisted about to face them. He brought up his pistol to return the fire.

Grant kept his finger's pressure tight on the trigger of his Sin Eater and watched as three rounds struck Thrush in the side of the head, sending both his uniform cap and sunglasses flying from his face.

The full force of the impacts hurled him backward. As Thrush fell, Grant absently noted a lack of blood. Pivoting on his heel, Grant aimed at the silver box and fired off the remainder of the clip. The Black Stone cracked and split into fragments. A ricochet whined around the room.

Then the only sound was the dry clicking of a firing pin striking an empty chamber. Flat planes of cordite smoke drifted through the chamber. Brigid let out a shaky breath, eyeing the shattered chunks of rock. "All of the king's horses."

The world staggered around them. They were buffeted by zigzag images of memories and experiences, which were-were not their own.

And with the wrenching dislocation came pain, a furnace of agony in their heads, their brains, their minds.

The wild tilting stopped as suddenly as it began. Grant and Brigid gasped, faces damp with perspiration.

"The fusion is weakening," Brigid said tightly. "Breaking the Trapezohedron might have had something to do with it."

Grant forced himself toward the door in reeling walk. "What about Kane? We can't leave until we know what happened to him."

Brigid joined him the corridor, and they drew on wellsprings of strength and started running, each footfall causing little flares of torture to scorch the inner walls of their skulls.

"He could have been forced out already," Brigid panted.

"Or chilled. Will he be dead here and alive in Cerberus?"

"There's no way to know." An undercurrent of anguish cut through her voice, but it could have been an effort to control the pain.

They retraced their route through the white, sterile, silent corridors. Even the sounds of their running feet was muted. As they reached the T junction, they saw a figure standing in the center of the intersection.

It was the Battle Class soldier, freed from its cell, and it swayed almost hypnotically. Brigid was irresistibly reminded of the sinuous movements of a king cobra, lulling its prey. The creature gazed at them, faced stretched in a permanent grin, opening wide its arms in the repulsive mockery of a human embrace.

Hefting his Sin Eater, Grant muttered, "I'm out of ammo. What about you?"

By way of an answer, Brigid extended her arm and the Walther spit flame and twiglike snaps. The predator was struck three times in the hip and torso. The impacts turned it this way and that, but it remained on its feet. Then the firing pin clicked.

"No choice but to backtrack," Grant stated, carefully sidling away.

They were astounded to see the creature move to cut off their retreat. Its jaws opened and closed, flecked with bubbles of saliva.

A voice spoke from behind them. "Standard rules of termination."

They snatched quick glances over their shoulders. Thrush moved staggeringly down the corridor, leaning heavily against the right-hand wall. He presented a more horrific sight than the Battle Class demon.

Both sides of his face were horribly distorted, punched out of shape, the flesh ripped and hanging down in scraps. Metal gleamed dully beneath the skin. He dragged a dead leg behind him.

He looked like a corpse that had refused to accept the fact of its demise, choosing a half-life over both a complete life or a total death. His huge eyes glittered with a feral malevolence far deeper than that of the creature scuttling toward them.

Thrush spoke one more word: "Implement."

The predator's scuttle instantly became a bound.

Grant thrust Brigid behind him and rushed forward, reversing his grip on the Sin Eater.

A long, talon-tipped arm swung high and swept down at his neck. Grant hurled his empty pistol, and the creature avoided it with an unbelievably swift movement of his narrow head. Then it was on him.

One clawed arm knocked his cap from his head and ripped deep furrows in his scalp. Blood instantly blinded him but he bored in, trying to get inside the lashing arms.

The razored spurs raked his back, shredding the cloth and flesh beneath it, flaying it to the bone. He heard Brigid scream. He snarled with savage joy as he locked both hands around the predator's neck.

"Master race, my ass," he snarled.

Chapter 27

Kane prowled the streets of Dulce in the deep, dark hours before dawn. Grant was not in his flat, nor Brigid in hers. Checking with the Chancellery, he learned they had gone out to the Purity Control Foundation the afternoon before, but they had yet to return.

A security alert, a complete lock down, was in effect at the facility, no one allowed in or out at the order of Field Marshal Thrush. Even Major Kane with a vitally important and disturbing report for the field marshal was not to be admitted.

By the time he had been airlifted back to the Dakota base, Kane had concocted a cover story that would withstand an initial, cursory investigation.

The horde of Roamers and outlanders had suspected a trap and laid one of their own. In the tension of the conflict, the Battle Class troopers had reverted to utter bestiality, driven mad by the blood and violence. They had turned on their own and even attempted to take over the OGRE.

Only Major Kane, the hero of the Calgary campaign, the knight of the Reich, had turned the tide. He couched his tale with enough colorful adjectives and exaggerations that suspicion had quickly turned to awed admiration.

He had been back in Dulce for over three hours, his injuries treated and bandaged, wearing a crisp new uniform, all dressed up with no place to go.

But he knew the fierce pain in his head, growing more intense by the minute would force him to go somewhere, whether he wanted to or not.

He tried to walk it off, appearing to pace purposefully but with no real purpose along the dimly lighted streets, not caring if he was seen by the Zone Troopers or not. He waited for dawn to color and brighten the sky, then he intended to bully or shoot his way into the facility beneath the Archuleta Mesa.

A sleet storm of blinding agony scorched through his head, and he stumbled against a lamppost, leaning against it, gripping the metal pole tightly as his anchor.

Finally after what seemed an interlocking chain of eternities, it blew itself out. His limbs shook and his breath came in labored wheezes.

"Major Kane," Field Marshal Thrush said flatly, peremptorily.

Kane looked up. At first, he saw no one, then a figure shifted in the mouth of an alley, at the far limit of the puddle of illumination shed by the streetlight. It was dark shape, blacker than the shadows.

Kane groped for something to say, wondering if there was any point in furthering the masquerade.

Thrush made the decision for him. "You still live. Not that I'm particularly interested in the details at the moment. I applaud your resourcefulness. It's very intriguing."

There was something in Thrush's voice, some odd

tone or note that made Kane's skin prickle. His hand strayed toward the butt of his Sin Eater.

"Is that a compliment, Field Marshal?"

"I did not mean it as such. However, you are free to interpret it anyway you wish. Kane, why did you come here?"

The question surprised Kane so much he examined it for a hidden meaning before replying slowly, "You more or less insured I would."

"Did I? How?"

"You threw down the gauntlet to me, you challenged me. Remember?"

"I—" Thrush broke off. He remained silent for so long Kane was on the verge of calling out to him.

Finally, in a low, rustling voice, like the beat of distant wings, he said, "Gaps in the memories I draw upon. I don't have complete access any longer."

"I have a question for you. Why did *you* come here?"

"A unified world...my priority. Bring the unproductive members to heel...all marching in unity." Thrush spoke distractedly, as if he were confused, lost, searching for a familiar frame of reference.

"It is the end of it now...my Battle Class breed defeated by human inferiors...word will get out...the possibility that humanity can fight back and win will spread...rebellions and revolutions...unity will be broken."

"Where are Baptiste and Grant?" Kane demanded.

The disoriented note in Thrush's voice vanished. "They are here. I brought them with me."

Kane's eyes narrowed, searching the murk beyond Thrush's dim figure. He saw nothing but shadows. He drew his Sin Eater. "Where?"

Propelled by kicks from Thrush's feet, two objects rolled like awkward balls from the wedge of darkness, stopping at the circle of light cast by the street lamp.

A sheathing of utter, soul-freezing horror covered Kane. He could only stare at the heads of Brigid and Grant. Beneath the crusting of blood on their faces, he saw how their features were stamped with defiant determination, as if they had died fighting and died hard. He saw the ragged, chewed flesh at the sheared off stumps of their necks.

He barely heard the gunshot and was nearly oblivious to the muzzle-flash briefly flaring in the mouth of the dark alley. The bullet took him low in the chest, its velocity bursting his internal organs, driving the air from his lungs, hydrostatic shock stopping his heart.

All the strength drained out of his limbs, and he felt the hot blood beat out of him with the last spasms of his heart. He knew he was crumpling toward the gutter, his pistol falling from his hand, uniform cap sliding from his head. He'd seen himself die in this same place before.

The pain in his head gave a great, last heaving surge, then Kane floated over his body, watching as Thrush nudged it with a booted foot before holstering his own Sin Eater.

The dying man with his face looked up at Thrush,

and his writhing lips formed one word before blood vomited out of his mouth. "Why?"

Thrush's head swung up, and his cast his gaze about like a foxhound sniffing out a scent. Then, tonelessly he said, "Another time, Kane. And most certainly another place."

Kane felt himself drawn with the suddenness of thought into extreme cold and utter darkness.

Epilogue

Lakesh looked into the three faces around the table and uncomfortably cleared his throat. Kane's clothes were rumpled; Brigid's hair hung askew; Grant's eyes were red with fatigue and something more than fatigue. Horror seemed to crawl across all of their faces like something alive.

"Is that all you remember?" he asked.

None of the three people answered in words. They restricted their responses to short, grim nods. Lakesh reached over to turn off the tape recorder.

Trying to sound businesslike, he said, "Best we get a full account of your experiences before the memories begin to fade in your minds."

"I don't think I'm liable to forget watching a hell spawn eating one of my eyeballs like it was a grape," Grant muttered.

The three of them had rematerialized an hour earlier, right on schedule. They had dealt with the period of disorientation and confusion better than Lakesh had projected, and after having them examined by DeFore, they had joined him in the cafeteria for the debriefing.

"The memories will fade," Lakesh assured them. "As your own identities and life experiences rise to the fore over the passage of time. In less than a week, I'd judge you'll consciously recall only fragments.''

"Even me?" Brigid asked, lifting the coffee cup to her lips. It trembled ever so slightly.

Lakesh didn't know how to answer the question, so he evaded it altogether. Throwing her a jittery smile, he said, "Despite it all, you're back here safe and sound and my theory has been proved. The mattrans can be adjusted to pierce not just linear space but sidereal.''

"Wonderful," Kane said with cold sarcasm. "An infinite number of places you can send us to so we can get ourselves chilled, over and over. I know I'm thrilled by the prospect.''

Grant shifted in his chair, stretching out to scratch beneath the edges of the cast on his propped up leg. "I'm so thrilled I'm never going to do it again.''

"We might have no choice in the matter, you know," Lakesh said quietly.

Kane's eyes blazed with a sudden revulsion. "To hell with that, old man. We don't know if we did any good on that casement, if we changed things. And if we did change things, we don't know they were for good or bad. The choice is ours, not yours.''

Lakesh kept calm and composed in the face of the outburst. "I never meant to imply that it was, friend Kane. Whatever changes your actions might have wrought, you did exactly what you claimed Balam— our Balam—said for you to do. Remember?''

Brigid intoned, "'His vigil is complete. Yours begins…to find a way for your people to survive, as mine did.'''

"He was talking about overthrowing the barons," Kane snapped.

"Then why did he give you the prime facet of the Trapezohedron?" Lakesh asked.

"You tell me."

"Whatever the entity known as Thrush is or isn't, it's obvious he exists in some kind of interdependent relationship with both the Trapezohedron and the Archons. I submit it's highly likely that Thrush might be responsible for the most of the acts we attribute— or blame—on the so-called Archon Directorate."

"What the hell is he, then?" Grant demanded heatedly. "Is he their agent, their ambassador, their policy maker, their enemy—what?"

"That probably depends on the casement," Brigid stated. "He implied as much."

Kane blew out a slow, disgusted breath, crossing his arms over his chest. "He's already done his deeds on this casement. The world is unified." The last passed his lips in a contemptuous whisper.

"Yes," Lakesh agreed. "But now you've brought yourself into direct conflict with him and his ideas of unity."

"You think he might want revenge?" Grant asked doubtfully.

"To employ one of his own euphemisms," Brigid said with a wan smile, "'the extraction of troublesome factors.' We were certainly that."

With a groan, Grant heaved himself out of the chair. "I've got to sleep on this. For a week or two."

He limped toward the exit. Domi waited for him

there, and neither Kane nor Brigid were overly surprised to see him slide an arm around her shoulders.

Lakesh pushed his own chair back and picked up the recorder. "Both of you should get some rest. Let your minds slow down in order to process all this new information."

He walked out of the cafeteria, leaving Kane and Brigid alone at the table. Kane covered his sudden unease by gingerly probing at the padded bandage on his hip. The wound twinged.

Casually, he said, "I noticed you didn't mention the method by which you and I achieved fusion with our analogues."

Brigid shot him an irritated glance. "I noticed you made that very same omission."

"Were you embarrassed or ashamed?"

"I might ask you the same question."

"You might," he pointed out, "but I asked first."

She stood up swiftly, the chair legs screeching on the linoleum. She started a little guiltily until she remembered they were alone in the cafeteria. Before turning away, she said quietly, "I'm not ashamed, Kane."

Just before she reached the door, Kane called out, "Baptiste?"

She paused, glancing back, but not meeting his eye. "Yes?"

He grinned at her. "And I'm not embarrassed."

With a toss of her red-gold mane she was through the door and gone.

In the Deathlands, power is the ultimate weapon....

JAMES AXLER

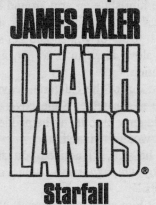

DEATH LANDS®

Starfall

Ryan Cawdor and his warrior survivalists jump into Montana territory, where they are joined by members of the Heimdall Foundation, an organization of whitecoats that investigates the possibility of alien visitation on earth.

Their paths cross with those of a Baron's sec men, who are searching for valuable debris from an abandoned space station that fell from the sky—the same "fallen star" that intrigues the Heimdall members.

While Krysty tries to fend off a telepathic mind assault, Ryan and his companions must find a way to deal with the sec men....

Take 2 explosive books plus a mystery bonus FREE

Mail to: Gold Eagle Reader Service
3010 Walden Ave.
P.O. Box 1394
Buffalo, NY 14240-1394

YEAH! Rush me 2 FREE Gold Eagle novels and my FREE mystery bonus. Then send me 4 brand-new novels every other month as they come off the presses. Bill me at the low price of just $16.80* for each shipment. There is NO extra charge for postage and handling! There is no minimum number of books I must buy. I can always cancel at any time simply by returning a shipment at your cost or by returning any shipping statement marked "cancel." Even if I never buy another book from Gold Eagle, the 2 free books and mystery bonus are mine to keep forever.

164 AEN CH7R

Name _____ (PLEASE PRINT)

Address _____ Apt. No. _____

City _____ State _____ Zip _____

Signature (if under 18, parent or guardian must sign)

* Terms and prices subject to change without notice. Sales tax applicable in N.Y. This offer is limited to one order per household and not valid to present subscribers. Offer not available in Canada.

GE2-98

A struggle for light and life against the tidal wave of the past...

STONY MAN™ 39

BREACH OF TRUST

A violent conflagration erupts when the Stony Man operatives are sent in to confront the Russian mob. The mission is tragically disrupted, leaving two dead, and leaving Stony Man with no choice but to fight this battle without restraint...or remorse.

Available March 1999 at your favorite retail outlet.